STEVEN TORRES

VENGEANCE IS MINE

This is a **FLAME TREE PRESS** book

Text copyright © 2022 Steven Torres

FLAME TREE PRESS
6 Melbray Mews, London, SW6 3NS, UK
flametreepress.com

US sales, distribution and warehouse:
Simon & Schuster
simonandschuster.biz

UK distribution and warehouse:
Marston Book Services Ltd
marston.co.uk

Publisher's Note: This is a work of fiction. Names, characters, places, and incidents are a product of the author's imagination. Locales and public names are sometimes used for atmospheric purposes. Any resemblance to actual people, living or dead, or to businesses, companies, events, institutions, or locales is completely coincidental.

Thanks to the Flame Tree Press team, including:
Taylor Bentley, Frances Bodiam, Federica Ciaravella,
Don D'Auria, Chris Herbert, Josie Karani, Mike Spender,
Cat Taylor, Maria Tissot, Nick Wells, Gillian Whitaker.

The cover is created by Flame Tree Studio with
thanks to Nik Keevil and Shutterstock.com.
The font families used are Avenir and Bembo.

Flame Tree Press is an imprint of Flame Tree Publishing Ltd

flametreepublishing.com

A copy of the CIP data for this book is available from the British Library
and the Library of Congress.

HB ISBN: 978-1-78758-648-2
PB ISBN: 978-1-78758-646-8
ebook ISBN: 978-1-78758-649-9

Printed in the USA by Integrated Books International

STEVEN TORRES

VENGEANCE IS MINE

FLAME TREE PRESS
London & New York

For Beatrice the Brave
and
Damaris the True

I love them both with all my heart

CHAPTER ONE

"That bitch," he said over and over again. He called her other names, worse names, but this was the one he kept coming back to, and he worked himself into a frenzy with it. Spit gummed up at the corners of his mouth, his eyes were wide, there was a vein that bulged its way down the center of his forehead. He clenched his fists so hard as he spoke that he had to shake them out to relieve the ache in them, but this only lasted a few seconds before the fists were knotted again. There was a drop of blood on one knuckle from where he had backhanded a table lamp across the room. He was used to letting people know about his displeasures, his angers, and the man listening to him knew Robert Meister had never been angrier.

"I want you...I want you," he sputtered, got control of himself and went on almost calmly. "I want you to destroy her. Make her pay. Make her sorry. And get me back my money."

"You want me to make her dead?" the man listening to him asked. This was the route he would have gone, but you didn't kill someone unless it was called for. It wasn't something you could undo or take back. People took it seriously. And it cost more.

The man laughed, and it came out like a dog bark. "Kill her?" he asked. "Lenny, there's no suffering in that. No pain in that. I want her to feel it. I want her to feel it bad."

"A beating?"

"You know what I want you to do," Meister said. He shook his fist at Lenny.

Lenny nodded slowly. He knew what was being asked of him. It wasn't just pain, but a pain that would never go away. If she lived to be a hundred, she'd still regret having meddled.

"That'll cost money," he said. "I mean...."

He didn't get to finish the sentence. Meister stopped him, putting a hand up then going into a desk drawer, fishing out a key, unlocking another desk drawer, bringing out a cashbox, picking up a change tray and pulling out a wad of fifty hundred-dollar bills. He tossed it onto the desktop.

"Get it done," he said. "Quick. And there's that much more when it's all over."

Lenny picked up the money and fanned it a second. He was thinking, calculating. For a more delicate job – a murder done right, for instance – he might need more money to get the best people. For rough work like this, he'd need someone without a conscience, without a soul. Often, they were the most useful people. Often, they were the cheapest. Disposable even.

"What if she goes to the police? This could turn into a bigger problem, no?"

Meister started breathing hard again, probably thinking about the trouble she could cause, the trouble she seemed intent on causing. He barked out another laugh.

"I don't think she'd do that. A lot of pride in that one. That little Puerto Rican spic bitch."

Lenny wanted to point out that this was a mostly Puerto Rican neighborhood, that he was Puerto Rican, but he stored that away. Decided to keep things professional.

"But what if?" Lenny asked. He wanted to know if there was more money coming in case things got messier.

"That bitch," Meister said. "If she goes to the police, I'll kill her myself. Tell her that. If she goes to the police, I'll kill her. First, I'll pick up her daughter from school, though. Tell that bitch that if she even thinks about the police, her little girl will get what she got. Worse. Then I'll kill them both."

Lenny wanted to say that this was going a bit far. One thing to hire people to do dirty work – it's what made the world go round – but it was another thing to do the work yourself. Amateur bullshit.

"You got it?" Meister asked. He was shaking his fist again.

"No problem. Consider it done. By this time tomorrow, she'll be as quiet as a mouse and out of your hair."

"Good."

Meister paced his office for a full minute, then noticed his audience was still there.

"What?" he asked.

"You got an envelope?"

"A what?"

"For the money." He held the bundle up.

★   ★   ★

Taking her was easy. She knew what she had done and who she had done it to. She looked over her shoulder when she should have looked straight-on ahead.

A quick punch to the nose, a hard shove into an alleyway, and she was stumbling, fighting to keep on her feet, three, four, then five steps, each step deeper into the alley and farther from public view. A green dumpster helped stop her momentum, but another push before she could set her feet, and she stumbled two or three more steps.

She found her feet and faced her attackers – she'd never seen them before as far as she knew. Her purse was still on her shoulder. This wasn't personal, and it wasn't a purse snatching. And there were two men with ski masks. "You don't have to do this," she said, thinking she was about to die and that her daughter would grow up without her.

"Sure we do," one of the men said.

He was stepping closer, forcing her to take steps deeper into that alley, farther from people who might see and say something.

He took another step. She had nowhere else to go. She let the purse slip off her shoulder. If it was a fight, she wanted her arms free.

"Mr. Meister sent us," the one in the background said. He was taller and thicker in the shoulders than the one closer to her. "He wanted you to know that what happens here is your fault, not his."

The closer man rushed her, threw a punch that missed her nose by a half foot as she leaned away from him. She threw two punches of her own – one caught him solid on the left cheek; the other landed on his right ear and hurt her like hell.

She hopped a step back. The guy she hit stepped toward her, his hands up like a boxer. He jabbed, but she leaned away again, shifted her feet, and when she came back at him it was with a kick straight to his crotch. Her father had told her a kick to the crotch was effective if you could land it. Landing it was the hard part. She landed it. The guy went to his knees with one hand holding his groin and the other hand up like he was asking for a time-out.

She pressed her advantage, hit him with an uppercut to the tip of his nose. She was about to give him another when the bigger guy punched her in the side of her head. She hit the brick wall sideways and slid down it to a sitting position. Then there was a hand on her throat, pulling her up. Dazed, she grabbed at that hand until she saw a knife blade shining and coming down toward her. She put her hands up to stop it, and the hand at her throat pushed her head up against the bricks behind her again and again, until she didn't know what was happening anymore.

* * *

For a little more than a minute, the two men beat her – kicks and punches, and when she had gone limp, they pushed her against the brick walls and concrete pavement, slamming her head and the rest of her against the surfaces. Then she stopped moving. Mr. Meister had wanted them to do everything to her – everything they could imagine, all the brutalities, all the humiliations. He wanted her violated; he wanted her face carved; he wanted her to have to live with his fury forever. But after the fight she put up and the force they used against her, neither man wanted to go further. Besides, there was the sound of sirens – not coming for them, but still, not far either.

When they were about to let her go, finally, one of them, stubble on his face, blood on the tip of his nose – her blood – he leaned in close to her right ear and hissed something. Her eyes rolled. She had prayed to lose consciousness throughout the beating, but she'd been kept from it – expertly perhaps. Now her eyes rolling back earned her a hand at her throat and a hard shake.

She focused on his lips.

"Remember, Elena, we know where you live. We know your husband. We know your daughter. One word to the police, and that's it. Your perfect life goes down the toilet."

He shook her again, lifting her partway by the lapels of her torn jacket, and she focused on his eyes – brown.

"What we did to you," he told her. "Best if you keep it to yourself. We can do the same to that little girl of yours. Maybe even worse."

He let go of her with another little shake, and she fell to her hands and knees. The men started to go and Elena kept her head down. Didn't want to see them walking away, didn't want to know which way they headed, just wanted them gone. One ran back to her a few steps and squatted next to her. It was the one she had kicked, the younger one.

"Just let this be a lesson to you," he said. "You don't tell your husband, you don't tell the police, and the next time you see Meister, you smile like nothing ever happened and do what he tells you. You understand?"

Elena nodded. He patted her back as though he cared for her, as though he could comfort her. Then he stood and walked off. Elena still had her head down.

A door opened and closed and beyond the door she could hear footsteps receding and the sound of cars. When she was sure they were gone, she slowly stood. The lone light bulb in the alley was underpowered, but it shone like the noon sun in her eyes, blinding her. She tried to smooth out her skirt or what was left of it. She saw that her hand was shaking badly, like she had Parkinson's. She shook it out, but that didn't help.

She reached with her other hand and saw that she'd been stabbed straight through it, the mark like a stigmata wound. Blood flowed and there was probably a muscle or nerve severed because the middle and ring finger wouldn't quite work, but it wasn't shaking so she used it to get her clothes back in order.

★   ★   ★

She knew the routine, but couldn't bring it to mind. There were things you were supposed to do right after an attack, a rape. A certain set of steps to be followed in a certain order. But this wasn't that. She was almost positive this wasn't that. Could she have lost a few minutes to unconsciousness? No. This wasn't that. It was a beating, a bad one. Kicks to her head and gut. And blood in torn panties. What was the routine for getting beat until you bled? Was it take a scalding hot bath, drink yourself to sleep and hope you never wake up again? Probably not, but it sounded like the most reasonable thing.

She didn't have unlimited options. There weren't that many people in the world she could trust with her life at a point when she was as fragile as she'd ever been – there was her husband, but he'd want to talk and ask questions and probe her feelings, and she couldn't handle that just then.

And there was her father. He'd want to protect her, maybe even want to strike out at the people who had done this to her, but he'd find his hands were tied, he was powerless, and he'd know exactly what she felt.

She turned toward her father's house; she could handle his reaction – his anger might heal her, she thought. Every few feet she braced herself against a car or the brick walls of a building. *Drunk*, people probably thought of her. *I wish*, she thought back.

★   ★   ★

When his daughter knocked, Ray Cruz was sitting on his sofa, watching a recording of a Jets game even though he knew the score from the news the night before. He wasn't even sure he'd heard a knock, until she knocked again, louder. The Jets had spent the first half of the game being humiliated, and were rallying to maybe score a few points, so he went to the door, but his heart was still sitting on the sofa, watching. His eyes turned to the set, his focus there, he didn't even bother looking through the peephole, though normally he would have.

Idiot.

He opened and looked at her and felt he knew what had happened, knew it all. She walked right into his arms and needed him to hold her, and he did the best he could.

He wanted to ask, just to be saying something, to begin making sense of things in the universe again; he wanted to ask her:

"Elena, Elenita, what did he do to you? What did he do?"

But he could see all the damage, or at least a lot of it, just by looking at her. And it would have been a stronger man than him, a much stronger man, who could get those words out without being strangled by them. If his life depended on it, he could not have spoken a clear word. He thought it was like he'd been stabbed in the throat and the knife was still resting there.

She went past him to the bathroom. The door shut, and he stood outside and heard the shower run at full blast. He didn't know what to do with his hands. He went from almost touching his face to almost putting his hands in his pockets and back again incessantly. He couldn't speak to her when he had her in his arms, and he certainly couldn't say anything to her while she was trying to wash herself of the whole experience. He knew that if what he thought had happened to her had happened to him, he would want the world to melt away and leave him alone.

Give her space, he told himself quietly a dozen times or more. He thought maybe it was a mistake, but he listened to his own advice.

He paced. There wasn't much to do until she came out of the

bathroom. The only constructive idea he could form was that he would kill Willie, her husband. It didn't occur to him that anyone else could have done all this to her. And he had never liked Willie. William, he liked to be called, as though it made him a man. He was a thinker, not a doer, and there was something fishy about people who talk that much shit.

Ray had just decided that for the sake of harmony within the family, he would kill Willie quickly; it'd look like an accident. Then he heard the water turn off in the bathroom and he went to the door. He wanted to claw his way in and hold her again, but *Give her space* ran in his mind.

He heard her sobbing and wanted to shout at her – *"Elenita, please!"* – because every sob was breaking his heart, killing him, and when she finished sobbing and came out, he might be lying by the bathroom door, broken and useless.

She started the water up again after a minute of sobs and whimpers that left Ray shaking throughout his body like a man about to die in the cold.

★   ★   ★

Her nose was broken, one of her eyes almost closed, her jaw bruised on both sides. Her nails were broken even though she took great pride in them usually. Her hair was a mess – jet black and long. Ray had no doubt it had been used against her, used to hold her down, to pull her whichever way she was wanted to go. There were the marks of fingers on her throat.

Mostly, it was the torn clothes. *She dresses well, my daughter,* Ray thought. *Never a slob, not even in grade school.*

The slit of her skirt – a below-the-knee skirt – was torn. Her blouse was torn – a sleeve almost completely off, buttons missing. Someone had grabbed her by the front of her shirt. It was a white blouse, and Ray could see her bra was torn. And yet....

She still had a gold necklace around her neck. It hadn't been ripped from her. It wasn't a mugging. Had to be personal. Had to be Willie.

He went into the bedroom and looked through the top drawer of the dresser. He still kept a few things from when her mother, God rest her soul, had been around. Her mother had been a smaller woman, and he didn't think anything would fit Elenita except a bathrobe Maria had used every morning to start her day.

He didn't check the bottom drawer. He kept a couple of handguns there, both Smith & Wessons – a small frame revolver with an ankle holster and a heavy .9mm with a waistband clip holster. There was extra ammunition for each. *Not like I would need more than one bullet*, he told himself. Willie was soft. An execution. One bullet behind the ear or maybe through the eye. Or maybe a knife to the gut. Ray knew where to find a man's liver. Or through the throat.

Ray was thinking this shit when the water went off again in the bathroom. What else are you supposed to think when someone has beaten your daughter and raped her and thrown her out of her own house? When your daughter comes crying to you like this? There are times when you've been kicked about as low as you can go and the only thing that you can see, the only step up you can take, is to plot revenge. *It's low, but sometimes it's all you've got.*

★   ★   ★

"I got a bathrobe for you here if you want it," he told her through the door of the bathroom. It came out weak, but it came out.

There was no answer for a minute, and he tried to think whether he had anything that she could hurt herself with while she was in there. He didn't have the old razor blades he used when she was little. He felt some relief, but it didn't cross his mind until much later that he had plenty of leftover medicines from when Maria had been sick three years earlier. Strong stuff. Probably wouldn't have been effective, but Elena wasn't thinking along those lines anyway.

He thanked god when she spoke.

"Okay. Leave it on the doorknob," she said. It was like music.

Maria used to leave towels and underclothes on the doorknob every time Ray forgot them. It was something they'd done in the family.

He left the bathrobe and went back to his room. He looked through the closet to see if there was anything else he could get Elena. Pulled out a shirt and a pair of jeans and then thought again and got out a sweater in case she wanted to go home. He laid it all out on the bed and went out into the hallway to wait for her.

The five minutes or so of silence from the bathroom were hard, but he forced himself to stay still and stay quiet. He could hear sniffling, and sniffling wasn't dying.

Ray had heard that crying was part of the healing process. It wasn't how he was raised, and he sure as hell didn't know if it was true. He was crying those five minutes in the hall – there was nothing else to do – but he didn't see that it did him any good. Maybe expressing the fact that your soul has been torn helps some people to feel better. For him, it just felt like his soul was torn. No improvement.

When she opened the door, she went straight into her father's arms again. No talking, no crying, just rest.

He walked her to the sofa, could have screamed because the TV was still on as though football mattered. He found the remote and shut it down. They sat holding each other. For Ray, it was enough at the moment. The revenge, the anger, it all dissolved. It wasn't needed, wouldn't be helpful just then. It was a while before he could think of something to say.

"Are you feeling any better?" he asked. He expected she would say no, but at least that would be the start of a conversation. He didn't know if conversation was supposed to be helpful like crying was. *People say it is*, he thought, but he couldn't think who had said it. Either way, he wanted information, wanted to hear her talk. If she was talking, she was surviving.

He was surprised when she pulled away a little to look him in the face, and she nodded.

"A little," she said.

He could take that. Progress.

"Do you want to talk about it?" Ray'd heard that line in movies. Maria, his wife, had never been much of a talker, not with him anyway. She'd been a good woman, and he'd been a bastard. That's how he summed up their relationship whenever it was brought up. Maybe that had something to do with it.

Elena thought about the question for a moment, then she shook her head. Ray couldn't blame her.

★　　★　　★

Time is supposed to heal wounds too, but it didn't seem to be working. They sat there for a good half hour and in all that time a cut on the back of her hand wouldn't stop bleeding.

"That needs to be stitched," Ray told her. Over the years, in his line of work, he'd made that assessment more than a few times.

She looked down at her hand and smiled. It was the most defeated smile he'd ever seen.

"It goes all the way through," she said. She held the hand up to show him. The three-quarter-inch cut on the back of the hand was duplicated on her palm like she had put her hand up when someone was stabbing her.

He wanted to pick at the wound, see if it really did go all the way through, but that wouldn't have helped her situation any.

"We should go to the emergency room," he told her. "They can set your nose too." She put her stabbed hand up to her nose and touched it.

"It's broken?" she asked.

"I've seen a few broken noses," he told her. "That's one of them. But don't worry. Nowadays with plastic surgery they can make you as good as new. Better, if you want."

"But they'll ask questions," she said.

He figured she was right on that point – didn't know what to say.

"True," he told her. "But then if you put it off for a few days, they'll ask questions then too, no?"

She didn't seem convinced.

"And that hole in your hand might get infected. Plus...."

He didn't want to say that she might want to do something to prevent sperm and egg from meeting.

"A D and C?" she asked.

Ray wasn't sure what she was talking about, but figured she knew. She had always been the smarter one of the two of them, he reminded himself. She had finished high school and gone to college. A real college, not the prison bullshit he'd gone to, to pass the time. He nodded.

"I don't need one of those, but can you take me home for a few minutes, so I can change?"

"But what about Willie?" he asked.

She looked at a clock on the wall.

"William won't be home from work for another hour or so, and Rosita is with the sitter until he picks her up. You're right though. The emergency room will take more than an hour."

"But, uh, Willie...."

He wanted to ask whether Willie had been the one to do all this to her. He hadn't considered it could be someone else even though there were a good four million other men in New York City.

"William? He doesn't know. Not yet. First things first," she said.

Ray tried to figure out whether she was protecting Willie from him or protecting him from himself or if some other guy was really responsible while she dressed herself in some of his clothes. If it wasn't Willie, if it was some stranger she walked past on the street who decided to follow her and take her, then the revenge he wanted was slipping away. Hard enough for police detectives to catch rapists when they had all the information. Ray'd have almost no chance, and he knew it.

He found a spring-handled blackjack in a kitchen drawer and

packed it in an inner coat pocket. Elena came out of the bedroom with one of his jackets on and his Jets logo knit cap, and they went out.

CHAPTER TWO

It was a short drive to the hospital. Neither one of them said a word. Ray had lots to say, but he kept it to himself.

Funny, he thought as he parked. *The most traumatic thing in the world can happen to you and eventually you stop crying*. He didn't think you were healed when that happened – that would mean you go back to normal. He thought your pain got plastered over like with a cast, or covered up like with a bandage.

Business was slow at the emergency room. There was a mother with a couple of coughing children, and an old guy who had fallen asleep. Elena jumped to the head of the line.

The nurse took her vitals and had Ray fill out some forms. She asked Elena a bunch of questions which all ended up being the same – what happened to you? The nurse kept looking at Ray with each question, and he knew she wanted to add, *"Did the old guy who brought you in do it?"* Ray understood her concern – he had a few scars on his face and his nose was one of the broken ones he'd seen that made him sure Elena had the same condition. There had been many times when people thought the worst about him when they saw him next to someone who had been stomped on. Often, they were right to think that way.

Elena didn't have much to say to this nurse except to point out injuries. She didn't want to talk about how she got them. Ray didn't think she would, but part of him wanted to hear the story too. She just wanted to get all this over with.

From the sadness in her eyes, the slump of her shoulder, the lead in her voice and the listless movements, Ray could tell that she was more tired than she had ever been and that she wanted to be doped up and put into a warm bed, and that she wouldn't want to crawl from under the covers for a long, long time.

Ray couldn't blame her. He thought of it as his job to make sure she got through this visit and got what she needed with the least hassle. Her knight in shining armor, even if he had arrived a little too late for the battle.

The nurse moved them to another room, looked at the chart, and told Ray that when the doctor arrived, he'd probably ask him to leave the room. Ray said he understood. The doctor could ask anything he wanted.

★   ★   ★

Dr. Warwick was a young white guy, maybe six feet and thin. He was reading a chart as he came in and looked at the two of them. He smiled at Elena – a grin, Ray thought. Looked like he thought this was a joke.

"*Hablas inglés?*" he asked.

"Yeah," Ray answered. "How about you?"

It took him a second to get Ray's meaning. He smiled even larger. *Just our luck to get Howdy Doody*, Ray thought.

The doctor introduced himself to Elena.

"I'm here to have a look at the hand and the nose and to examine you for possible other trauma. Dr. Rosen is one of the attending physicians on duty right now, and he'll be down in a little bit to help you with…any potential…female troubles. I'm going to have to ask you to change into a hospital gown and you, sir, I have to ask you to step outside the curtained area."

He pointed Ray to a plastic chair, and when he sat in it, Dr. Warwick pulled a curtain around Elena's exam table. He stood next to Ray while Elena changed, then he went in to deal with her.

Ray leaned forward in his seat to listen. There were times when Elena yelped during the exam. Ray jumped out of his chair and told her it was all right through the curtain. After a few minutes, Dr. Warwick left the room to get something.

Ray moved over to her side and asked if she was okay.

She smiled at him, and even though it was a weak smile, it meant that she could smile again.

"I'll be okay, Daddy," she said. "I just don't want to talk about... things."

"They can't make you," he was telling her as Warwick came back with a little pushcart.

He pointed Ray back into his chair and took the cart behind the curtain.

"You have a couple of injuries that I'm going to have to put a few stitches into," he told her, and he introduced her to the needles he was going to use on her, and the injections he'd have to give to numb the area. Even with the local anesthetics, Elena was whimpering for a part of his time with her. At one point he told her that she had to stop being such a baby. It sounded like he was kidding with her, but Ray heard it and put his hand on the blackjack he had with him, and if she hadn't stuttered out a laugh for him, Warwick would have caught that blackjack to the side of his head.

Dr. Rosen came into the room, checked the chart in his hand, and went behind the curtain after giving Ray a glance. He was an older man, a few years older than Ray, balding, glasses hanging around his neck. His presence gave Ray more confidence about Elena being treated right, but one look from him made Ray feel like he had been pegged for a criminal.

"Has Dr. Warwick discussed the issue of reporting this incident?" Rosen asked.

Warwick jumped in. "I thought I'd leave that for you to explain, given that you'll be dealing with the...the female troubles."

Ray pictured the grin Warwick had on and the sour look Rosen probably gave him.

"Well, just so that you're not caught unaware, we are required to call in the police whenever we suspect that there has been a sexual assault."

"No police," Elena said. "I wasn't raped."

"Are you sure?" Rosen asked.

She wanted to say she was one hundred per cent sure. She was almost positive she had not lost consciousness during the ordeal. Her bra had been torn, her panties too. She didn't remember how that had happened. Still, "I'm sure," she said.

"Well, whether you speak to them at all is, of course, up to you, but we have to notify them and they invariably want to speak to the patient. You understand, don't you?"

"No police," Elena said again. This time, her voice was only a little more than a whisper.

"Don't worry, Mrs. Maldonado. The police officer they send will be someone experienced in these matters, and remember, you don't have to answer them."

"No police," Elena said. This was the weakest voice. Ray got out of his seat and in another second he would have pulled back the curtain and smashed in Rosen's skull. What was it with doctors? Why couldn't they ever listen?

"Don't you want them to catch the man who did this?" Warwick asked. Ray couldn't figure out if Warwick had been trained to be so insensitive, or if it came naturally.

Elena whispered something her father couldn't hear. Apparently neither could the two doctors. She repeated herself, just loud enough.

"I already know the guys who beat me," she said.

★   ★   ★

It's hard to know what to do when a nightmare becomes reality. And when the reality becomes a hell.

When Ray thought a man had violated her, he felt like he'd been defeated in something – after all, if you can't protect your closest relative, your baby girl, what good are you? But then to hear from her that it wasn't just a simple assault, that it had been two men or more. How is that information supposed to fit into your world?

★   ★   ★

Dr. Warwick left the room along with his cart. Dr. Rosen examined Elena for a few minutes, then he moved her to another examination room. Ray followed along, but this room was smaller, and he had to wait outside. A police detective arrived about fifteen minutes into this exam. About fifty years old, six feet tall, a few pounds heavier than his doctor would have liked, hair that threatened to flop over his eyes if he didn't look after it. He stood next to Ray and sized him up for an ex-con in two seconds. That was fine by Ray.

"This supposed to be your daughter?" he asked.

"She's supposed to be everything I've got," Ray said.

"And you know she's got to speak with me?"

Ray shrugged.

"If she feels like it," he said.

He was quiet for a half minute. Ray wondered if he had sounded more hostile than he intended, but didn't really care if that were so.

"If she doesn't have anything to hide," the detective started and left it at that.

After a minute of silence, he started up again – stuck his hand out for Ray to shake.

"Detective Jack Carver," he said.

Ray took the hand and shook it once.

"Elena's father," Ray answered.

"Well, look. We both want exactly the same thing. Believe me. We both want to get the asshole that did this to your daughter. Can we agree on that?"

Ray nodded.

"Good. Then we can work together on this and maybe get somewhere. I need her to talk to me. To tell me everything. That might be very difficult for her, but with your help, she can get through this, and I can get the information I need."

He sounded reasonable – just two guys talking. But then, it wasn't his daughter in there with Dr. Rosen.

"Mr. Carver, let me tell you something. If Elena wants to talk with you, she will, and I'll hold her hand through the whole thing. If she doesn't want to talk…then that's it. I know my girl. If she wants to do something, it gets done. If she doesn't want to do something, you're out of luck."

"But let me tell you something, Elena's father. If she doesn't talk to me, then the creep who did this to her can do this to other women. Understand?"

Ray nodded and shrugged.

"True, but they're not my daughters," he said.

"Ah, but that's where you might be wrong. God forbid the guy comes back at her, but if he does, you'll be sorry she didn't co-operate with the police."

Ray didn't say anything to that. He could have told Carver he was planning on keeping a close eye on his child, and if this dude came by again, he'd drop him to the ground and make sure he never got up. He wanted to give Carver this much information: it was more than one guy and it wasn't her husband. But he kept that to himself too.

After another minute, Carver told Ray to stand up and give his name. Ray thought about telling him to go to hell – he had paid all his debts to society already. He was a citizen like anyone else. But that would have been the hard way and Carver looked tired. Not as tired as Ray, but tired. Jerking his chain didn't look like the right way to go.

"Ray Cruz."

"Any ID to go with that?" Carver asked. Ray never could figure out why more cops didn't just cut to the chase and ask for the ID first.

He pulled his driver's license from his wallet and handed it over. Carver studied it and handed it back. Then he walked away. Ray knew what he was going to do, and he hoped Rosen would do what he needed to do quickly, but he didn't have that kind of luck.

★　　★　　★

Carver came back ten minutes later at a quick pace. Ray was still standing, his back against the wall, and Carver walked right up to his face and tried to fix him with a stare like Ray was going to start crying or something. He pulled back a few inches to say what he had to say.

"I got your sheet," he said. "Had them read it to me over the phone at the reception desk."

Ray shrugged again; he wasn't about to applaud.

"When you were twenty-two you went up for seven years – manslaughter – kicked some joker in the ribs a few too many times in Sal's Bar on Tremont. I remember that place – tough joint."

He stopped talking and looked at Ray like he should say something.

"Youthful indiscretion," Ray said.

"Uh-huh. When you were thirty-five you did another three for...." He looked down at his notepad. "Let's see. Assault. Broke a man's arm. And his jaw. And one of his pinkies. And a rib. Let me guess. Another 'youthful indiscretion'?"

"Midlife crisis."

"Uh-huh. You trying to be funny, Mr. Cruz?"

Just then Dr. Rosen opened the door and stepped out. He looked at each of the men and nodded Ray over to an empty room across the hall. He couldn't tell if it was a diversion tactic to let the detective slip into the room or if he really wanted to tell him something important, but he went with him. Carver went in to speak with Elena.

★   ★   ★

"I can't go into the full details of the case, but I'm hoping that as her father you'll have some influence with her on a couple of issues that I think are important."

Ray thought Rosen already looked older than when he had first met Elena; maybe it was just a trick of the imagination.

"First, she mentioned going back to work, and I told her she should really take some days off. She made no promises. She needs rest, not just mentally and emotionally, but physically. She needs fluids – it'll help her heal. Plenty of water. And I really think she could benefit from speaking to someone about this event – if not a psychiatrist or therapist, then maybe a priest or minister. Maybe her husband. One way or the other, it's my experience that patients benefit greatly from unburdening themselves. Maybe she could speak with you."

Ray smiled, almost laughed. Dr. Rosen might know a lot of things, but if he thought Ray had some hidden therapist skills, he was deluded.

Ray shook his hand and thanked him for the talk. Then he went to see what damage Carver was doing.

*   *   *

There he was standing over her as she sat on the edge of the exam table. He was in her space like she was a criminal he was trying to sweat a confession out of. She looked up when Ray opened the door, and he could see relief in her face.

Carver took a step back from her, giving her some room to breathe. "This is ridiculous," he said.

"What is?" She took his bait. If she had been her father, she would have just agreed with his assessment and gathered up her things to go.

"This. You got attacked, maybe you got raped – I've dealt with women who didn't know they'd been raped. Terrible things. But you're actually helping the guy who did this to you. I could catch him if you gave me half a chance, but...." He tossed his hands up and let them fall slack to his sides. He shook his head.

"I just can't, detective." Elena was looking down, guilt dripping from her words like she had done something wrong.

"Let me guess. He said that if you tell anyone or call the police that he'd come back and kill you, right?"

Carver put his hands to his hips waiting for the answer.

Elena looked up a second with a face that told her father all he needed to know about her answer to the question. He didn't doubt Carver read it too.

"Well, let me just tell you that they all say that, but there is one thing to know about these rapist bastards...."

"I wasn't raped."

"If you say so. But they're all cowards at heart. That's why they make their chickenshit threats...."

Elena got up and started to gather her clothes. She was still in her hospital gown.

"Detective, I really can't," she said, and she motioned toward the door. Ray opened it for him.

"Well, here's my card in case you want to talk. I'm pretty sure my boss is going to want me to pursue this further, so I'll probably be in touch even if you're not interested," Carver said, then he stepped outside.

Ray followed, closing the door and giving her a few minutes of privacy to get dressed.

"I'm guessing the police academy didn't do sensitivity training back in the day when you were starting out," he said.

"Nope. They just taught us how to catch bad guys."

"And they haven't sent you to take a workshop or anything?"

"You're complaining about how I treated your daughter, Mr. Cruz? Because if you are, I'd say I think you're misplacing your anger."

He walked away, and Ray had no doubt that the detective would get a lot more information out of the doctors than he ever would.

*   *   *

It was while Ray was driving away from the hospital with his Elenita sitting in the passenger seat next to him that he remembered this was the same hospital where his daughter had been born, where he had held her for the first time – a mop of black hair, pudgy cheeks that almost but not quite closed up her eyes, and hands that jerked out as though she were looking for something in the blur of light.

He had let some tears escape back then, tears of joy. Not at all like the tears as he drove.

*   *   *

Looking out the passenger-side window at the cold city streets and the cold city people on them, Elena remembered being driven down the same road four years earlier. She held her own daughter that day.

She remembered, too, what Dr. Rosen had told her an hour earlier. The baby she had learned about the week before and loved even then would never come to fruition.

"It wasn't meant to be," Dr. Rosen said gently.

She caressed her now-empty belly and for the moment was glad she had not yet told anyone of the life growing inside her. A life, now extinguished.

CHAPTER THREE

The drive to Elena's apartment wasn't that far, but Ray took a long way around, trying to give her more time to calm herself. Not that she looked that upset to him. She looked more beat. Maybe she was thinking things through – going over what had happened to her. That was one of the things about the past – no amount of thinking changes anything. Any way she sliced it, she'd been attacked. He told her this when they parked.

"You can't change it, *mi'ja*," he said. "It won't go away. The man who did this...the men...they're out there...."

This made her start crying again, but it was a quiet cry. He put his hand on her knee, and she took it in both hands and put it up to her face for a caress. At some time or other each of the fingers on his hand had been broken, some of them accidentally, but Ray had never thought they were rough until then.

He kissed the top of her head.

"*Mi'ja*, if you don't want to talk to the police, then that's fine. I don't like talking to them either...."

She looked up at him with a smile, and he stopped his talking a moment. He wanted to savor that smile for her sake and his.

"I don't like talking with them, *mi'ja*, but if you don't talk with them, then talk to me. I...I want to protect you. *Entiendes*? If you know who did this, you can just give me a name and I'll—"

She put up a hand to cut him off.

"Please. *Papi*, I can't."

That was all she said and the smile disappeared and the tears came back in full force. Enough to drown her. Ray put the car in gear and drove around a little more.

He wanted to tell her something he'd heard in a movie once or twice and that he'd found to be true. *"The best defense is a good offense."* Kill the bastards who did this and they wouldn't be hurting her again, not her or her family.

And he wanted to tell her not to worry about him. He didn't know if what might happen to him was passing through her mind at all, but she didn't have to concern herself with any of that. He could get killed, he could get beat, or he could go to jail. Those were the bad possibilities if he handled the guys who had done this to her. He'd never died before, but he'd done the rest and wasn't afraid.

They'd lost the parking space by the time he got around to the front of her building again. He double-parked.

"Are you good to go?"

She nodded, and they both got out.

They had worked out a plan about how to handle things. Ray would go in first, talk to Willie, explain things, then she'd go in. Just as he was about to open the door with Elena's key, he figured out it was a lousy plan. Better than nothing, but it didn't take into account his granddaughter, Rosita. She'd have questions, she'd be scared, she'd want to sit in Mommy's lap and pick at her stitches.

★　　★　　★

Willie was at the door as Ray opened it. He tried to look past his father-in-law, but Ray rushed him back in.

"Where's Elena?" he asked.

"A bad thing happened to her," Ray said.

He was looking right into his son-in-law's face to see how he'd take the news. If he didn't show the right amount of concern, the right level of surprise, Ray still had a blackjack in his coat pocket.

"What?" he asked. "Is she okay?"

It was a little hard to read his face. Ray wanted to be sure, absolutely sure that Willie wasn't involved, that his little girl wasn't just protecting him for god only knows what reason. Normally Ray would have thought it would be easy to tell if Willie was concerned or not, but Willie was a self-centered asshole. What didn't pinch his toes wasn't really his problem. Ray had no doubt the train of thought would go like this: *"Elena got the shit kicked out of her, but why wasn't she around to make my dinner?"*

It took him three seconds to figure out Willie wasn't involved with her attack. If he had done anything to her, he would not really want her father walking in through his door. He would have hidden or grabbed a knife. Ray had told him on his wedding day that if he hurt his baby girl, Ray would kill him. A lot of fathers-in-law probably say that or something like it, but Ray showed him the handguns. Nothing like a .9mm pointed at your nose to make a hypothetical situation seem more real.

"Is she in the hospital?" Willie asked.

"We were there just a little while ago. Look, there isn't any nice way to say this, so I'm just going to spit it out and you're going to understand, then you're going to help Elena with anything she needs like a good husband."

"And what would you know about being a good husband?"

Ray took a step back. He had stepped in close to make his point and to keep his voice down. Since Rosita wasn't running around, he figured she might be taking a nap, and it would be the best thing for everyone if she slept through the night.

He wagged a finger at Willie.

"Let's just keep focused on Elena here," he said. "She's going to need your support."

Then Ray told him why.

★   ★   ★

Outside, Elena leaned against the hallway wall. She caught herself touching her belly and stopped. She could always truthfully say she'd been kicked in the gut, but she wanted to avoid the issue altogether.

"You've lost a lot," she whispered to herself, then her mind turned to what more she could lose.

*   *   *

It took three minutes for Ray to get through the story and to add emphasis to the part where Elena might not want to say anything about what happened and that it was important that he respect her wishes. For once, it looked to Ray like Willie had empathy for a fellow human being. He needed to take a seat to absorb all that he was told, and by the end of what Ray had to say, he was leaning forward with his hands on his knees and his breathing had quickened and the breaths out were a bit ragged. He was angry. Good.

Ray opened the apartment door and waved Elena in. She entered sheepishly, as though it weren't her home too. As though she had done something wrong or something to deserve the treatment she had gotten.

He wanted to hold her and reassure her, but she went straight into Willie's arms, and Ray found himself a seat.

"My god," Willie said. "Who did this?"

She shook her head. She didn't look at her father, and he thought for a moment that maybe she wasn't afraid to tell him in particular, she was just afraid to tell anyone at all.

"Okay," Willie said. He stroked her hair and they moved to the couch. Ray figured it was about his time to leave. They had healing to do, and he had to think.

Ray gave his daughter a kiss and told her he'd be back and that she could call him day or night.

"I love you," he said. "But rest."

If nothing else, being with Willie seemed to calm her, make her feel better, and Ray was comfortable leaving her side for a time.

In the car, he sat and tried to go through what he knew. It wasn't much.

Elena worked from eight to four most days, but sometimes she worked longer hours if there was a need. Problem. She was at his door at about four o'clock. She didn't drive herself, so she must have gotten out early. Why? Asking her boss was another problem.

Ray wasn't sure what she did exactly – office stuff for a law firm. Not criminal law – contracts. Maybe real estate. One way or the other, talking with lawyers was only a little better than talking with detectives.

Besides, it was late. He'd drive by the offices but didn't think there'd be anyone to answer his questions until the next morning.

And what if Elena went to work? If she didn't want to talk with her father, she probably didn't want him snooping around. He wasn't about to ask questions with her there. Even if she didn't go to work, if she took a few days off, he wasn't sure how he'd get answers out of lawyers without them knowing he was her father and reporting back to her. And he certainly didn't want to let them know something bad had happened to her if she was calling in sick with a head cold.

Anyway, what did he want information about her for? It might help, but what he really wanted was information about the guys who had attacked her.

*   *   *

She knew the guys who had done this to her. She knew them, but she had never told her own father about them. If they were hoodlums, bad men, if they were bothering her for whatever reason, would she have told him? This was the type of problem he was used to cleaning up for people. Over the years he had worked for a lot of guys and the job often included giving troublemakers incentive to go away.

When Elena was in the seventh grade, she liked a boy for a short time, but it soon soured. Happens. But then the boy started to bully her. It made her cry for days. Finally, she told her father about it, and he had a talk with the boy – that's it, a nice quiet talk. After that, he left her alone.

He told his daughter, "If anyone bothers you, bullies you, hurts you, let me know, and I'll take care of it. That's what fathers are for.

It's what they do." She understood, but that was a long time ago. She could fight her own battles now. Usually did. But this was a two-or–more-on-one street fight.

She had a husband now. Maybe she told him about her troubles and he dropped the ball. With Willie it was easy to imagine.

But who would do such a thing to his daughter? Why? How did she happen to know about men like this? And what kind of men would attack her like this? In broad daylight?

This sounded like a job to him.

When something happens on the street, the people know. They may not have the full details, you might have to put together a lot of pieces, and there might be a lot of bullshit tossed in, but the information is there.

Who do you ask? Depends on what you want to find out about. How do you approach them? Depends on who they are.

$$\star \quad \star \quad \star$$

Lenny Acevedo was an asshole. He had started working the muscle game about ten years earlier, but the only talent he brought to the job was his willingness to do the dirtiest work. He had hurt children, grandparents, and he had raped women. He collected his fees for all this.

When Ray first knew him, Lenny was a coke fiend who somehow kept his shit together well enough to get the jobs done. He had even worked for Fat Tommy just like Ray. Now he had stepped up to crack and, from what Ray knew, he was getting sloppier – hiring the cheapest subcontractors – and getting less work. He supplemented by stealing.

He used to hang out in Sal's Bar, but they'd been burned out years ago. By Ray, actually. They'd done something to dis Fat Tommy, and Ray got the call. The deed was done late at night – no one got hurt; Sal got an insurance check and moved to Florida. Now Lenny hung out at Tino's. This place had more lighting and fewer fistfights but the usual backroom business.

Lenny was at the bar hunched over a drink when Ray came in. He was holding on to the glass on the counter and staring down into the drink like it might escape if he didn't pay attention. Good time to stick him if someone wanted him dead.

Ray clapped him on the shoulder as he took the stool next to him, and Lenny nearly jumped out of his chair.

"Do I know you?" he asked. Ray guessed that was his way of giving himself time to think his way out of trouble, but if he was waiting for his brain to help him out of a jam, it might be a while.

"I think you do know me," Ray said. He pointed to his nose. Ray had broken Lenny's for him about four years earlier.

The bartender came over.

"Just a water," Ray told him. He didn't look happy to be pouring it, but Ray tossed a five in his direction and that made things better.

Lenny stayed quiet and sipped at his drink. He was hoping Ray'd go away. That maybe this was a coincidental reunion. Ray, of course, didn't have any other plans for the night.

"I need a little information," Ray said.

"Buy a dictionary," Lenny answered, then he laughed into his drink.

There was a strong urge to pull out the blackjack and slap Lenny with it, maybe a few times. If it had been Sal's Bar from way back, Ray probably would have, but he didn't know Tino – hell, he wasn't even sure if there was a real person named Tino. Don't start trouble in a place you don't know.

"Look, Lenny, I didn't say I wanted free info. I'll pay," he said. He pulled out five hundred-dollar bills. That perked Lenny up a little.

"What kind of information?" he asked.

"A woman was beaten, maybe even raped, about three or four this afternoon."

"What's her name?"

"None of your business."

"Okay, any idea where this happened?"

Ray figured it was probably closer to where she worked than where he lived. He told him.

"Probably the Hunt's Point area."

Lenny rolled his eyes. If a bad thing was going to happen to someone, Hunt's Point was a likely spot for it.

"Anything else you can tell me?"

"It was more than one guy."

Lenny took a drink. Seemed to Ray to be running things through his mind. Maybe he was. Maybe he was just thinking about how high he could get on five hundred dollars.

"Is she connected in any way?" he asked.

"Like the mob? Gangs? No. Definitely not."

Lenny shrugged and finished his drink. It was like he was warming up to detective work and had hoped that there was a connection he could trace to make his job easy.

"I know a few people in Hunt's Point. Leave the money. I'll make a few phone calls."

"Bring me something I can use," Ray told him. He put the hundreds he'd pulled out on the counter and showed Lenny several others.

Lenny got up to go, but he turned to Ray.

"This client you're working for? They got fat wallets?"

"They got enough to put me on their side."

"But they don't know who set them up?"

"You ask a lot of questions, man. Let's just say, I'm looking for all the info I can get before I go to work on these guys."

Lenny looked back at his empty glass and then back at Ray. "I thought you got out of the racket. Retired," he said.

"I got bills to pay," Ray told him, then he left.

★   ★   ★

Talking with Lenny helped clear Ray's head, not a common side effect of meeting Lenny. Figuring out what he wanted to tell him and what he didn't want to tell him helped Ray sift through what the whole thing looked like to him.

Elena wasn't directly involved with anyone in what the newspapers correctly called the Underworld. Ray'd spent decades in that world, and it was exactly like the land of the dead as far as he was concerned – nobody had a heart that still beat, nobody had a connection to life. Hollow eyes and souls everywhere.

Elena had never been involved with any of that, but her father was. Or had been. But even when he had racked his brains, he couldn't think of a single person in the life who would come at him through her. Besides, he'd gotten out when Maria went sick three years earlier. And except for himself, everyone he knew of in her life was on the straight and narrow and had always been that way.

Then there was the issue of *where* she'd been attacked. Not near his house. Ray lived in a quiet neighborhood. The Hunt's Point area was about a mile away, but not so quiet. Apartment buildings – low rent to reflect the care the landlords were willing to put into them – on one side and factories and warehouses on the other.

In the Sixties and Seventies the police from the 43rd had gotten into so many shootouts and altercations with the citizens – there'd been so many murders and assaults – that the precinct was referred to for a long time as 'Fort Apache'. Then in the 1980s the buildings around the precinct had been demolished and the lots left vacant because no one wanted to spend a dime building in the neighborhood, not even the city, that the community referred to it as 'Little House on the Prairie'. In some areas of the neighborhood, crime had gone down, but mostly because no one lived in those spots. If they did, they kept safe by staying indoors after dark.

Still, there were abandoned buildings, acres of lots filled with rubble and rusting cars, and streets so desolate that you could commit any sin in the middle of them – twice – and no one would know. Even if they did, they wouldn't care.

Those desolate streets were the best place for dealers and prostitutes, but Ray had been to Elena's job before. It was in the best part of Hunt's Point, near the six train. Not great, but no place for an attack between the door of her office and the steps leading down into the subway.

This bothered him. She would have had to have gone out of her way to find a spot secluded enough for someone to attack her. Was that what she had done? Why?

*   *   *

Ray drove by Hunt's Point knowing full well it wasn't going to tell him anything. He went past the law office. It was a small place with some signs in the window. The gate had been rolled across and the lights were off.

There were people in the street – a couple of homeless guys, a couple of prostitutes, a pair of young lovers walking hand in hand. Closer to the train station, there was another couple arguing loudly – sharing with everyone.

He parked and walked from her office to the train station. Not a single spot to do anything that took longer than a few seconds, not at four in the afternoon, at least.

He was about to go down into the subway, but he knew that station well enough. There was a live token booth clerk, there were cameras, and there were crowds at that hour.

He wandered the area for a little longer. Wandering didn't bring him any insight; it just got him tired and cold. He wound up back in front of the law offices where Elena worked. He put his hand on the gate and stared inside. If a cop had come by, he'd think Ray was planning to break in.

He gave the gate a shake. He tried to think of a way he could blame the people who worked there – they should have walked her to the subway, or given her more work to do so she'd have come out later – but nothing he could think of satisfied him.

Somewhere in the city, there were guilty people. That much he was sure of. And he'd make them pay – that also was written in stone.

*   *   *

He sat in his car in front of his daughter's apartment building, watching. The lights in her apartment were on until late – past midnight. The radio told him it was in the single digits outside. Inside the car, it wasn't much better. Ray had sat waiting for people on a lot of jobs. He'd gone through worse.

He planned to sit outside and protect her from there. If anyone suspicious came along, he'd be right there to deal with them. But at one in the morning a guy went into the building – a young guy, maybe twenty, wearing nice clothes, probably coming back from a club. A little after two in the morning, a couple of women went in together, also well dressed, laughing with each other, maybe a little tipsy. At three a guy came out wearing blue coveralls with grease stains. He rubbed his hands as soon as he came out and looked up and down the street. He spotted Ray, strode over to a beat-up Datsun and drove off. A half hour later Ray began to nod off. He put his car in gear and drove home. The guys who had done this to his little girl weren't stupid enough to try something in her own apartment building, and he had a big day in front of him.

CHAPTER FOUR

Lenny Acevedo waited outside the office, sitting in the chair the secretary had pointed out to him, biting at the flesh around his right thumbnail and spitting out bits. His right leg jogged in place. The secretary tried to ignore him, but it was hard when he sighed.

"Did you tell him it was important?" Lenny asked.

"Sir, you heard me announce you. I told him exactly what you said. It's only been three minutes."

Lenny nodded like what the secretary had to say was going to calm him. Finally, the secretary's phone rang once, she picked up, said "Yes," and turned to him.

"You can go in now."

Lenny sprang out of his seat, but he calmed and strode to the office door like he was already bored of the meeting he had been waiting for. He closed the door behind him.

"We got a problem," he announced when he'd crossed half the room.

The office was large. Five paces to get to the first piece of furniture – a pair of leather-back chairs for people to sit in and face a giant desk – mahogany maybe. Meister sat behind the desk, his jacket off, leaning back. There was a smile on his face, but it was frozen on.

"What problem? I saw the picture of the work your guys did. Looked fine to me."

"She hired someone to look into this…thing."

"What?"

"She hired someone to—"

"I heard you. She didn't go to the police? She hired someone? Who? A lawyer? Private detective?"

"No, no. Nothing like that. I don't know how she did it, but she got hold of a guy who used to work muscle back in the day, Ray Cruz."

"And you know this because...?"

"He came to talk to me. Laid down a few hundred. I think she's got a stash though, and I wouldn't doubt she's ready to lay down a few thousand to get at the guy who set her up."

"But she knows I sent those guys, right?"

Lenny shrugged. "I guess so."

"What do you mean, you guess? The whole attack was about sending her a message. Did you do it or not?"

"Yeah, of course we did," Lenny said.

Meister leaned back in his chair a little.

In truth, Lenny wasn't positive the guys he hired told her anything. He stayed out of the alleyway, acting as a lookout.

"She got hit in the head a lot," Lenny said. "Maybe she forgot."

"Hope not," Meister said. "Was that all you wanted to tell me – I should be on the lookout for this loser, Ray?"

Lenny nodded, but he didn't rise from his seat.

"The thing of it is, I don't know Ray Cruz all that well, but I know he's smart and he's nasty. I worked protection years ago for this guy, Billy, and Ray...."

Lenny trailed off there. The smile that had crept onto his face evaporated. Meister leaned forward in his seat. Lenny might not be interested in telling the story, but Meister wanted to hear it.

"What?" the man asked. "What did Ray do?"

"I hid Billy. In New Jersey. But Ray, he asked the right people the right questions. He found out. I think he paid a cop. Anyway, he got to Billy."

"And?"

"He killed him. Broke my nose and my wrist too."

Lenny hung his head and touched his nose.

"Well, this Billy didn't sound so smart. If I had to run, I sure as hell wouldn't go to Jersey. Cold as it is outside, I'd head for Hawaii."

Meister leaned back and smiled again. Tossed his hands up in the air as though to say this was a simple puzzle to figure out and Billy must have been an idiot to get himself killed.

Lenny tried to smile too.

"What?" Meister asked.

"Nothing."

"What?"

"Just remembering Billy. Ray made an example out of him – beat him with a pipe. Broke his neck with that pipe."

Meister leaned forward again, thinking. A hand went up to his own neck.

"You find this guy and get him to back off. This Billy guy was an idiot. Ray paid a cop? Well, I already beat him to it. I got a few cops of my own that wouldn't mind a little extra cash. Get this Ray off my case. Hell, I'll even pay him more than he's getting from that bitch. I don't give a damn how much she's paying him."

Lenny thought about it a moment. Sounded good to him.

"Ray Cruz," Lenny said. "He's probably going to be over where the girl works – you know, talk to people in the neighborhood, shit like that."

"You said his name is Cruz, right?" Meister asked. "That was her name before she got married." He sat back again. There was trouble on his face, but Lenny didn't want it to be there. He didn't want Ray working this job for personal reasons. He didn't want this girl to be his daughter.

"Still," the man said, "Cruz is a pretty common name for you Spanish people, no?"

Lenny thought about that a moment, then he smiled and nodded, but the smile was weak and the nod was barely visible – almost like he was thinking about something else entirely. Like how to leave New York if things turned out as bad as he thought they might.

★　　★　　★

For Elena, the night had been horrible. She wanted sleep, but every movement woke her with pains and each waking moment reminded her of misery. She thought, somewhere near four in the morning, that it wouldn't be a sin to go to the kitchen, find the half bottle of wine in the refrigerator, and drink it down. Not a sin, but not a long-term cure, and when she awoke, it would be to a ringing hangover to go with the mild concussion Dr. Rosen had diagnosed for her already. So every time she woke up, she counted the minutes off on the display of her bedside alarm clock until she drifted again.

She was out of bed before the clock rang and in the kitchen before William got out of bed.

"What are you doing?" he asked. It should have been obvious. Eggs were frying on the stove.

"Making breakfast," she answered.

"But…" he started. He didn't have a plan for what to say next. He wanted her back in bed, resting, but he assumed that wasn't about to happen.

She turned to him and made sure he gave his full attention.

"I'm still her mother. I'm still your wife," she said. Then she turned back to the eggs.

"Go get yourself ready. And dress Rosita."

William wanted to hug and kiss her and let her know everything would be all right, but he nodded his way out of the room.

By the time William got Rosita ready for breakfast, the food was on the table, and Elena was back in bed, the bedroom door shut. She didn't want Rosita to see her. Not yet. Not with the bruises she carried. Not right before heading to school.

★　★　★

Ray came over to see Elena for a few minutes. He entered the bedroom. She smiled at him. It was weak, but there weren't any tears.

"You look like a wreck," he told her. One of her eyes had fully closed and the bruises from the night before had only grown and become darker.

Elena almost laughed at the comment, but caught herself. The laugh would have hurt her ribs.

"You should see the other guy," she said. There was a smile on her face.

"Yeah?"

Elena nodded.

"I got in a few punches like you taught me."

She threw a soft jab into the air.

Ray smiled. When she was little, he'd taught her how to snap out a jab using his upper arms as punching bags. He knew the strength she had.

"And I landed a kick to the groin. Knocked him to his knees. Like you taught me."

Elena's smile faded, and Ray's smile melted.

"The fight went downhill from there," she said.

Ray held her hand in silence for a moment.

"Listen. I'm going to do something for you," Ray started. He wanted to tell her about his plans for talking to as many hoodlums and whores as it took to find out who had done this to her and about what he planned to do with the information. He wanted to say that in a few days' time he'd have killed everyone involved with the attack on her and that she wouldn't have to fear anything ever again.

The look on her face told him she was afraid of what he might do.

"I'm gonna get you some plane tickets. Send you off to Puerto Rico for a few days. You, Willie, Rosita. Maybe a couple of weeks at your grandmother's house."

Ray's mother was dead, but Maria's mother had a farm in Puerto Rico, and Elena had spent many summer weeks there while growing up.

"*Abuela* hates you," Elena reminded him.

"So? She loves you. I didn't say I'd go."

"I can't go like this," Elena said.

Ray nodded. He understood. Elena didn't want people on the island to know what had happened. He didn't want them to know either. It wasn't that there was anything to be ashamed about, but who wanted to have to repeat the story over and over?

"I'll book a hotel in San Juan. Your *abuela* will never know you were even on the island."

Elena reminded him of Rosita's need for schooling, William's job, her own responsibilities.

"Nothing is going to fall apart because you take a few days off. Rosita's as smart as any kid. She'll catch up. *Es mas*, a week off might give the other kids a chance to catch up to her."

"And William?"

Ray didn't know what William did for a living. Couldn't imagine him being effective at anything. He shrugged.

"I'm sure he can take a few days. This isn't a normal circumstance," Ray said. "I'll get some flexible tickets, you guys will leave in a couple of days if everything can be worked out. You'll relax, get some sun, get out of this winter bullshit we got here in the city. You'll feel like a million dollars."

Elena sighed. He had almost worn her down.

"And while you're away, I can clear things up over here," Ray said.

Elena knew what he meant and sighed again.

★   ★   ★

Elena did not go to work. Willie and Ray both thought this was a good thing. Rosita was told that her mother was very sick – contagious. Couldn't see her – shouted out her goodbyes that morning through the bedroom door. Ray stayed while Willie took Rosita to the school bus stop. Kissed Elena goodbye when Willie returned.

Elena staying home was the only difference. She still wouldn't say a word about what had happened to her or why.

"I can't speak about it," she said. "I want to tell you everything

I know. Those guys that beat me? I'd love for you to visit them and straighten them out. I want to fight back."

"Just give me their names," Ray said.

"I've seen them around before. I don't know everyone's names."

"But you know some names, right?"

"Yes."

"But you won't tell me?"

"Not yet," she said.

"Maybe soon?"

She nodded.

The desire to speak, to accept the defense her father was offering, was great. She wasn't defeated by the attack, though it almost extinguished her soul. She wanted to fight back. Nothing would have made her happier than to talk to Ray all about the man who had sent them, but that wasn't going to be possible.

There was Rosita to consider. Also, she knew her father wasn't the type to get his revenge in some subtle way. He'd get caught, wind up on death row, and it would be her fault. She would endure, keep her mouth shut.

And she didn't want to know what Willie would do with the knowledge she had stored in her heart. What if he merely shrugged? Or told her she should have fought back harder?

Silence was best; necessary even, because if everything came out, the reasons why she had been abused in this way, she'd wind up having to talk with the police and what she had to say might just get her locked up. Even that threat didn't scare her.

Meister probably thought he had accomplished something with the attack he ordered. Little did he know.

★　　★　　★

When Detective Carver came around again for a second try at prying information from her, Elena didn't even bother to see him. Willie had taken a few hours in the morning off from work and spoke to the detective at the front door, not letting him in even when asked.

"I just figured that if I could get a timeline started – I know when she was in the hospital, but if I had a better idea about when, exactly, she was attacked and where this happened, I might be able to put together a few pieces of the puzzle without having to bother her for things like a description."

"She still doesn't want to talk with you," Willie said.

"Okay, but that's the beauty of it. She doesn't have to. She could just talk with you, then you could tell me what you find out. She never has to talk to me at all."

"Well, she hasn't told me anything like what you're asking."

Detective Carver rubbed his forehead. He completely understood Elena's desire to keep a low profile – if he were a victim, he wouldn't want to talk about it, but then he wouldn't need to talk about it with anyone to make sure the bastard paid.

"Any chance she'd come down to the station house, take a look at some mugshots?" Carver tried.

Willie pursed his lips and shook his head. "Not today," he said. "She needs to rest."

Detective Carver tossed his hands up and surrendered.

"I'll be back tomorrow unless the precinct gets something else for me to track."

Willie shrugged. Carver could come back as often as he wanted, but if Elena didn't want to see him, that was it.

Carver left, sighing.

*   *   *

Later, when Detective Carver had left, Willie prepared to go to work.

"You'll be okay?" he asked Elena.

"Go," she told him. She didn't want to be the object of pity and there was a chance she could finally get a few hours of sleep.

Willie left the apartment building and didn't notice the two men in suits sitting in a car parked across the street and a few dozen yards away. They watched as he left.

"Is that everyone?" Meister asked.

"Father, daughter, husband. That detective. Should be about it. She might have a friend over, but I doubt it. She's pretty private."

Meister nodded. "Then get up there," he said.

The younger man exhaled. Then he got out of the car and made his way up to Elena's apartment.

The doorbell rang, and Elena got up to answer it, almost happy for the interruption. Sleep was staying away from her, frustrating her.

"Who is it?" she asked through the door.

"Mark Langan," he announced quietly. He didn't need the entire apartment building hearing his name.

The door didn't open immediately and Elena didn't say anything. Langan tried again.

"I know what happened yesterday," he said. This, also, was quiet. The door still didn't open. "We need to talk about it, Elena."

Langan looked around. There was the sound of someone's television coming from somewhere on the floor. He hoped it was enough noise to mask what he had to say.

"Elena. Look. Worse things can happen to you. Your family," Langan said. The lock came undone.

★ ★ ★

Ray went to the law office where his daughter worked, and walked past it. It was a bustling place – the lawyers were the best dressed, he figured, then the secretaries or paralegals. Maybe fifteen or twenty people went in and took up positions or went straight to offices in the morning. Ray wanted nothing more than to go in, speak to whoever was Elena's boss and ask some simple and direct questions – did Elena have enemies on the job, among the clients? Had anyone threatened her? Had there been any psychos hanging around the office or outside of it? Had anyone noticed anything that might give him a clue as to who had done terrible things to his daughter?

But how could he ask any of this if Elena had called in with bronchitis?

Besides, he didn't think a bunch of lawyers would want to talk to him, if only because they wouldn't want to open themselves up to accusations of negligence.

Still, Ray thought, Elena had fought back. He saw the scabs on her knuckles – if some guy tried to stroll in with bruises to his face, Ray would drag him out and get some answers. He didn't think any of the lawyers had done this, but he didn't know that for sure.

Plus, there was a chance that if a couple of thugs were hired to do this to his daughter, they might come in to pick up their payment. Of course, he didn't think lawyers normally met with the thugs they hired in their offices, but it was possible.

He tried to think of some story he could tell to get himself inside the offices and within reach of answers. Nothing came to mind, just like it hadn't come to mind all the previous night.

He was about ready to give up on the idea of talking to the lawyers – there were plenty of dope dealers and streetwalkers for him to interview. He stood a few doors down from the law office, staring at it like it might speak to him.

"Cruz," Detective Carver said, nice and loud, clapping him on the right shoulder. "What the hell are you doing here?"

"Just standing," Ray answered.

"Ah, well, no law against that, right? Unless you're thinking about going in to talk to one of the lawyers in there. You weren't going to do something stupid like that, were you, Cruz?"

Ray didn't say a word.

"Good, because I just came from your daughter's apartment. She seems to want to bury this whole thing, leave it in her past. Now, I'm going to pursue it – I normally work homicides, but it's been slow the last couple of weeks. If you start stepping on the toes of people I need to speak to, we're going to have troubles, you understand me?"

Ray nodded.

"Good. Now I'm going in there, and I'm going to ask some questions, and when I come out, I don't want to see you loitering. Got it? Good."

Carver strode over to the law office and entered, his black trench coat flowing out behind him. He never looked back.

★   ★   ★

Carlos Alvaro, Lisa Soto, Charlie Pilar, and Carmen Escobar all owned legitimate businesses in the area between Elena's job and the train station she would have headed to if she were going home. Ray talked with each of them, asked them to find out what they could, left them each a couple of hundred dollars, but none of them had anything to say that could help him.

From those legitimate business owners, he moved on to speaking with dope dealers and streetwalkers, but for three solid hours and a thousand dollars, he got nothing. Nobody knew anything. Nothing had been heard the evening before.

Tired, disgusted with himself, he went into a diner for a late lunch. The waitress looked as tired as he felt.

"Bacon cheeseburger," he ordered.

"How do you want it?"

"Huh?"

"How do you want it?"

"On a plate," Ray said. The waitress rolled her eyes.

"I mean do you want it well done? Medium? Bloody?"

"Well," Ray answered, and as soon as the waitress turned away from him, a thought came to mind and he left the diner as fast as his aching feet would carry him.

"Blood," he said out loud once he was on the street. "She was bleeding."

Elena must have bled a trail, he thought. It would show how she got to his apartment. If he traced it back, it would lead him to where she was attacked.

Ray walked the sidewalk outside his apartment building a dozen times before he noticed a drop of blood. She had come at his building from the south – the direction she'd have traveled if she came from work. Finding a second drop of blood was as hard as finding the first, but it got easier as the afternoon wore down to a nub and the temperature dropped.

With three-quarters-of-a-mile worth of blood drops and smears on the walls, he was in front of the office where she worked. He looked through the glass of the front window. A receptionist looked back at him, and he moved on, thinking it was only a matter of a few seconds before she got spooked at him and called somebody, maybe the police.

Elena could not possibly have been attacked in the office. At the time she was attacked, the place would have been crawling with lawyers and clients. He walked slowly past the law office, trying to think things through. He stopped a couple of doors down.

To hell with it, he thought. *I got the gun – if I want answers from them, I can get them.*

He turned and was about to head back to the law office, pull out the revolver and start asking questions. If someone needed shooting, he'd provide that service. A smudge caught his eye.

The store he stood in front of, a *cuchifrito* selling fried everything, had a palm print of blood on the window in front of the *alcapurrias*. He walked a little farther, found more drops. Three doors down from the end of the block the drops led into an alleyway. From the head of the alley he could see piles of garbage bags and two five-yard bins.

The blood ended in front of a steel door with a single light bulb above it and a sign tacked onto it – *KEEP OUT*. There was blood on a spot of the brick walls. There was long dark hair mixed in with the blood on the bricks. Ray understood precisely everything.

The bastards who did this got Elena into the alley somehow, shoved her into this wall, they did what they did to her, then they left her. The owners of the place probably had no idea what had happened. Maybe they didn't notice the blood and hair. Maybe they did. In a neighborhood like this you'd only call the cops if there was something valuable missing, maybe not even then.

Ray went back around to the front. It was a restaurant serving Spanish food – rice, beans, pork chops. It wouldn't be busy for another couple of hours, when work let out for most people at five. Ray went up to a counter where four waitresses in white blouses and skintight black pants were talking. One of them broke conversation and took a step toward him.

"I'm looking for the manager," Ray said.

"He's not here," she said. "Can I help you?" Worry was swallowing her face whole.

"I know you have security cameras for the front of the store. I need to see the videos for yesterday."

Her face registered the strangeness of his request.

"There's no videos," she said. "Just a storage room."

"But I need to see."

"Why?" She looked like she was half inclined to lead him to the back. The other half of her probably wanted to call the other waitresses over for advice.

Ray pulled a wad of cash from his pocket and peeled off a hundred-dollar bill. She reached out and took it from him and gave a glance over at the other waitresses. They weren't paying attention.

"And I'll give you another one when I'm finished seeing the video," he said.

"There's no video. Cameras only for show."

"Fine, just let me see the back rooms."

He followed the waitress down a corridor, through a storage room and past a small office with a desk and a chair. The tour ended at a room with a heavy door. The padlock on it was hooked through its latch, but not done up. It would be the room closest to the alleyway. Ray hoped it would have a video recorder.

The room was maybe fifteen feet long but only six feet wide. The walls were down to the studs and there were a dozen pieces of Sheetrock leaning up against the right-hand wall. There were a few pieces of lumber and a couple of five-gallon cans of joint compound. There were buckets with tools, and there was dust over everything.

"Wait here," Ray told the young lady who'd led him. He walked into the room alone.

There wasn't much to learn from seeing the room where he had hoped there would be video recordings. Nothing to tell him who had done it or why.

He took a last look around and held out another hundred-dollar bill.

"You guys hear anything going on in the alley yesterday, maybe three-thirty?"

The girl shrugged and shook her head. "There was a lot of music on yesterday. Anyway, sometimes the workers are working here all day and we don't hear anything up front."

She took the hundred, folded it up and tucked it away. She smiled at him and for a moment she reminded him of Elena from a few days earlier and before tragedy. He wanted to caress her face but checked himself and walked out.

Darkness had fallen on the city and a snow was starting. He stuffed his hands into his jacket pockets and walked home.

*　　*　　*

Later that evening, Ray, tired as he was, went over to see his daughter. He had no plans to share with her what he had found. Maybe there was a connection between the restaurant and the attack that Elena could make clear to him, but he knew she wouldn't want to talk about that. He'd figure it out for himself. For now, it was enough to be near her.

Elena and Willie were having one of their low-key arguments. The ones that simmer but never boil. Probably the best type of argument to have with Rosita asleep in her room. Ray felt the tension in the way Willie answered the door. Ray didn't know what it was about, and he wasn't sure what to do to end it. Ideas came to him, but nothing Elena would approve of. Whatever the fight was about, his presence calmed things. Not the usual effect for him.

He sat on the sofa near his daughter. She was in a bathrobe and had her legs up, her knees almost at her chest. It didn't look like a comfortable pose. She looked sleepy.

If the TV had been on, Ray would have been happy to watch anything, but it wasn't and he felt like a fool sitting between husband and wife in the silence.

"How was your day?" Ray asked Willie. It wasn't much of a conversation starter, but he didn't feel he deserved to have the question ignored. Willie felt differently.

Ray ignored Willie back.

"You feeling better, *mi'ja?*" He turned his back on his son-in-law and focused on Elena.

She shrugged.

"The police were here. Right after you left," Willie threw in.

Ray glanced over at Willie then back to Elena.

"They bother you?"

She started crying and used the sleeve of her bathrobe to wipe tears away. Ray reached out and put a hand softly on her knee. He didn't want to make things worse, but couldn't keep himself from touching her.

She shook her head. She wanted to tell about the other visit, the one from Mark Langan, but she knew that if telling about the guys who had actually hurt her was bad, then talking about Mark Langan and how she was involved with him, working for him, was even worse.

She shook her head again – cleared her mind. She wiped her eyes and her nose and stood, putting her feet into slippers.

"Where are you going?" Willie asked.

Elena pulled herself up to her full height.

"I'm going to get a glass of wine," she said. Her voice was slurred a little.

Ray could tell she was not sleepy, just a little on the drunk side.

"That's your fourth," Willie said. The edge in his voice clued Ray in. This had been the source of tension.

Elena pointed at her husband, jabbed her finger like she was aiming to take out one of his eyes.

"I have been beaten. I have had to hide myself from my daughter because I look like this. Like this." She pointed to her face and its bruises. "I'll drink a fourth glass, a fifth glass, and anything else the hell I want," she hissed. Then she turned for the kitchen.

Willie started to get out of his seat, but Ray reached across and put a hand on his knee.

"What?" Willie asked.

"Let her have her drink," Ray said.

"So this thing can turn her into a drunk?" Willie asked.

Ray nodded.

"One bender doesn't make a drunk," he said.

"Oh yeah? How many does it take?" Willie said. He started to get up again.

"Three. Look. She needs to get through today and tomorrow and the next day," Ray said. "Whatever it takes to get her through. Let her have her drink. Let her sleep it off. The headache in the morning will keep her from doing it again."

Willie wasn't sure he agreed, but it didn't matter much anyway. By the time he got to the kitchen, Elena was mostly done with her wine. A short while later, she was tipsy and ready for sleep. Ray saw her into bed and prepared to leave.

"Look," he told Willie at the door, "I'll see if I can talk to this detective, get him to ease up on her. Maybe if he doesn't come around for a few more days, she'll get a chance to relax a bit. Heal."

"That detective doesn't like you, Ray. Don't do us any favors," Willie said. The two men looked at each other for a second, then Willie closed the door.

CHAPTER FIVE

At a little past five in the morning, Ray stood in front of his bathroom medicine cabinet, staring at himself in the mirror. He'd gotten about an hour and a half of sleep. The rest had just been tossing and turning and aching to be doing something. He got up exhausted, but there was no point in staying in bed anymore. There wasn't a point to staying in the apartment at all. His daughter had sat in the living room after the attack, showered in the bathtub. The whole place gave him the worst memories.

In his sleepiness he thought for a moment about counting the scars on his face, but he stopped himself.

"Self-indulgent bullshit," he whispered.

Besides, there was work to do.

Finding out about the men who had beaten his daughter meant scraping the bottom of the barrel, and he hadn't heard the scrape yet. He hadn't yet talked to Israel Mendoza.

★   ★   ★

Along one stretch of Bruckner Boulevard there were three shops in a row that offered to fix or replace auto glass, headlights and side-view mirrors. They'd also fix flats if they had the stock or charge your battery – but glass was their bread and butter. Each of the shops had, for a long time, been owned by one man – Samuel Ortiz.

Sammy had been wiry and greasy – always dirty and in torn clothes, though Ray had done some petty jobs for him and knew he had money. He sold and installed car parts, and when business slowed, he hired some homeless guy or drug addict to go around the neighborhood and smash lights and windshields in the night. The next morning, he'd have a line of people looking for parts. He got a piece of just about every car stolen within five miles of his shops, and in the South Bronx, that was a lot of cars. He usually sat on a high stool in front of Sammy's Fixit and counted money.

Israel Mendoza was one of the drug addicts Sammy hired. He was the best of the bunch. Most drug addicts would smash windshields all in a row – ten or twenty cars all on one block. That got the police involved, and though there was no way they could tie the broken glass back to Sammy, that didn't stop them from hassling him – not something he needed. Israel – Israh to his friends – was more inventive, smashing a window on one block, cracking a taillight a block over, wandering the neighborhood and getting the results without the police ever being called.

Of course, Israh had other jobs around the neighborhood – delivering packages he wasn't supposed to open or scaring little old ladies into moving out of their apartments, things like that. These odd jobs kept him in the know.

Ray walked to Sammy's Fixit, his hands buried in his jacket pockets, his head down against a cold wind. Sammy wasn't out front. Instead, there was a young man just inside the garage. He was tall and thin, and his hair was almost to shoulder length. He had a clipboard and perked up when Ray walked in. The name patch on his coveralls said he was *SAMMY JR*.

"Your father around?" Ray asked.

"He died."

"Sorry to hear that," Ray said. He hadn't actually spoken to Sammy Senior in a few years. Wasn't really all that sorry. Still, the news was a little bit of a conversation stopper.

"Is there something I can help you with? Need auto glass?" Sammy Junior smiled.

"No. I'm looking for a guy that used to work here – Israel Mendoza."

The smile on Sammy Junior's face melted away.

"Why?" Sammy Junior asked.

"Well, that's between me and Izzy," Ray said. He pulled a hand out of his jacket pocket and tossed it palm up as though Sammy Junior should be able to see that this was none of his business.

Sammy Junior folded his arms across his chest, clipboard still in hand.

"Well, Israel works for me. He's working for me right now, so if you want to talk to him about personal stuff, maybe you should come back during his lunchtime."

The muscles in Sammy Junior's face were working overtime – twitchy almost. He didn't want to, but Ray smiled at the young man. Clearly, he wasn't used to talking tough. The smile didn't make things any better.

"Maybe you should leave now," Sammy Junior said. He unfolded his arms and pointed at Ray with the clipboard. Ray thought about slapping the clipboard to the ground, but restrained himself. Sammy Junior wasn't the one who would need slapping around.

"Look, mister," Ray started.

Just then Israel Mendoza came walking into the garage with a bag of McDonald's food in one hand and a tall soda in the other. He wasn't wearing headphones, but was humming to himself anyway and had his head down. Something made him look up and whatever happiness was on his face fell off of it.

"Oh shit," he said. He dropped the bag and the soda and turned around at a run. Ray went after him.

Because of all the trucks that came by to drop things off, the sidewalk in that area was cracked, crumbled and in some spots nonexistent. It took Israel Mendoza ten steps to stumble. Ray caught up and pushed him, knocking him to the ground.

"No, no, no, no, no," Israel kept repeating like it might help keep Ray from hurting him. He huddled his arms to his chest and Ray pried the right arm away from Israel's chest and forced it straight. Then he gave it a little twist.

"Ow, ow, ow."

"You shouldn't have run, Izzy. I just want a little information."

"I don't know anything. Swear to god."

"I'm gonna call the cops on you," Sammy Junior said. He was standing a few feet behind Ray as Ray pulled Israel off the pavement by the twisted arm.

"Don't do that," Ray said. "Me and Izzy just need to talk for a few minutes."

"Call the cops, Mr. Ortiz," Israel shouted. Ray twisted his arm some more.

He dragged Israel back to the garage and looked around.

"Hey, Izzy. Remember that vise Sammy used to have bolted down on a table? Where is that? Oh, and that blowtorch. You want to tell me?"

"I didn't do nothing," Israel said over and over again. His legs gave way under him and Ray wound up holding the entire man's weight by the twisted arm.

"You remember the last time, Izzy? You took something from Fat Tommy. Opened one of those packages. I really beat the shit out of you then. Oh, and there was an open wrench too. Pretty good for smashing stuff."

"Please, Ray. I...I didn't do anything. Swear to god. I don't know anything about anything. I didn't take anything. I...I...I just work here. Mr. Ortiz...."

Sammy Junior had gone into a tiny cubicle he called his office at the far end of the garage and was on the phone with an emergency operator.

"Put that phone down!" Ray shouted, and with his free hand he pulled a revolver out of his jacket pocket. Sammy saw the gun over the cubicle partition. It was aimed at him. He put the receiver back on its cradle and ran his fingers through his hair.

For the moment things in the garage were quiet – Israel even stopped whimpering.

"Good," Ray said. "Now, ever since Sammy died, I don't know where everything is here – the vise, the torch, things like that. Still, I came prepared for this conversation."

He waved the gun.

"Now. Everyone stay calm. That way only Izzy gets hurt. Understand?"

Sammy Junior had his hands in the air as though this were a robbery. For all he knew, it was.

"Okay then. Now, Izzy, you ever play 'Twenty questions'?"

Israel nodded, but he started to whimper.

"Good. We're going to play something similar. I call it 'Answer my questions or I'll shoot you, you stupid dopehead piece of shit.'"

"I'm clean," Israel said. He was crying now and shaking.

"What?"

"I'm clean and sober," Israel said. He struggled to control his voice. "Clean and sober. More than a year."

Ray rolled his eyes.

"Clean and sober? Good for you. I don't care if you're the next pope. Answer my questions or I'm gonna leave you with very few usable parts. Understand me? Good. Now, a lady got jumped a couple of days ago. Two guys or more – probably muscle. I need to find out who did this and who paid them."

"I don't know," Israel said. His voice had all the tension of knowing this was not the answer the man with the gun wanted.

"Wow. That is such a wrong answer," Ray said. He pulled on Israel's arm and pressed the gun to his wrist. He cocked the hammer with his thumb.

"Wait, wait, wait. I might know someone who knows something."

"So, what are you waiting for?"

"Are you going to hurt her?" Israel asked.

"I don't hurt women."

"Yes, you do," Israel said. There was a puzzled look on his face.

"All right, you caught me. Let's just say, I won't hurt her if she doesn't run."

Israel, his arm extended out in a weird angle, a gun pressed to his wrist, ready to blast his hand off, thought about his answer.

"There's this girl, Marla – she's a black girl. Prostitute. Maybe twenty, really big on top. She works over on Southern Boulevard. She said yesterday that something nasty happened. Woman got attacked by two guys, maybe raped. Said she thought the TV news might come by, but they didn't. Maybe that's who you want to talk to – Marla."

Ray thought about it for a moment.

"You know what happens if I go to Southern Boulevard and I don't find Marla? Or if I find her, but she says you're lying?"

Israel nodded.

"All right then," Ray said, and he let Israel go with a shove.

Ray waved his gun back at Sammy Junior.

"Don't get any bright ideas," he said.

He started to walk out of the garage, then turned back. He pulled four hundreds out of his interior jacket pocket and threw them at Israel's face.

"Go get yourself some crack," he said. Then he left.

Israel let the money fall to the floor, and he didn't rub his wrist or show that he had been hurt in any way. Only when Ray was long gone did he move at all, stooping to pick up the money.

"Asshole," he said.

⋆   ⋆   ⋆

"I know something," she said.

It had taken Ray most of the day to find the woman Israel had told him about.

She told Ray her name was Marla, but that it could be anything he wanted. He was tired, and he imagined she was at least as tired. The sun was an orange smudge low in a cloudy sky. The day was raw, snow falling lightly, but enough to get you wet and freeze you if you stood outside. Most of Marla's job was spent standing outside.

Marla folded the two hundreds Ray handed her.

"Let me just say, I know two dudes did some nasty shit yesterday. I don't know both their names, but one of them is this Dominican guy. His woman is out here sometimes when that dog turns her out for a few tricks."

Marla looked around as though she were looking to see who was in hearing distance or forgetting she was talking with someone. Ray peeled out three more hundreds. He'd hand her all he had if the information was good enough.

Marla took the money, folded it in with the other bills.

"I wasn't holding out for more money," she said. "Just trying to remember what that asshole's name is. His wife's name is Mary. She got a little boy. Her husband, though, she don't call him by his first name. She calls him by his last name. And he got a white SUV with BORI-Q or something on the rear window."

"That makes them a Puerto Rican couple," Ray said. It was more to himself than to Marla, but she answered him anyway.

"Well, whatever. Tomato, tomahto. His name...I know it starts with *V*."

She looked around again then looked up.

"Vasquez?" Ray suggested, trying to jog her memory.

"No. More like Vegas."

"Vega?" Ray asked. This was as close as he'd come to anything resembling a lead. He didn't get the feeling he was being strung along. He'd given her money before asking anything. Marla shook her head.

"Nah, *V* at the beginning, *AS* at the end, but I can't think...."

"Vargas?"

Marla's face lit up with recognition.

"You got it. Anyway. That's his name. That's what she calls him anyway. Her boy's name is Cheetoh, some shit like that. Anyway, that Vargas dude is one mean bastard. Best to stay away from him if you know what I mean. He be out here at three in the morning to pick her up, drag her into his car by the hair, and it's more than one john I seen him bitch slap. Always angry, that guy. Gonna give himself an ulcer."

Ray pulled out another five hundred.

"Any idea where they live?" he asked.

"Nah, not really," Marla answered, putting the bills with the others. "But Mary comes walking and she comes from that direction. Not too many buildings over by that way."

Ray pulled out a few hundred more, didn't count the bills, and handed them to her. She didn't hesitate to take them.

"What's this for?" she asked.

He was already turning away.

"Stay safe, Marla," he tossed over his shoulder.

★   ★   ★

Finding the building Mary Vargas and her little boy, Cheito – nickname for 'Little José' – lived in was easy. Like Marla had said, there weren't too many buildings in the direction Mary walked from. Her apartment was on the sixth floor out of six in a building that was supposed to have a working intercom and a front door that locked to keep out evil.

Ray got the name off the mailboxes in the lobby, climbed to the sixth floor and stood with his ear to the door for a few minutes. Mary said a few things to Cheito in baby talk and sounded happy. Cheito didn't have much to say, and it didn't come through the door clearly, but Ray guessed the boy was a year old or so. He jogged back down the stairs and into the darkness of the night. He had passed a small pharmacy a block or two away.

At the pharmacy, the only thing that looked like it might be an appropriate toy for a small boy was a brown teddy bear that they'd put out for Valentine's Day though it wasn't even Christmas yet. He bought it and pulled off the heart-shaped balloon it was hugging, dumping it in the trash.

"Mrs. Vargas," he called through the door when she asked who it was. "My name is Jay. I know your husband, José."

He had guessed the man had named his son after himself and asked somebody on the second floor to confirm.

"He's not here," she said through the door – nobody's fool.

"Oh, I know. I can wait.... It's important."

He smiled for the peephole but couldn't tell if she was looking at him. From the voice coming through the door, he figured she was a small woman. Maybe not even able to look through the peephole.

"I don't think he'd want you to come in," she said finally.

Ray moved close to the door so he wouldn't have to shout.

"I owe him some money. Please. I need to pay. You...you don't know what he's like when he's angry."

For a full minute there was silence. At last, the dead bolt came undone. Ray knew he could push his way through whatever chain was on the door, but he didn't want to make that kind of scene. There wasn't a big chance anyone would call the cops or even care if they heard a scream coming from Mary, but better not to risk it.

The door opened, the chain still on. Mary was probably a little less than five feet tall and definitely less than a hundred pounds. She had short dark hair and someone had gifted her with a black eye exactly the size of a man's fist and turning purple. There was a cut in her lower lip as well. Obviously, she did know what her husband was like when angry. She put her hand out for what she expected to be an envelope. Ray could have dropped the teddy bear, grabbed her arm and yanked. He could have hurt her until she undid the chain, but there was no point in that.

He offered her the teddy bear.

"A little something for Cheito," Ray said.

What mother could resist? It was too large to go through without undoing the chain. Once the door was opened wider, Ray let himself in. Mary moved out of his way, not knowing how to resist his advance even though he wasn't using any force.

"Can I see the boy?" Ray asked. "I've heard a lot about him."

"Well..." Mary started, but Cheito toddled up to Ray and took hold of his pant leg. Ray took him up into his arms and nuzzled his neck until the boy started laughing and drooling.

Mary closed the door, locked it.

"Can I get you something to drink?" she asked.

Halfhearted hospitality.

"Yes, please," Ray answered. "Maybe a little *café con leche*?"

Mary looked at him, but Ray didn't return the favor. He kept his eyes on the boy.

"Coming right up," Mary said at last. She didn't know how her husband was going to take to her having let some guy into the apartment. She'd have to ask to see proof that this man, Jay, knew her husband. She went into the kitchen to get the coffee ready and pulled a fillet knife from a drawer, kept it close.

"You said you owe José money?" she called out from the kitchen.

"More than two grand, but I finally got it," Ray said. He walked over to the kitchen doorway, spotted the knife on the counter first thing. He was still holding little Cheito with one hand. With his free hand he pulled out a roll of almost thirty hundreds.

"You could just leave it here," Mary tried. "I'll tell him who left it. Tell him you brought Cheito the doll too."

Ray told her he didn't want to impose.

"I just want to make sure everything is even between me and him, you understand?"

Mary nodded.

★   ★   ★

It was two cups of coffee later when José came up the stairs to his apartment; the look on Mary's face changed from worry to fear and Ray knew José was home before he put his key to the lock.

"What the...? Who the...?" José didn't know how to react. There was a man he didn't know sitting at the dining room table with his child sitting on his lap. Mary was also seated. There were cups of coffee on the table like his wife and the man had been sharing the latest neighborhood gossip.

"Hey, just the man I wanted to see," Ray started. He stood, still holding Cheito, Cheito still holding the bear.

"Who the hell are you?" José asked. "Who the hell is this?" He turned to Mary.

"He owes you money," Mary said.

Ray pulled out the wad of cash on cue and spread it out on the table.

"It's all here," Ray said. "Every last penny."

It was a fair amount of money and when someone spreads cash like that out on your kitchen table, it's hard to stay upset. Even if you are upset, it's hard to do anything about it if that someone is holding your son. José kept looking from Ray to Mary and didn't know what to think or do.

"Now," Ray said, getting José's attention. He had his hand back in his jacket pocket. If he had a thick coat on, it would have been impossible for José to be sure whether Ray had a gun in that pocket or was just bluffing. The jacket was thin however, and José knew a handgun was being pointed at his son's belly, tickling him, in fact.

"Now, I think you and I have a bit of talking to do, so I think it's best if we leave Mary and Cheito here and we go out to El Coche maybe, get a bite to eat. What do you think?"

José wasn't sure what to say. He had a gun of his own. It took a few seconds, but he decided that leaving was exactly the right thing to do. As soon as they got down the stairs to the street, he'd turn around and make Ray eat the gun in his pocket. He'd make him sorry.

"Yeah, man," José said. "Whatever. Let's get this show on the road. Don't wait up," he said to Mary as he turned and opened the door.

Ray put Cheito down, kept his hand on the revolver in his jacket pocket, threw a little wave to Mary and the boy and went out.

★   ★   ★

José played along for a flight of stairs, kept his hands away from his sides and in plain sight. The old dude with the gun wasn't gonna do anything to him until he had him someplace quiet. Maybe not even then. A lot of people threaten, but most don't have the balls to do anything. José had the balls. When they got to the last landing, he was going to turn around on this old bastard and smash him in the face. Wouldn't know what hit him. Be on the ground before he even thought about pulling out his gun – if it really was a gun. For all he knew, he was being held hostage by an old guy with a water pistol.

Then he'd pull out his own gun, stick it in this guy's gut and pull the trigger. Nobody would call the police. Nobody would give a shit. This was the Bronx. Happened every day.

★   ★   ★

On the fifth floor there was an apartment with a TV blasting out the theme song to a *Mission: Impossible* repeat.

"José," Ray said as they started the next flight of stairs.

"What?"

"Look at me when I'm talking to you, you little shit."

José turned to face Ray, and Ray slapped him in the jaw with the revolver.

José fell backwards on the stairs, reaching for the handrail to steady himself but missing it. He felt like his face had exploded and didn't even notice landing on his ass on the steps or hitting the back of his head on the tile floor of the landing.

When he opened his eyes a fraction of a second later, Ray had the barrel of the revolver pointed straight at his nose.

"Don't fight me," Ray said. Then he smashed the gun onto the crown of José's head four times, with savagery though the first hit had already drawn blood.

★   ★   ★

The rest of the stairs were a blur. José didn't remember getting out to the street or having his wrists taped together, his ankles taped together or his mouth taped closed with duct tape wound around his head, pulling on a thousand hairs. He didn't remember being dumped on the back seat of a car, but that's where he was when things started to get clear.

Ray was in the driver's seat and looked back at José through the rearview mirror.

"Hey! You're awake," Ray said. "Thought you were going to die on me. You don't know how mad that would have made me. Anyway. You're going to behave, and we're going to talk. You tell me what I need to hear, and this won't be any more painful than it needs to be. *Me entiendes*?"

José started to struggle. He kicked at the door.

"You do that again, and I'll need to stop this car," Ray said. "Believe me, you don't want me to do that."

José did it again. Ray pulled over, put the car in park and pulled out the blackjack he'd been carrying since the night Elena showed up at his door. He got out and opened the door José had kicked.

"Are those steel-toed work boots or just regular ones?" Ray asked. José tried to kick him. "No difference. This is going to hurt."

José tried to kick again, but Ray caught the feet in mid-flight. He held them still – last thing he wanted to do was bring the blackjack down on his own hands. He raised the blackjack over his head, caught José's eyes and the terror in them, and brought the blackjack down with all his might. The pain of the ankle breaking, pulverizing really, knocked José out for the rest of the drive.

★　★　★

Ray drove down Vyse Avenue. The night was black as pitch with snowflakes coming down from out of the darkness. The air was just cold enough for the snow to stick to the windshield. Ray parked and waited, watching José in the rearview mirror. He looked peaceful.

They were parked in front of a stretch of land used by the city of New York as a landfill and a transfer station. They weren't far from the East River – it could be heard in the quiet of the night.

"Time to make the donuts," Ray muttered to himself. He got out of the car, went around to the door of the back seat passenger side. He opened it and leaned over José's face.

"Naptime is over," he said and slapped José's cheeks. The man woke up. Ray pulled the tape partway off José's mouth so he could talk.

"What? Who are you?" José asked. Ray answered him by dragging him out of the car and onto the sidewalk by the collar of his jacket. When José's feet hit the concrete, pain shot through him and he screamed. Ray lifted him a little then threw him down. José's head hit the pavement with a crack.

"Son of a bitch!" José roared. He was angry and tried to raise himself to his knees, but his ankle punished him for the attempt.

Ray squatted next to José and moved close. José tried to lash out, but with his hands behind his back and a leg that wouldn't stop stabbing him with pain, he could only curse.

"You want to keep talking?" Ray asked. "You want to keep talking, that's fine by me. I got all night, I got this blackjack, and I got plenty of patience."

José calmed himself in fits. If Ray had moved in any closer, José would have bitten him.

"Good," Ray said. "Now, I got a few questions. You tell me what I want to hear, you might even make it out of here alive."

"You are so dead," José said. It was the first thing he was able to say calmly. "So dead. You have no idea who I am, mister. I got people."

"Uh-huh. You got people who don't give a shit about you. Even your son is too young to know you, and that wife of yours? You better believe she'd forget you in a second."

"You don't know shit," José said, but the words had lost some of their fire.

"That's why I'm here, José. I want to learn. You understand me?"

Ray turned José onto his side and dragged him a couple of feet, propping him up against a chain-link fence. He held José's chin in his hand and stared into his face. José was unnerved by this.

"What?"

"I heard on the street that you and another guy did something nasty to this woman a couple of days ago. I need to know the name of the other guy," Ray said. His voice was calm – all business.

"I didn't do shit," José said. "You heard wrong, old man."

Ray kept his eyes on José's face and everything he saw there told him José was lying. He'd read faces just as ugly many times before – he knew how the muscles worked in a lie and how they worked in the truth. He knew which way José would turn to look first if he were lying, and that's exactly what José did.

Ray shook his head slowly. "You don't want to do it this way," he said. "I'm going to find out that guy's name even if I have to break every bone in your body to get it."

José was about ready to laugh in the old guy's face, but it didn't come out. Instead, he looked up and down the road. Ray followed his eyes.

"What? You think the police are going to come by and do something to help you? You think Five-O is gonna come down and save your ass from me? Well, I'll tell you that Five-O ain't patrolled this area at night since before you was born. Believe me. They don't give a shit what happens out here. They find bodies in the river or in the dump all the time. Now just tell me what I need to know and we'll be cool."

José looked at Ray, sizing him up.

"I ain't telling you shit," he said. He had somehow made a calculation that Ray wasn't going to hurt him, not badly.

"That's disappointing," Ray said.

He pulled the blackjack out again and dangled it in front of José's face.

"I had this specially made a few years back. It's a foot long, there's a spring in the handle and there's a round piece of iron in the leather here. I broke your right foot with one swing. I'm gonna break your left foot with another swing. You know what happens if I miss your foot and hit the sidewalk instead? No? I'll chip the concrete. Now, don't move."

José looked Ray in the face, and miscalculated.

"I ain't afraid of you," he said. Ray saw the muscles working in the face and knew it was a lie.

"Maybe not," he said. "But this is still gonna hurt like a mother."

He raised the blackjack over his head and brought it down on José's left shin an inch above the rim of the boot.

★   ★   ★

"I didn't want to have to do any of that," Ray said.

He tried to sound sincere. In truth, he hadn't felt much about it one way or the other. He'd broken José's left shinbone, his right kneecap, and absolutely crushed his right shoulder with three quick whips with the blackjack.

"Now, I asked you a question about who you were working with the other day. Let me know and we can finish this."

José had howled when his shin broke, but he hadn't been able to get back enough air to make much more than a loud whimper with the other injuries. He was sputtering. Tears rolled down his cheeks, and drool dangled from his chin. If there was a time when he wasn't afraid of Ray, that time was over, and he had learned his lesson.

"I need to know who you were working with, and I need to know who you were working for."

"I don't know who we were working for. I...I didn't get the job."

"Fine," Ray said. "Just tell me who you were working with. Then this can be over."

José continued crying. Ray waited a minute, then gave José a light tap on the thigh with the blackjack.

"You need a few more smacks?" Ray asked.

"I can't...I can't tell you. He'll kill me."

Ray smiled and shook his head.

"Kill you?" he repeated. "What? You think I'm planning to let you go? Nah, that's not how this is gonna go. Trust me. You're dead already."

José was gasping for air, sobbing uncontrollably. He didn't know if the last swing of the blackjack had broken anything – Ray had surprised him with a smack straight to the gut. It felt like the hit had just about stopped his heart.

"You're gonna tell me what I need to know. Then I'm gonna kill you. The only difference is whether I go back to your apartment and kill your little boy too. Little Cheito. That's it."

José writhed for a moment more. It made Ray roll his eyes. He had beaten one guy – father of a man who owed Fat Tommy money – for hours one morning. Used an iron pipe. The guy hadn't cracked. Never did say where it was his son was hiding. José wasn't that tough.

Ray put the blackjack on the sidewalk and reached into a jacket pocket. He slid out a cheap Bic lighter and squatted next to José again. Pulled at his hair to get his attention.

"I'm an old man. I don't have the energy I used to have. Now. I'm going to ask you one more time. Then I'm going to turn you around and put this lighter to your fingertips. I'm not going to stop until your nails pop off. Then I'll ask you one last time. If you still hold out, I'm going to pop you in the top of the head with the blackjack, throw you into the East River and drive over to your apartment. You understand me?"

José nodded. He'd heard every word.

"Don't hurt my little boy," José said. It came out as only a little more than a whisper. "Don't hurt him. He didn't do nothing."

"Let me tell you something, José. Something before I kill you. That woman you hurt was my daughter. You understand me? She was my daughter, and she didn't do nothing to you either. So, honest to god, I don't give a shit about your kid. Understand me?"

José nodded slowly. He was crying still, but breath was coming easier.

"Good. Now, who were you working with? Where do I

find him?"

"Manny González," José said. "That's it. I never find him. He finds me."

Ray stayed squatting next to José. He wondered whether to believe this piece of news and what else to ask.

"No phone number?"

"He calls me," José said.

"What about tattoos, scars, what does he look like?" Ray asked. He didn't want to finally have a name without being able to verify it – Manny González wasn't that unusual a name, and he didn't want to kill a bunch of wrong Mannys just to get the right one.

José gave a description – height, weight, skin color, everything down to how he dressed and what kind of car he drove: Buick.

"She clawed the shit out of him," José added. He had composed himself. "She got in a couple of shots on me, too."

Ray couldn't think of anything else to ask. He figured he'd been told the truth, or as much of it as he was bound to get from José. He stood up and towered over José. The wind picked up, and the snow fell faster now. It covered everything, José's broken legs included.

He put away the lighter and brought out the blackjack again.

"Any last words you want to say? Maybe something for your son?"

José shook his head slowly. "Tell Mary she can look in the top shelf of the closet now."

"Your stash?"

José nodded.

"Anything else? Maybe you want to pray?"

"Is it gonna do any good?"

Ray shrugged.

"You don't have to do this," José said. He was starting to blubber again. Ray didn't have the stomach for it.

"I'm her father, José. Believe me. I have to."

José looked up at Ray for a moment hoping for pity, then he bowed his head, and Ray raised the blackjack high over him.

★ ★ ★

Once, when Elena was about fourteen, she asked her father if he had ever killed a man other than the one he had gone to prison for.

"No, baby," Ray said. "The people I work for, they got other people for that – specialists. I just rough people up sometimes. Put it this way: if I rough them up, then nobody has to bring in the specialists."

He caressed her cheek as he lied, but he never knew whether she had believed him.

CHAPTER SIX

By the time Ray took care of José's body so that it wouldn't be found for a week or more, it was near midnight. Too late to visit with his daughter, so Ray drove straight home. He was more completely exhausted than he remembered ever having been.

In the vestibule of his apartment building, he walked right past the bank of mailboxes and was starting on the first stairs up before thinking more clearly and turning back. He grabbed three or four pieces of mail and carried them up without looking.

The apartment was dark and quiet, and he thought about turning on the TV or at least some lights, but didn't. He wanted sleep more than anything, but it would take some time for him to calm. Outside the living room window there was a streetlamp that shed just enough light into the apartment for him to see his way around furniture. He moved closer to the window and held up his letters one by one – the light bill and two credit card offers. He stooped to pick up a business card that had fallen out of his hand.

"Ramona Esposito, Special Agent, FBI."

There was a phone number and tiny print writing on the back.

I would appreciate speaking with you concerning your daughter. I will return – 8:00 a.m.

Ray turned on a lamp and scrutinized the card and the seal of the FBI on it. It refused to make sense no matter how much effort he put into it. It was another hour before he gave up trying to figure out what the Feds wanted with his daughter. He'd give Elena a call in the morning.

★   ★   ★

The phone rang at six in the morning. Willie.

"What?" Ray asked.

"Where were you last night? Don't you check your messages?" Willie asked. "Why do you even have a recorder?"

"You want to get to a point, Willie? It's six in the morning."

"The FBI was here last night, asking questions."

"What kind of questions?"

"About the attack, Ray."

"Shit."

"Exactly. They kept at her for a half hour. They wanted to know all the details, and they wanted to know who did it."

"What'd she say?"

"Nothing, just like with the NYPD, but she cried for an hour and woke up a half dozen times last night at least. We had to explain it all to Rosita...."

"You what?"

"Relax. We just told her Elena had been hurt, none of the details. Still, that had Rosita bawling too. I tell you, we were a wreck last night."

Ray was silent a minute. He couldn't make sense of FBI involvement in an assault case.

"I've been trying to figure out why the FBI would take an interest in Elena...."

William paused, maybe hoping Ray would volunteer something. He didn't.

"You used to work with gangsters, Ray, didn't you?"

★   ★   ★

It wasn't exactly true that Ray had worked with gangsters. Not the Edward G. Robinson types anyway. Fat Tommy had been his main employer for a bunch of years. But Fat Tommy was just fat, not connected – a go-between for go-betweens and a lot of little business ventures on the side. He had a couple of other guys who worked for him, but never anything like the muscle needed to be a gangster.

Ray had also done a lot of freelance work. There were drug gangs – punks, he thought of them – that needed to get control of one corner or another of South Bronx real estate. There were Albanians who bought up apartment buildings then wanted the tenants to clear out. There were Russians who wanted Albanians to get the message that they weren't going to move. Twice he'd worked for actresses who needed stalkers to get a message. Union leaders wanted to send messages. Administrators sent messages. Angry husbands sent messages. Fathers and mothers sent messages. Everyone in New York City wanted somebody to get hurt. Ray helped fill that need.

But all of that was years in his past and if the FBI was worried about it now, they were the only ones. Even guys whose legs he'd broken had moved on.

"I'll talk with her," Ray told Willie. He meant it.

★   ★   ★

Ray got ready for the day – a shower and shave, clean clothes, a breakfast of eggs and sausages with toast – a hearty meal because he had never spoken with the FBI in his life and thought they might want to take him to some branch office for questions and that might take the better part of the day.

There was still time before eight in the morning, so he pulled a kitchen chair over to the living room windows to keep watch. When the Feds arrived, he'd talk to them – talk all day if they required it. No point in avoiding them. But he'd do it outside of his apartment. He'd go out to greet them. If they wanted a peek at his apartment, they'd need a warrant. Probably not too hard for them to get given that he was an ex-con, but unless the body of José Vargas had already been found, they didn't have probable cause.

The street below was busy. People rushed off to bus stops and train stations. Kids were dragged along behind parents rushing to get them to school before starting their own day. Everyone was bundled up tight, and those who came out of the building across the street with their coats open closed them up quickly. It was bitter out; Ray didn't doubt that. His feet were under the old cast-iron radiator. His knees were warm, but he noticed he had shoved his hands into his jeans' pockets.

Three minutes to eight in the morning, a dark late-model American-made car parked across the street, though with alternate side of the street parking rules that should have been risky. Ray watched a young woman – short, with short hair and in a smaller version of the trench coat all G-men used to wear in the movies – pop out of the driver's side and put a sign on the dashboard.

Ray put on a Yankees jacket, gloves and a baseball cap and left the apartment. He was locking up when he heard her footsteps a floor below.

He jogged down to meet her.

"Ray Cruz," she said. She looked a little startled to see him and held up an ID holder in one hand. Her other hand was stuck out in front of her as she stopped on the stairs. She wanted to shake hands. Ray ignored the gesture.

"In the flesh," Ray said. "I'm guessing you're Ramona?"

"Special Agent Esposito. Were you going somewhere?" she asked.

"I was going to save you the trip of coming up all these stairs. We can talk in your car."

"Well, we're closer to your apartment now," Agent Esposito tried, but Ray ignored that too and kept walking down the stairs. She followed him.

"All right," she muttered. "Car it is."

They hit the cold air outside and the air hit back. Even with gloves on, Ray knew it wouldn't be long before he was wishing he'd invited the FBI lady into his apartment instead. He took a good look at her as they walked.

"What?" she asked.

"Are you from the Bronx?" he asked.

"Florida."

"But maybe we met before?"

"I don't remember every face, Mr. Cruz, but I definitely don't remember yours."

★　★　★

"Buckle up," Agent Esposito said as soon as Ray got comfortable in the front passenger seat.

"Why?" he asked, but he was already reaching the seat belt across his chest.

"We're not going to sit out here in front of all your neighbors," she answered and she put the car in gear and pulled out.

Several minutes later, neither of them had yet said a word. Ray was beginning to think he should have tried skipping out of his apartment an hour earlier. Finally, she pulled into a supermarket parking lot and found a spot far from other cars.

Agent Esposito turned in her seat to face Ray. She was about thirty; her face seemed hard to him – like she'd been in some fistfights or done a lot of drinking – but she was pretty, he thought, but he didn't like to think it. After all, he wasn't planning to say anything important to her at all.

"You're probably wondering why the FBI is concerned with your daughter." She paused to give Ray time to react. He hadn't actually wondered about that angle at all since the night before. Not until the moment she mentioned it.

"After all," she went on, "an assault is usually just a local matter, not a federal one." She paused again, but Ray still didn't have much to say. The pause lasted too long.

"You can cut out the dramatic bullshit. You want to tell me something," he said, "then say it."

Agent Esposito faced forward again.

"I didn't want to reach out to you at all. My boss said talk to you, so here I am. Let me just say that your daughter has actually been working with me and several other agents on a case. She knows people, she has access to facts. Somebody got the idea she was out to hurt them. They hurt her first."

"You got her mixed up with something and this is what she got?" Ray asked. He turned in his seat to face Esposito, but that didn't make her look at him.

"She got beat because of you?" Ray demanded.

"She came to us, Mr. Cruz. Look. There isn't much that I can tell you about this. It's still under investigation, and I swear to you that I... we don't know the full details. We've got a very short list of people who might have been behind the attack. We are definitely working this just like she was a federal agent. But we're having a hard time working the case. You want to know why, Mr. Cruz?"

She looked back at Ray. She looked upset. Her lips were pressed together thin.

"We're having a hard time because you're out there throwing around money, pushing people around and scaring the people Elena worked very hard to get information on."

"People are getting scared?" Ray asked. "Good. I'm glad."

"Wrong attitude, Mr. Cruz. One of these people did this to your daughter. One. But you're scaring away a whole group. This means they might all decide to move to the tropics or to Europe and then we can't touch them."

"That's your problem," Ray said. "You might need to extradite them to get some justice. I just need a plane ticket."

"Brilliant," Esposito said. "And what are you going to do? Hunt them down and shoot them like dogs?" She didn't need to make air quotes to let the sarcasm drip from her voice.

Ray shrugged and looked away.

"Well, let me point out something, Mr. Cruz. Whoever did this, he did it to get information out of her, but he also wants to keep her quiet. They want her to stop snooping. Right now, that's what the FBI wants too. We weren't expecting this...this level of escalation."

Ray shook his head. "Then let me find out for sure who did this—"

"No."

"I can get you the name and you guys can pick him up and—"

"No."

"But I'm not even talking about—"

"Mr. Cruz. Listen to me. If you keep pushing, they might feel like they need to kill you."

"I don't give a shit," Ray said.

"And they might feel like killing your daughter...."

Agent Esposito let the words hang in the air a moment. So did Ray.

"That's right, Mr. Cruz. They attacked her. They want her quiet, but there are other ways to keep her mouth shut. The same guys who beat her might be paid a little more to kill her."

Ray looked out the window and smiled a small smile. At least one of the guys would not be bothering her again. He planned to make sure the other attacker was also disabled by the end of the day.

"What are you smiling about?" Esposito asked.

Ray shook his head.

"People have to pay," he said. Sounded like an observation, not a threat.

Agent Esposito rolled her eyes and sighed. She put the car in gear and a few minutes later she was pulling up in front of Ray's apartment building. Before he got out, he spoke.

"Was that all you wanted to say to me?" he asked.

She sighed again.

"You keep digging, and they'll kill her. Possibly you first, but her for sure. And that is going to be on your head."

She looked out through the windshield as she said this, as though already thinking about the road in front of her. Ray got out, and she pulled away before he had taken a step from the car.

★　　★　　★

In his apartment, Ray was hungry for another breakfast. His hands had a tremble to them as he made his coffee; he tried shaking them out, but it didn't help.

He tried to think through what Esposito had said last. That it would be his fault if his daughter got killed. He felt like he was skating on a razor edge, and if he wobbled one way or the other, Elena would die. If he did nothing, she could be killed. If he didn't do enough, fast enough, she could be killed. He was flailing his arms and an ocean wanted to drag him under. He was climbing a mountain and a landslide was headed for him.

The milk he was heating for his coffee boiled over, and he dashed the pot and coffee cup into the sink, breaking a plate.

⋆   ⋆   ⋆

Ramona Esposito let herself into a small apartment ten blocks from where she had dropped Ray off. She shrugged out of her coat, dropped her purse near the door and went to sit on her bed. Stood up again to get the hip holster off and tossed it onto her pillow. She sighed heavily, thinking, rubbed her forehead then picked up the phone. She dialed a number from memory and waited. A man answered.

"*Papi?*" she said.

"Hey. How's it going? Everything all right?"

"Uh, not everything."

"What? This Elena girl still won't co-operate?"

"I think I can break her down...."

"You only have until this coming Monday."

"I know, I know, but...."

"What? Something else?"

"You ever hear of this guy named Ray Cruz? I heard on the street he used to work muscle in the neighborhood."

"Ray? Sure. He worked for me for years, but he's retired now. Like me. Why?"

"He's involved here."

"Involved? How?"

"He's Elena's father. Thinks he can still use his muscle to figure out who had her attacked."

There was silence on the other end of the line for a moment, and Ramona thought her father had hung up on her.

"She's his daughter?" the man asked.

"Yeah, and he's a pain in the ass...."

"Listen to me, Mona. I know Ray. He's not about to stop. Not for any reason. Look. You're better off just pulling out of this. Let everyone else take the heat. That Meister bastard and that Langan guy."

"I've put more than a month into this. I'm not about to pull out of it now."

"Then you better handle Ray."

"You mean kill him?"

There was silence on the line for a moment. Esposito repeated herself.

"If you can," her father answered her.

It was Esposito's turn to be quiet a moment.

"I think I know someone who would do it," she said.

More silence, then her father asked, "You haven't mentioned me, have you?"

Esposito didn't bother to answer. She hung up and looked through the nightstand drawer, found a pint of rum.

★   ★   ★

Ray was coming down the steps at the front of his apartment building. He knew exactly where he wanted to go, who he wanted to see. Detective Carver wasn't on that list, but there he was, standing at the bottom of the stairs, waiting. Behind him, a few feet away, were two uniformed officers. It didn't look good. Probably not a social visit.

"I looked for you all last night," Carver said. He was still in the same trench coat he had worn the day before and the day before that. "You're a very hard man to find."

Ray shrugged. As a policy, he kept his mouth shut whenever a detective started to chat him up. It was a strategy that had worked on many occasions.

"Well, we got a complaint about you. Now, didn't I tell you about bothering regular citizens?"

Ray shrugged again. He'd talked to a lot of regular citizens in the past thirty-six hours. He was planning to talk to some more today. Maybe even kill one of them.

Detective Carver pulled out a notepad and flipped through a few pages.

"One Samuel Ortiz says you came to his auto glass fixit shop and roughed up one of his workers. Israel Mendoza."

Carver put his notepad away.

"What have you got to say about that?"

"Never touched him. Israel and I go back a long way. I really doubt he would say anything like that about me."

"Mr. Ortiz called in the police. Israel Mendoza has some nasty bruising on his arm."

"Maybe Sammy did it."

"The boss beat his own worker then called the cops and said it was you? Why would he do that?"

"Maybe he hates me."

"Hates you? Why?" Carver asked.

"Maybe he hates Puerto Ricans," Ray said. He looked down the street as he said it. Sign that he was bored already.

"Hilarious, Cruz. You don't want to talk to me here on the street, fine. I'll just haul your ass in."

With that, Detective Carver motioned to one of the uniformed officers and that man brought out handcuffs. He made a sign in the air for Ray to turn around.

★   ★   ★

Ray went into a precinct holding cell and sat next to a guy who looked terrified. He was shaking and sweating and he seemed more worried about the fact that there were bars around him than by Ray's presence.

It was two hours later when Detective Carver came to fetch Ray and bring him into an interrogation room.

The room was bare except for a long table bolted to the floor and three chairs.

"Sit," Carver said, and Ray did.

"You want to tell me what you're bothering a scumbag nobody like Israel Mendoza for? You think he had something to do with the assault?"

Ray leaned back in his seat and folded his arms across his chest. "I thought maybe he knew something. Back in the day, a lot of things went past Izzy, and a few dollars or a hand around his throat and he'd tell you."

"So, you're admitting to talking to him?"

"Talk," Ray said. "Not beating him or anything."

"And the bruises? They looked pretty fresh when I talked to him."

Ray put his right hand out like he was going to reinforce a point he wanted make, but he had nothing to add.

"Well, let me tell you. I took his statement, and he was plenty shook up, but then I don't get paid to care how a guy like him feels. He's got a rap sheet that goes on for pages. His boss is another thing. He owns a legit business, pays his taxes, the whole bit. He's pushing Izzy to press charges because he didn't like how you behaved in his shop. Told you bothering citizens was going to be bad for you."

Detective Carver took the seat across the table from Ray. He rubbed his face with both hands then pulled out a little notepad from his shirt pocket, flipped through a few pages then looked up.

"So, what did Izzy say?" he asked.

Ray laughed out loud.

"You're stuck, huh?" He didn't wait for an answer. "Izzy didn't have squat to tell me. He said he's clean and sober now. Doesn't know what's going down on the street anymore and doesn't want to know."

Carver looked back at his notes.

"So, he didn't mention a black prostitute named Marla who works over by Hunt's Point and who's got big ta-tas?"

Ray shook his head.

"I told you what that little mutt told me. Clean and sober. Doesn't know nothing. But if you're telling me about this Marla, that's interesting. What is she supposed to know, exactly?"

"Marla? Very funny. Think I'll track her down and find out," Carver said. "Get up."

"You gonna keep me?" Ray asked.

"Yep. Might not charge you until tomorrow. Hope you didn't have plans."

★   ★   ★

Back in the holding pen, a six-foot-tall transvestite with broad shoulders had been added. He sidled up to Ray and away from the frightened man.

"That guy gives me the creeps," he said. He had on heavy makeup but a five o'clock shadow was beginning to show through. Ray stared at him.

"What?" the transvestite asked.

"That guy's no match for you."

"You know about fighting? What are you in for?"

"It's kind of a frequent flyer thing for me."

★   ★   ★

Five hours later, Detective Carver returned to the cell, opened it up and motioned for Ray.

"Get out," he said. He didn't look happy, not that that was Ray's problem.

"What happened? Izzy see the light of day and tell you it was all a mix-up?" Ray asked as he sidled past Carver and out the holding cell door.

"Izzy's dead," Carver said. "He went on a bender, got some heroin. OD'd."

Ray paused a moment at the news.

"What about Marla?" he asked. But Carver was already walking away.

CHAPTER SEVEN

The best part of the day had been spent sitting with law enforcement people answering their questions or not. A waste. Ray had a solid lead – Manny González. He didn't think José was the kind of guy to tell a lie with his last breath, so the chances were good that Manny was really out there waiting to catch a bullet.

But if Manny was the leader José made him out to be – if he had the information about who hired him and why – then he was probably smart enough to keep an eye on José for a few days after the attack. Make sure he didn't talk to anyone about it, didn't otherwise screw up in send-your-ass-to-Rikers kinds of ways. José disappearing the night before was likely to send Manny running for cover or just plain running. Ray needed to talk to him before he got wise and got out of New York. Six hours spent with Carver threw his game plan out the window.

Plus, he wanted to make sure José's wife wasn't missing him too much. Help her out with a little cash. Something to keep her happy for a few days at least. He didn't think that would be so hard, but again, getting there early, before she thought there was anything more than a bender wrong with her husband was key. Carver had ruined that as well.

After leaving the station house, Ray hailed a gypsy cab and went to see José's widow. It wasn't the most urgent thing he had to do, but it was the easiest. Then he could concentrate on Manny.

★   ★   ★

"He's not here," Mary Vargas said. Once again the chain was on the door, the door cracked open only a few inches, Mary sticking her nose into the opening.

"Oh, I know," Ray said. "I know where he is. I just have to give you a message from him."

He hoped this would open the door all the way and get him inside and out of the hallway, but that wasn't happening.

"I don't want to say where he is," Ray added, looking around as though someone in the building might overhear and give a damn. "I can give you the message if you let me in."

Mary thought about it a moment before giving in and opening the door all the way.

Ray went in and started talking quickly.

"First of all, José says he's caught up, can't come back here for a good long while. He might be able to call you in a week or two, but it might be longer."

"What happened to him?" Mary asked. She put her hand to her lips and looked concerned. Ray wondered if she were acting. He couldn't imagine actually liking an abusive man. Even he had never raised his hand to his wife though there were plenty of other things to regret.

"I can't tell you everything. Let me just say he got the wrong person upset, and now he has to spend some time away. Maybe even a few months."

"A few months?" she repeated. She didn't seem too concerned. Probably this had happened before.

"Well, he left you the money that I brought last night, and he has more money that's supposed to come in. A guy named Manny, Manny González, owes him a few thousand more, but I haven't heard from Manny in a while. Any idea where he might be?" Ray tried. He didn't think Mary knew anything at all about Manny, but there was a chance.

"Sure," she said.

"Really?" Ray couldn't keep the surprise out of his voice.

She gave Ray an address a few miles from where they stood.

"And you're sure it's the same guy?"

Her description matched the one José had given the night before.

"He's not a nice guy," Mary said. "Not at all. And, oh, my god, his wife…she's wicked."

Mary held her hand to her chest as though her heart were about to stop from the contemplation of evil.

"Bad people, huh?" Ray said.

"Wicked, wicked, wicked," Mary answered, and Ray thought that if anyone was a connoisseur in these things, it would be Mary.

"Well, I'm supposed to collect the money from them to bring it to you," Ray said. "Hope I find them."

"Well, his wife is always there. She babysits. But she won't give you a dime. Cheap."

Ray shrugged and put his hands up as if to say that things were out of his control. He was about to leave, but remembered something.

"Almost forgot. José wanted me to show you his stash. He said it wasn't much, but you might need it."

"Oh, I know where it is," Mary said, then she put her hand to her lips to check herself. "Don't tell him," she added quietly.

"Nah, nah, don't worry. Look, he can't come back for a good long while anyway, we'll keep it our little secret," Ray said.

He got a kitchen chair and took it to the bedroom and retrieved the shoebox for her. It was heavy and Ray figured that was a good thing. Inside, it held three thick bundles of cash laid on their side – fifties and hundreds with a couple of small stacks of twenties on top. Rough guess? Fifty thousand. Maybe twice that much. On top of it all was a handgun – a compact semiautomatic, seven in the magazine and one in the chamber. A thinking man's getaway stockpile.

"Oh, I'm supposed to take this to José," Ray said.

He was improvising as he lifted the gun out of the box by the handle, pinching it as though it were dirty. He dropped it into his jacket pocket without Mary caring for more than a glance. She kept her eyes on the money that had become hers.

"Don't talk about this money to anyone," Ray said. "Use it little by little. José might not come back for a while."

He was already headed toward the front door. She stopped him with his hand on the doorknob.

"Is he still alive?" she asked. Ray couldn't tell what answer she wanted to hear.

"Last I saw him, he was," Ray lied. "But he really did piss off the wrong people. I'd say if we don't hear from him in a week or two, you might want to take that money and the baby and move out of here."

"My family has property in Puerto Rico," she said. It probably wasn't meant for him. He answered anyway.

"That sounds very nice," he said.

★   ★   ★

It was fully dark out by the time Ray got to the address Mary had given him, and he was tired. A lot of sitting and waiting and walking and talking and a cold that had seeped into him as soon as he left what had been José's apartment. The temperature hadn't been too bad while the sun was out, but it had plummeted with the coming of night.

The intercom panel for Manny González's building was outside. Ray scanned the names and found the right apartment. He gave it a buzz. There was really no plan. He hadn't even bothered to bring his car along with him, and he wasn't sure how he would handle two people at the same time.

Nobody answered the buzz anyway. The apartment was on the second floor, and Ray took a few steps from the building to see if he could figure out which one it was. Four apartments had windows facing the street. One apartment was totally dark. He figured that was the one he wanted, and he stored that information away. No idea what good it might do him in the future.

There was no point in hanging out in front of the building so that he could be remembered by passersby later. He walked a few blocks back the way he came and took a seat in a *cuchifrito*. It was one of the better-quality places and he ordered a big meal – fricasseed chicken, yellow rice, red beans, fried plantains, a wedge of avocado, a salad in case there were any empty spots inside him and a tall Corona to wash it down. Somebody might shoot him before the night was over, but he wasn't going to die hungry.

He ate slowly, tried to savor the food and thought about the chances that Manny González and his wicked wife had gotten wind of what happened to José and decided that it was best to get the hell out of the city. Usually a good meal lifted his spirits, made him optimistic even in the worst of times, but even after he had murdered the half chicken on his plate, he felt like he'd blown it. His little pointless dance with Carver had meant Mr. and Mrs. González had had enough time to take a hint – maybe they heard something on the street, just like he had heard about José – and they were gone. It didn't much matter where they'd moved off to – Brooklyn, China – one way or the other, he had no good connections anymore and finding them might be impossible if the FBI, NYPD and whoever paid Manny were looking just as hard as he was.

It was past eight in the evening when he shoveled the last of the rice into his mouth. Outside, fat snowflakes were falling, sticking.

He paid his check and was about to leave. Two uniformed officers walked in, and Ray sat back down. He felt nervous for the first time since his daughter had come to him – unequal to the effort he needed to make. He waved a waitress over and asked for a coffee. The only place he didn't look was where the officers took a seat.

The coffee, more than his bladder needed really, calmed him a little. He paid a second time and left without ever having looked at the police and without them noticing him in the least.

*   *   *

The lights were still out in the apartment Ray thought might belong to Manny and his wicked woman. He leaned on the intercom buzzer as well. No response. He walked a few blocks off and tried again but with no luck. He became truly afraid that he had missed his opportunity, and he worried about what Manny might do if he thought the woman he had beaten was hunting him down.

It was past nine now. The snow was slowing down, but the cold was sharper, and Ray hadn't had a good feeling from his toes since leaving the *cuchifrito*.

Ray was about to walk a half dozen blocks to the nearest train station. A young black man came around the corner, his hands buried in his pockets, his face almost completely covered by the hood of his parka. Ray called him over.

"You live here?" he asked, pointing up at the building.

The guy shook his head and was about to keep going.

"I need some information about someone who lives in there. Can you help me out?" Ray asked. He held up a fifty-dollar bill and the young man gave him his full attention.

★   ★   ★

It took ten minutes, but the information was what Ray wanted to hear, and that made it almost as good to Ray's ears as sworn testimony.

"They out clubbing. The baby's at apartment 3B."

"And you got the description?" Ray asked.

The description the teenager brought back was the same as the one José had given him the night before, down to the scratches Elena had given out.

Ray peeled out a couple more fifties and the kid took them happily and jogged away, probably late for whatever party he was headed to.

★   ★   ★

There was no use in waiting, but he waited anyway. The snow stopped and the wind picked up instead. Ray watched the door of the apartment building from a half block away, shuffling his feet to keep warm. It didn't help. Nobody entered the building or left it for the next couple of hours. Nobody was stupid enough to be on the street at all.

At midnight, the *cuchifrito* turned off its lights, closed its doors, and the staff filed out. The owner rolled a gate across the front of the store and padlocked it. He eyed Ray for a moment, but Ray ignored him. Then the man moved on. A few minutes later, Ray did too.

★   ★   ★

Back in his apartment by one in the morning, Ray summoned the energy to step into the shower, but it was a close call. He wanted to dive straight under a pile of blankets, but he thought a hot shower would warm him. It didn't. He set the shower to scalding, and he was still shaking as the water coursed over him.

He got into sweats and got out flannel blankets – three of them. He kept them folded lengthwise and got under six layers. He lay facedown and put his pillow over his head. He started to think he might wake up sick, but he was asleep before he could come up with the word 'pneumonia'.

★   ★   ★

For a fraction of a second, he was awake. He thought he had heard something, and then he did. The swish of a baseball bat cutting through the air above him, on its way down.

The first thud hit him square between the shoulder blades, and there were a few others that caught him on the back, then there was one that smacked his left thigh. Hands grabbed his ankles – he wanted to kick them away, but his legs weren't of a mind to do him any good.

He was pulled off the bed. He tried grabbing on to the headboard, but missed. Instead he caught hold of the mattress but that didn't last long. The next whack was at the back of his head. The pillow took most of the blow, but what was left over nearly knocked him senseless.

Next, he was sitting on the floor near the bed and someone hit him good and proper on the right side of his face with something – not the bat, maybe a knee. Then he felt a rush of air go past his ear – the bat again, someone trying to smack his head off his neck like it was a golf ball on a tee. He tried to kick and caught the bat on the backswing with his thigh – not good for him. He tried kicking again and caught a small bookcase he kept near the bed. It toppled, everything crashing – books, a change bowl, a small lamp. It hit someone on the way down.

"Jesus Christ!" someone yelled.

Ray reached out, tried for the lamp. Heard the rush of air again, put his left hand up and caught the backswing again. His hand broke – probably a couple of bones. The knee again, smack to the bridge of his nose and he knew it was broken and draining blood. He found the lamp – one of those little metal ones that clip on to tables. The baseball bat scraped his chest – more pain than any other hit so far – then the knee caught him in the forehead, scrambled his brains though they hadn't done him much good yet in this fight.

"Enough!" someone shouted, and Ray heard the hammer on a gun being cocked back.

"You," the man said, "have been snooping a little too much."

The barrel of the gun was pressed hard up against Ray's forehead.

"Now it's time for me to kill you and—"

Ray whipped the lamp up and caught the gun hand. There was a roar. He whipped it again and caught the man's knee. The man stooped, Ray didn't know why, but even with only one eye open and with the darkness all around, Ray knew this was an opportunity. He whipped the lamp up and caught the man across the face, hard.

There was a stutter step back, and the man went out the bedroom door and fell down in the living room of the apartment – Ray heard his coffee table getting knocked over. It didn't survive.

Then the rush of air again. This time, the bat didn't go past. One hit to the back of his head and he was out.

*　　*　　*

"Cruz. You can't be having your friends over at two in the morning." It was the superintendent of Ray's building, crouching over him, shaking Ray's head by the jaw, waking him. The super's bathrobe was open.

"They're not my friends," Ray rasped out. Sounded like the cold he was waiting for had started early.

"Well, whoever. You look horrible. If they're not your friends, then who the hell was that running down the stairs?"

"Amateurs," Ray said. He tried to get up, but sitting on the floor was about as good as it was going to get just then.

★   ★   ★

Ray drove himself to the same hospital he had taken Elena to a few days earlier. Same emergency room, same triage nurse. This time, there was no skipping to the front of the line. It was an hour before he was seen. The nurse sent him for X-rays and that was another hour.

"Two bones broken in your hand, broken nose, no fractured skull," she told him.

She was cold, and he knew she remembered him from his first visit. She didn't like him and held a grudge. Thought he was a rapist.

"We'll need to set the bones in your hand," she said. "Dr. Warwick should be around in a bit."

"Warwick's the young Howdy Doody-looking guy?" Ray asked.

The nurse looked at him with what was almost a smile, but that faded fast. She sighed.

"I can set it for you, but it's not fun," she said.

Ray thought about it a moment.

"That Warwick was an asshole with my daughter," he said. He offered her his hand.

She gave him a shot to numb his hand but told him it wouldn't really do much good. Dr. Warwick came down to 'oversee', but he admitted he'd only ever seen the process once before.

She clamped Ray's five fingers, the clamps each having a lead wire that fed through a pulley and, at the other end, a bucket of water.

"Ready?" she asked.

Ray's hand was in the air; he held on to the arm with his good hand. Before he could nod to her, she let the bucket drop, pulling straight the broken bones. He winced.

"Son of a bitch," he muttered to himself a few times, his eyes glued tight against the pain.

He didn't pass out. He just wanted to.

CHAPTER EIGHT

The guys who had attacked him in the middle of the night may have been amateurs, but Ray knew that it didn't take a professional to pull a trigger. The streets of New York were filled with people who thought they had what it took to kill – many of them were right. The cemeteries of New York were planted full of the victims of amateurs.

When he went out to his car, he looked over his shoulder every few steps. Failing to kill someone doesn't mean you just give up and go home. Sometimes the killer learns from his mistakes and tries again.

With his hand in a plaster cast and tape over his nose after Dr. Warwick had tried smushing it back into place for ten minutes without much to show for his efforts, Ray drove himself to his daughter's apartment.

"Jesus, what happened to you?" was Willie's greeting.

Ray walked in past Willie.

"Where's Elena?" Ray whispered. It was seven in the morning.

"In the bathroom."

"And Rosita?"

"Still sleeping. What happened to you?"

"What do you think happened? Someone tried to kill me."

"Then why aren't you…. How did you…. What happened?"

"A couple of guys came to the apartment and beat me with a baseball bat and put a gun to my head."

"And?"

"And what?"

"They didn't pull the trigger?" Willie asked.

"I'm here, aren't I? Look. I fought back and they ran. End of story."

"Did you get a good look at them?"

"It was the middle of the night. They didn't turn on the lights. It was pitch black."

"Then how do you know they had a gun? Maybe it was just a pipe or something."

Ray pulled a small revolver from his jacket pocket, held it up for inspection using thumb and forefinger.

"They left it behind," he said.

Willie didn't have any more questions. He looked around as though he thought someone could be watching them through the walls.

"You should probably take this," Ray said. "You might need it."

"But what if...?"

"What?"

"What if the police are looking for it?"

Ray wanted to say something about probable cause and the fact that the police had none if they wanted to search Willie, but he kept it to himself and pocketed the handgun again.

Elena came out of the bathroom in a robe and slippers. She was drying her hair with a towel when she spotted her father. She came over to where he stood and looked puzzled.

"What happened?" she asked. She reached a hand out to touch the two stitches that had been sewn into his right cheek.

"We need to talk," Ray said. He was quiet and clear. The last thing he wanted was to make his daughter feel like there was something to be worried about.

★   ★   ★

"So, you're saying they might come here next?" Willie asked.

Ray wished there was some way he could tell his daughter's husband to go away and let the adults talk in peace, but he didn't think that would be helpful.

"I'm saying these people are motivated," Ray said. His voice was even. "They want something, and I think they'll do anything to get it. Consider taking a vacation, *mi'ja*."

Elena looked down as though her toes might have answers. Maybe they did.

"I can't just leave," she said.

"What?" Ray asked. "Why not? Nothing is more important than keeping some distance between these guys and your family."

"I can't leave town," Elena said. She looked up and repeated herself.

"You can't leave town? What did the police warn you about...?" Willie started and the answer clicked into place in his mind. "You're kidding?"

Elena didn't say anything, but she didn't have to either.

"Was it that Detective Carver?" Ray asked.

Elena didn't look up.

"Or that FBI lady? Esposito?"

Elena reacted to this.

"Esposito?" she said. "You know about her?" She looked over at her husband, and he raised his eyebrows in an imitation of innocence. Ray glanced at him and rolled his eyes.

"She left her business card in my mailbox, showed up early yesterday morning."

"What did she want with you?" Elena asked.

"She...she told me to stop asking questions," Ray said. It was the truth, and he didn't see how it could hurt.

"Was that it?" Elena asked.

Ray racked his brains. He didn't want to let anything slip that might hurt his daughter, make her more anxious than she already was. Couldn't think of anything.

"Pretty much," he answered. "There are people that want you to stay quiet. The FBI is investigating, but they're not sure who had you attacked. If I keep asking questions, she said those people might get even more nervous. They might hurt you...more."

Elena rubbed her face with both hands.

"But if you get on a plane and go away for a few days.... Maybe just two days, you can get away from all of this hassle and...."

"I can't," Elena said.

"But I'm not saying that you hide from the FBI. You can still testify in a trial or give evidence or whatever. Just take a couple of days off."

"I can't."

"Sweetheart," Willie broke in. "You can't help the FBI at all if...." He didn't know how to finish.

"It's not testimony they want," Elena said.

"Who? The FBI?" Willie asked.

Elena rolled her eyes.

"What do they want?" Ray asked. In his mind, the people with the greatest wants were the ones who had ordered his daughter attacked.

Elena looked at her husband then her father, deciding what she could say, what she could keep to herself. Spoke. Said, "I took something."

Ray looked up at Willie, and Willie looked back.

"Give it back," Willie said. His voice was gentle.

"I can't," Elena answered. "I don't have it anymore."

"What did you take?" Ray asked. He knew of course. The only thing worth torturing someone for was money.

"I took money," Elena said. "A lot of it."

"I'll pay it back," Ray said. "I've got savings."

"Seven million," Elena said.

She looked up at her father. Ray wanted to ask her to repeat herself, but couldn't think of a good reason to do that. He had heard her clearly enough. He looked at Willie instead. His eyes were wide, his jaw had dropped, and he'd pretty much stopped breathing.

★   ★   ★

There was no use in trying to pry more information out of Elena. She took millions from someone, and she repeated several times that she no longer had the money. If she told who she had stolen from, it'd be easy to figure out who had paid to have her beaten, but Elena wasn't about to let that information slip.

"But if you tell us, we can help," Willie said.

He was pleading. It wasn't attractive, but Ray was satisfied to finally see him take an active part in trying to defend Elena.

"You can't help," Elena said.

"But the police…" Willie went on.

Elena waved him off, got up and went into her room. Ray and Willie stayed seated on opposite ends of the sofa a moment.

"She has to talk to us," Willie said.

He was making an observation about what constitutes rational behavior. Ray nodded. He wasn't paying attention to his son-in-law. Never had. He was trying to think through Elena's reactions to the questions. When did she flinch and what would that mean? It was hard.

"Grandpa, what happened?"

Rosita stood at the threshold of the living room, ten feet away, rubbing sleep from her eyes. There was her grandfather with his arm in a cast and his nose taped.

Ray stood up, tried to smile.

"I fell," he said. Wanted to continue with *"out of bed,"* but he checked himself.

"I fell down the stairs in front of my apartment building."

Ray motioned with his broken hand, putting it out in front of himself as though trying to break his fall.

"I hit my face," Ray continued. "It was bad."

Rosita walked up to him and touched the cast lightly. She looked up.

"Does it hurt?" she asked.

Ray shook his head.

"Nah, sweetie. Only if I fall down again."

Rosita seemed satisfied with the answer, but she tickled his fingers protruding from the cast. That did hurt, but not enough to make Ray show his pain. She reached an arm up and Ray stooped so she could put it around his neck. That was also painful, but she gave him a peck on the cheek. Then she turned around and went back to her bedroom.

"You should leave," Willie said.

Ray nodded.

"I'll be back tonight," he said.

"What for?" Willie asked.

Ray ignored him and went out the door.

★   ★   ★

Ray had more to think about than he could easily handle. He drove himself to a diner in Parkchester to have breakfast. The Gold Eagle Diner was bound to be getting close to empty after the rush of people who had stopped for coffee and something on their way to the train station for the morning commute.

He found parking in front of a movie theater that had been converted into a church with enough space inside for a hockey rink if they'd wanted to go that way.

After putting in his order for eggs and ham, he asked the waitress for a pen. He needed it for sorting out his thinking on napkins.

"This ain't a stationery store," the lady told him.

She raised an eyebrow and waited for him to respond. He was tempted to try out his cast on her. Instead he pulled out a five-dollar bill. She folded it away and pulled a blue Paper Mate from somewhere in her hair, turned on her heel and went in back to hand in his order.

He pulled out several napkins from the napkin holder, used his left thumb to hold one down.

There were several questions he wanted answered. For the moment he wasn't worried much about Manny González. He'd given Manny thought already and knew what was going to happen to him if he didn't get wise first and run like hell. Instead, he thought about who had nearly snuffed out his own candle the night before.

No doubt that it was related to what had happened to Elena – the guy with the gun had told him it was about the questions. Not some revenge for putting José in the river. Now all he had to do was be on the lookout for a guy who looked like he'd been hit across the face with a lamp. And a guy who carried a baseball bat like Reggie Jackson.

He wondered if Manny had been one of the guys – probably the one with the bat. He didn't think a hired punisher would be as much of a talker as the one who put a gun to his head. No difference. He'd be having a talk with Manny soon enough.

He wrote on a napkin, *Manny and gun guy*. Then he scratched through *gun guy* and put in *Lamp Man*.

Then came the trouble with the missing millions. She took them, but didn't have them. Hardly made any sense. If you grabbed up a few million from someone, you knew they'd be angry. You used some of that money to get the hell away.

The waitress returned with his food. It was then that he noticed his hunger, and he went after his eggs and ham with knife and fork as though they'd done something to him. He used the thumb and index finger of his cast hand to stab the food and hold it down for the knife, then switched the fork to his right hand.

This bothered him. In his time working he had often been asked to get answers from people. Some of them had been hard cases, others had been creeps, others had been regular citizens who had stepped over a line and he made them want to retreat. The trick of it all was that he had never had to force answers out of someone with his hand in a cast and fresh stitches on his face. He looked like shit and he knew it. How could he intimidate someone if he looked like he had been recently beaten down himself? A handgun could help, but there were limits to what you could do with one onto the street or in an apartment.

Over coffee, he went back to the missing money. It gave him something to go on, but not much. If this was all about the money, then it had to be connected to her job. A law office, even a tiny one like where she worked, could have clients with millions. Why she would feel the need to take them, he couldn't tell, but then....

Elena was working for the FBI. That was strange enough, but what if they asked her to transfer some funds? Maybe they told her to take money and hand it over to them.

The certainty that this scenario made sense lasted less than a minute. Why would the FBI have her do something like that? How would something like that happen without her bosses knowing at the law firm? The first step for a client would be to complain to her superiors, no?

It made his head hurt and the coffee was weak; even a second cup did nothing to make him think clearer. He grabbed his napkins, folded them into his pocket, left a tip and walked out of the diner.

★   ★   ★

There were two things that wouldn't help Ray as he looked for Lenny Acevedo at ten in the morning – besides the fact that he might still be in someone's bed. There was the cold. As soon you stepped out on the street, the wind whipped you across the face and made your eyes tear.

Then there was the way Ray looked. His eyes were fully raccooned, his arm in a cast, his nose broken, and the stiffness in his walk had nothing to do with him being a tough man – tenderized was more like it. He had given Lenny five hundred dollars, but he knew that wouldn't buy much without a threat of violence – Lenny didn't just keep his ear to the ground because of the cash. He also feared Ray might tear that ear off his head if he didn't do as asked.

Not that Lenny wouldn't fear him anyway. Lenny was a coward and he knew the stories about Ray – seen some of them go down with his own eyes. Seen some of the aftermath of Ray Cruz off his leash. Right in front of his eyes, in Sal's Bar, back in the day, Ray had smacked a guy down with a punch to the side of the head and when he was down and drooling, Ray had knelt on the man's right arm, taken out a blackjack and whacked that man's right hand like the hand had done something wrong. No one knew what it was about; no one wanted to know. Last anyone heard, the hand was amputated.

Still, a broken arm was a broken arm, and Lenny might see that as a weakness. He'd think he could get away with anything and walk out untouched. But then, Lenny had a weakness of his own, and Ray knew all about it.

As bad an addict as Ray knew Lenny to be, he couldn't think of a future – even just a day – without drugs. Ray didn't know where Lenny lived, but he knew where he bought.

★   ★   ★

Lenny packed. He had more work for Manny and José to do, had called Manny's home and found out that José hadn't been heard from in a while. Worse, somebody had tried to kill Ray Cruz. Failing to kill that man was a mistake someone was going to pay for, and Lenny didn't want to be around when the bill came due.

So, he packed. Pants and shirts and underwear for three or four days into a gym bag along with enough money for three or four months and a handgun – nothing fancy, but it'd be enough, even for Ray.

His hands shook. He was pretty sure Ray knew nothing about what he had done to arrange for the attack on Elena Maldonado, and he wanted it to stay that way.

He needed something to take the edge off. The radio had told him it was about twelve degrees out, and he could hear the wind. He could go out to get a hit, but he needed to think clearly. He went into the kitchen, found a pint of Bacardi, uncapped it and gulped down a quarter of it. It would take a few minutes for the drink to calm him, but it would do the trick.

He put the cap back on the bottle tight and packed it in his bag. Almost as important as the gun. He sat on the edge of his bed, tried to figure out if there was anything else he needed to leave New York and where he wanted to go. Philadelphia sprang to mind even though he'd never been and didn't know anyone there. He didn't get a chance to think about it.

There was a pounding on his apartment door that caught him off guard and made him jump up to attention. He grabbed the gun out of his bag and headed for the door. He approached it with caution. He knew that if it was Ray Cruz coming to get him, it would be better to shoot him through the door than give him a chance at getting in.

"Lenny Acevedo, open up," a voice shouted through the door.

He took a peek through the peephole – looked straight at a police badge.

CHAPTER NINE

Nicanor Gomez – Nicky – had been selling drugs for about the last ten years. He had been arrested fifty times or more, but had only done about a half year of jail time. He wasn't a big player on the drug scene by any stretch, and he wasn't violent as far as the police knew, so for the most part they left him alone. Ray had worked for him on a couple of occasions when rivals set up shop a little too close to his territory.

On Longwood Avenue, just two blocks from Ray's place and across the street from the subway station entrance, there was a row of three-story apartment buildings with the first floor of each taken up with a storefront of one kind or another. The combination of apartments and stores kept the sidewalk fairly busy even on a bitterly cold morning. Ray checked to make sure that Nicky wasn't actually on the street – there was a teenager in a parka dancing a jig to stay warm – then he went into a grocery store that may have been fifty feet long but only about twelve wide. Nicky sat on a milk crate at the back with a couple of friends.

"Hey, Ray," Nicky pretty much shouted when he recognized Ray coming toward him. He held a hand out. "No see, long time."

He was wearing shades and a big smile. Ray took his hand and shook it briefly. Then Nicky pulled his shades down past his nose to look at Ray without the filter.

"The hell happened to you?" he asked. He was serious – not a normal state for Nicky most days. Ray couldn't tell whether it was because he was truly concerned or because he was afraid Ray had come to start trouble.

"I'm looking for Lenny Acevedo," Ray said. "Has he come by today?"

"Did he do that to you?" Nicky asked.

Nicky was usually streetwise though he often joked around. Normally, he wouldn't have pried into Ray's business – especially not when Ray had a broken arm and a mashed face. Ray cut him some slack. He liked Nicky. Somewhat. He stared.

Nicky collected his thoughts. He nodded for his friends to take a walk and they did.

"Haven't seen Lenny today. He was around yesterday. You know where he's living now? He's about a half dozen blocks from here. He's got an apartment over on Southern Boulevard past that Irma Cava joint. Don't know exactly, but he told me about that maybe two weeks ago."

Ray thought about that for a few seconds, looking down at his feet to concentrate. He understood drug dealers like Nicky. They wanted to make money. He never really understood addicts. Why would Lenny get chatty with his dealer? It wasn't like Nicky Gomez made house calls or deliveries.

Nicky got nervous at Ray's silence and cleared his throat.

"Lenny might come by later today. He usually does. Want me to tell him you were looking for him?"

Ray was distracted. He was wondering how long it would take to locate Lenny with the vague address Nicky had for him.

"Nah," he said. He shook his head slowly.

"It'd be no trouble," Nicky continued. "I'll just say you came by and—"

"You tell him I was looking for him, and I'll come back and hurt you," Ray said.

It didn't matter that he had a cast on one arm and a bandage over his nose and stitches on his face. Nicky held his hands up in surrender and turned his face to one side, flinching as though waiting for a token smack that he would take rather than try to get his friends to help him deal with Ray.

Ray reached out with his good hand and patted Nicky on the shoulder.

"Relax," he said. "Just don't talk to anyone about me looking for Lenny."

"No problem. No problem," Nicky said. The words came out as almost a sigh. "Want me to let you know if he comes by?"

Ray nodded.

"I'll be around," he said.

He started to walk away, but Nicky had a brilliant idea.

"You spread a little love, and I can get some boys to take a look around for Lenny."

Ray thought about that long enough to get Nicky nervous again. Sending people out to look for Lenny would probably help in finding him, but it would also alert Lenny and the element of surprise would be gone. He shook the idea off.

"Just keep your mouth shut until I come back. If he comes by, just try to get an idea of where he's planning to spend the day."

"No doubt," Nicky said, and he saluted Ray. It almost made him smile.

On his way out, Ray stopped at the front counter of the grocery store, got a Pepsi and a bag of Funyuns. He stepped out onto the sidewalk. The teenager across the street stopped his dance just long enough to hand off a tiny package to a guy who had pulled up in a Camaro. The car was off in a few seconds, then the teenager was back to dancing. Ray started walking away toward Lenny's new apartment, but he hadn't taken five steps when he heard a car pulling up behind him.

He took another step or two. If it was Carver again looking to arrest him for something, there was nothing wrong with waiting until he heard a car door open. He wasn't about to panic. He threw a look over his shoulder at the car. Sure enough, Detective Carver. In the car with him was Lenny Acevedo.

Ray knew Lenny had ridden in plenty of cop cars in his day, but this was different. Lenny was in the front passenger seat. He didn't look nervous to be in the car; in fact, it looked like he was smiling – not a big smile, but enough for Ray to see. Ray kept walking, slowing down a little. He tucked his cast up against his chest. Didn't want it to be seen.

Lenny turned to Detective Carver and the two men shook hands. Lenny put his hand on his heart, promising something, then he finally got out of the car and went into the grocery store at a jog.

Ray stood at the corner not a full hundred feet from the door of the store. He turned in at the recessed doorway of another store and watched the detective's car idle from over the top of a pay telephone. Carver went to reading from a notepad. A few seconds later, Lenny came out and climbed back into the car. They drove off, neither one of them ever looking in Ray's direction.

★   ★   ★

Ray tried to keep the car in sight, but it wasn't easy. Around the corner and down the block, Carver stopped for a red light. Ray wanted to jog to catch up, but there were parts of his body that wouldn't let him do that.

Carver had pulled away when Ray got to the intersection, but Ray looked over his shoulder and found a gypsy cab coming up on him. He waved it down.

"*A dónde vamos?*" the driver asked.

"Just go straight," Ray said, adjusting himself low in the back seat. "I'm looking for a dark four-door – a detective's car."

"*Mierda,*" the driver muttered. "I don't want trouble."

"There he is," Ray said.

He used his cast arm to point out Carver's car. They were passing a bus stop across the street from a public library and a city bus pulled out right between Carver's car and the taxi.

"Sorry," the driver said.

"Not yet you're not," Ray answered under his breath.

The driver got the idea to make a charge past the bus on the left-hand lane, but Carver had slowed down considerably. The taxi had to get back into the right-hand lane in front of the car they were following. Ray sank lower in the seat.

"*Mierda,*" the driver repeated.

"You got that right," Ray said out loud. "Look. Just don't lose them. Get back behind them when you can. You understand me?"

"I understand."

The driver pulled back into the left lane, slowed to let Carver pass, then cut back in behind the detective.

"Are you trying to get him to see you?" Ray asked.

"No, no. I just want to get behind him."

Ray tried to think of something constructive to say, but nothing came to mind, and he didn't want to waste his energy. They rode smoothly for a minute. Ray had sunk so low, he couldn't see out onto the street anymore. He hoped Carver was still in view.

"How's it going?" Ray asked. As soon as the words were out, he had an answer.

The taxi screeched to a dead stop.

"What happened?" Ray asked.

"He stopped," the cab driver said.

"And you almost hit him?"

"Almost."

"Go around him, you asshole."

The driver stopped again at the end of the block, fifty yards from where Carver had double-parked, went around the corner and dropped Ray off. Ray took a look. The car had only the detective in it. At a payphone, Ray called 911.

"There's a guy with a gun," he said.

He gave an address and was told a squad car would be around in less than a minute. The response surprised him a little. He didn't know the police gave guarantees like that, but he only had to wait half the time before he heard sirens.

From the corner, he watched as the squad car went past Carver toward the address Ray had called in. Carver threw his hands into the air, but put his car in gear and drove off, following the squad car to the emergency call.

Ray's top speed was a little less than a fast walk. Every time he tried to break out into a jog, some part of him screamed. When he got into the vestibule of the building, he was grateful to be out of the cold and face to face with Lenny holding on to a fully packed gym bag.

If there had been time, Lenny would have reached into the bag and gotten out the gun, but he didn't recognize Ray until Ray had grabbed him by the front of his jacket as he hit the last step and dragged him off the stairs and pushed him up against the foyer wall. His head hit with a crack.

"Hey, hey, hey," Lenny said. There was anger in his voice – he thought someone was stupid enough to mug him and he was carrying a brick's weight in cash.

The anger didn't last.

"Ray? The hell happened to you?"

Lenny was a couple of inches taller than Ray. Ray left his feet, headbutting Lenny hard to the bridge of his nose. Lenny's eyes crossed, and he closed one. The nose might have been broken – again – but at least he wasn't tasting the flood of blood he'd swallowed the last time Ray did this to him.

"Pay attention, Lenny. I'm paying you hundreds of dollars for information and now I see you're in a detective's car, talking. You got something to say? Why ain't you talking to me?"

"Ray, I was going to give you a call, but—"

Ray headbutted Lenny again. Still not much blood, it wasn't as hard a hit.

"I'm telling you the—" Lenny could see he was about to get headbutted. "I mean, look, I just got the information – it's nothing, really. I was going to talk with you, but this cop, he came and picked me up first. Said I had to go with him. Couldn't really say no. See what I mean?"

"So tell me now," Ray said.

Lenny hesitated, and he could feel Ray was about to launch into his nose again, tried to think what to say. Nothing good came to mind.

"Tell you what?" Lenny opted for.

Ray launched straight for Lenny's nose, Lenny hit his head on the wall behind him trying to avoid Ray – bounced right back into Ray.

The blood flowed then. It trickled down his throat and down his face.

"You want to keep playing?" Ray asked. "I can do this all day."

"Wait," Lenny said. "Wait, wait, wait."

"Wait for what?" Ray asked. Then he felt the cold metal of a gun's muzzle pressed up against the back of his neck.

"You harassing my witness, Cruz?"

Carver grabbed Ray by the jacket collar, pulled him away from Lenny, slamming him into the opposite wall. Ray's hand hit the plaster hard and broke again, maybe not even in the original spot.

"Get into the car, Acevedo," Carver barked out.

"He hit me," Lenny said.

Carver would have rolled his eyes, but he didn't want to take them off Ray.

"Just go to the car. I'll take care of Cruz."

Lenny shook his fist in Ray's face.

"You would have been so dead," he hissed and went outside, gym bag in hand.

For a full minute, Carver and Ray didn't move. Ray spoke first.

"You going to arrest me or shoot me? I'm getting tired of being pinned against the wall."

Carver stayed quiet for another half minute like he was trying to make up his mind. Ray wished he could at least look the detective in the eye, but his face was smushed against the wall.

"What is wrong with you?" Carver asked. "Am I going to have to kill you so I can investigate your daughter's assault? Jesus, Cruz, the only potential lead I have and you break his nose. How am I supposed to interrogate him now? Anytime he gets uncomfortable, he can scream police brutality. What judge isn't going to believe him? Now I gotta finesse him – offer him immunity and shit like that."

"You could let me handle him," Ray said. "I'll get all the answers you need."

"Yeah, or I could just haul your ass in. That way, Lenny can't say a word about brutality."

"Maybe I could scream about police brutality. If the judge'd believe him, they have to believe me," Ray said.

"Yeah, or I can just get you to Rikers. They got plenty of inmates who could use a bitch with a cast on."

"They can try," Ray said.

The steam had run out of both men. Detective Carver let Ray go slowly, taking a step away like he thought Ray might try to hit him. Ray stood straight. Even that little motion of righting himself hurt like hell. He wiped the spit from the corner of his mouth with his sleeve.

"You going to arrest me?" Ray asked. He knew there was plenty of cause if Carver wanted things to go that way.

"Nah, you'd only get into more trouble trying to take your tough guy bullshit into lockup. Probably get yourself banged up too. You and your daughter'd be a matched set."

"Can you tell me what you think he knows?" Ray asked.

"What? You think we're partners now?" Carver asked. "You are exactly the last person I would tell about anything on this case. Understand me?"

Ray shrugged. There wasn't much else to do.

"What about talking to Lenny?" Ray said. He'd go to jail if it made it easier to get the truth out of Lenny.

"I can handle that. I'll just tell him that if he doesn't talk, I hand him back over to you, so you guys can finish that conversation you were having. He'll talk. If he has anything to say is another issue."

Carver started to leave; Ray took hold of his arm lightly.

"Why'd he get that bag? Where does he think he's going?"

"I told him I'd take him to the train station after he tells me everything – Grand Central."

"You still planning to do that?" Ray asked.

"Never was planning on it," Carver said. "I figure, if he doesn't have any good info, I'll cut him loose and on his own. If he knows something, it'll be a while before he gets out."

Ray didn't know whether to believe him, but he didn't have much choice. They went out together and Lenny was hugging himself, trying to keep warm outside next to the detective's car. Carver opened a door to the back seat and Lenny got in. The detective took the driver's seat and quickly pulled away and into traffic.

Ray stood for a minute, trying to think over all he had seen and heard of the relationship between Lenny and the detective. It took that long for him to realize Carver hadn't bothered to check what Lenny had in the gym bag, as though he had no reason to fear that he might be carrying a weapon.

CHAPTER TEN

Ray walked back toward the grocery store on Longwood Avenue. There was something else that bothered him about how Carver had handled Lenny. The more he thought about it, the worse it looked. Before Ray came on the scene, before they knew he was watching, Lenny rode in the front seat like a friend. After Ray makes it known he's watching, Lenny has to take the back seat. It was like Detective Carver choreographed that detail – to make Ray think he had no connection to Lenny, no relationship other than cop and crook. And there could only be one reason to try so hard to make Ray think that.

Ray went past his own car and into the grocery store where Nicky Gomez was still sitting on a milk crate telling a joke. The guys around him were already laughing when Ray walked in.

"And she's the girl who had the biggest one I've ever seen," Nicky finished up.

He had his hands out in front of him like he was going to catch a watermelon. The guys at his side cracked up into even louder laughter, then they looked up at Ray and quieted down.

"We need to talk," Ray said.

The guys on either side of Nicky looked at him and he nodded. They left, going over to the far side of the store.

"What happened to you?" Nicky asked.

"What did I tell you the last time you asked me?" Ray asked.

"Nothing," Nicky answered.

"Now how about I ask the questions?"

"Yeah, but—"

"But what?" Ray wasn't in the right mood for negotiating with Nicky.

"But your stitches popped. You're bleeding."

Nicky motioned to his own cheekbone. Ray put a hand up to his face and wiped away a smear of blood. Carver forcing his face into the wall probably did this to him.

"I'll be fine. I just want to know if Lenny came by or not. If he didn't, can you give me any clues about where he might be, where he's been hanging out, who he's working for these days?"

Ray pulled out a thick wad of cash and held it all up for Nicky to see. He knew Nicky – knew he didn't want to get involved in other people's troubles, but he had his price. It wasn't all that high usually.

Nicky stared at the wad a moment, then shook his head.

"Lenny ain't been around since yesterday," Nicky said. "And I don't really keep track of where he hangs out. I kind of just sit tight here. Lenny comes to me. Understand?"

Ray nodded and put his money away. He wanted to take a couple of minutes to try and figure out why Nicky was lying to him, but he wasn't sure the reason even mattered. He sighed.

"I'll come back later," he said. "Let me know if he comes by and try to get him to talk a little."

"Got it," Nicky said. He pointed at Ray with forefinger and thumb in the form of a pistol, pulled the trigger. Ray smiled at him. It couldn't have been a happy smile, but Nicky didn't notice.

He headed for the door, and Nicky's bodyguards went back to take their seats again. Ray stopped at a refrigerator on his way out. Paid for a beer at the counter. It was early, but then Nicky wasn't likely to hold that against anyone who wanted a drink.

The storeowner put the bottle in a brown bag, and Ray tightened the bag around the neck of the bottle. He walked back to Nicky.

"One more thing about Lenny," Ray said, stepping between the seated bodyguards.

"*Di'me, hermano,*" Nicky said, smiling like he was already thinking about his next joke.

Ray smacked the bottle into the mouth of the guard on his left, then smacked the one on his right. Then he did it again. All so fast,

Nicky only had time to fall off the milk crate he was on. His smile was gone.

The guards were on the floor holding their faces. Ray took a quick look behind himself to make sure the store owner wasn't getting any ideas, but the store owner just looked back at him, scared.

Ray gave Nicky a kick with his heel.

"Get up," he commanded, and Nicky scrambled to get to his feet.

"You lied to me," Ray said. Then he smacked Nicky in the ear with the bottle and Nicky went down again. This exposed the crown of his head, and Ray took advantage of that.

For a moment, Nicky lay on the floor, balled up and holding the top of his skull, feeling for blood and finding it. Ray stood there. There was a sound, a whine he couldn't identify. He looked at the store owner again, but the man was frozen to his spot, wide eyed, but not whining, not unless he was a ventriloquist. The bodyguards had stopped holding their faces. He could tell they were thinking about standing up, fighting the old guy with the broken arm, but they were convincing themselves that there was nothing to be gained by the attempt. If they had their guns out, they'd be shooting him dead, but they didn't and weren't ready to try.

The whining stopped for a moment and started up again with a deep inhale; Ray identified it – Nicky was crying like a grumpy toddler.

"You kidding me?" Ray asked. He looked up at the ceiling, hoping Nicky would compose himself. "Get up."

"No," Nicky answered. "You're just going to hurt me."

"If you don't get up, I'll kill you," Ray said.

The whining stopped. Nicky slowly got to his knees, then to his feet, keeping his hands on his head, gently touching his broken scalp. Ray noticed Nicky's ear was flaming red. He also noticed there was a handgun stuck in the waistband of Nicky's pants which was exposed now. And he noticed that Nicky had wet himself.

Nicky squinted as though the fluorescent lights were too bright for him.

"You pissed yourself?" Ray asked.

For a second, Nicky lowered both hands to his crotch. He didn't touch, just wanted to cover himself up – cover his shame. The stain wasn't nearly small enough to be covered that way. He put his hands back on the top of his head.

"Tell me what you know about Lenny," Ray said.

★   ★   ★

At a stoplight, Detective Carver adjusted his rearview mirror to get a look at Lenny in the back seat of the car. Lenny had half curled himself into comfort, using his gym bag for a pillow. After a minute of arguing, he'd fallen asleep, and now he was snoring. Carver readjusted his mirror.

They were headed south toward the 138th Street Bridge. Carver was wondering how he'd gotten stuck with such a waste of human flesh in his back seat when someone honked a horn. He took his foot off the brake, but checked himself. The light hadn't turned. Instead, there was a watch commander riding shotgun in the squad car that had pulled into the lane next to him. The lieutenant made a whirling motion with his hand, telling Carver to lower his window.

"What you got there?" the lieutenant asked.

"Some homeless guy. Taking him to shelter so he doesn't freeze to death."

The last thing Carver had considered was that he might have to explain why Lenny was in his car.

"What are you, the Salvation Army? Don't you have any cases to work?" the lieutenant asked.

Carver opened his mouth to say something, he wasn't sure what, but the light changed, and the squad car pulled away. Carver put a light foot on the accelerator, let the watch commander pull ahead and watched as the squad car made a turn and disappeared. Carver readjusted the rearview mirror at the next red light. Lenny was still sound asleep in the back.

★   ★   ★

Before leaving the grocery store, Ray took the paper bag off the beer bottle, pinching the bottle between his cast and his chest. He balled up the bag and threw it at Nicky. Then he walked out, not looking back.

On the street, even though there was a wind blowing and he knew it was bitterly cold, he felt like he was burning up. He wanted to go home and get into bed and lie there – nothing else, just lie there. It wasn't yet noon. In the time since midnight, he'd been beaten – almost killed – and he had braced Lenny, and smacked down a drug dealer and his two bodyguards. Busy man.

Yet for all the beatings, what had he learned? Lenny, a drug addict, had bought drugs. He thought he was leaving New York, so he had bought several days' worth. Ray could have guessed all that without having smacked Nicky with a bottle.

And Lenny knew something. Ray was sure of it. Carver was an asshole, but he knew his job. If he was talking to Lenny, it wasn't to shoot the breeze. But whatever Lenny knew was going to be processed by the police. Nothing Ray could do about that. Lenny had slipped through his fingers and taken whatever information he had with him.

And what if Carver made some sort of deal with Lenny? Gave him a light sentence in exchange for testimony or, even worse, put him in some sort of witness protection program for crackheads?

Ray got to the driver's-side door of his car and took a look back at the grocery store. Nobody was watching him. Probably just glad he'd left without killing anyone. He pinched the beer bottle between his chest and the cast again while he dug in a pants pocket for the car keys. He got them out and swung the door open, clipping his cast hand. The bottle slipped and shattered at his feet with a dull pop. Pain rocketed through his hand and arm, and he closed his eyes for a moment, standing in the cold.

"Who am I kidding?" Ray said aloud, and a woman walking past him looked his way before hurrying on.

He sat in the car, the doors locked around him, the key in the ignition, and doubt eating at his soul.

"What's the point?" he mumbled.

He knew there were a lot of people he could bribe or beat – he could even kill people – but he wouldn't be changing the fact of what had happened to his daughter. He wouldn't be finding the one person who had ordered her attack. Carver had more resources – Carver had warrants and a badge and a gun he could use in plain daylight if he felt like it. Ray didn't have any of that. He didn't even have the use of two hands anymore. The wad of cash in his pocket was a little over three thousand dollars, but it was the last he would be easily able to get his hands on. Some jerk had convinced him to put his money into CDs at the bank, and he'd have to cash one in with a penalty if he needed more – the penalty was nothing; leaving a paper trail was a different story.

The teenager who had been trying to keep himself warm while waiting for customers on the sidewalk across from him stopped his jig and crossed to the grocery store. He went in, and Ray figured that whatever else he did, he had better get the hell out of there before Nicky or one of his bodyguards started hatching something stupid.

★   ★   ★

A pothole woke Lenny from a dream where a beautiful woman lay naked on a bed, her arms at her sides, her legs together as though she were waiting to be wrapped as a mummy. He was sitting on the edge of the bed with clothes on, looking at her. He also was waiting.

"Where are we?" he asked Detective Carver.

"Look out the window," Carver said.

Lenny did as he was told. He could tell they were crossing a bridge, but other than that, he had no clue. He fell asleep again. Minutes later, another bump in the road.

Outside, there was a two-lane road in what Lenny figured was 'the country'. He checked his watch. Unless he'd slept twenty-four hours, they couldn't have gone that far from the Bronx. He reckoned an hour had passed.

"Where are we now?" Lenny asked.

"Jesus, Lenny. Look. Out. The. Window."

Lenny tried again. Trees, trees, trees, no landmarks unless he was missing something or going blind.

"This ain't the Bronx, is it?" he asked.

"Does it look like the Bronx?"

"So, where are we?"

"Lenny, shut up. I'm trying not to get lost here."

Lenny sat back and fell asleep again. Didn't wake up again until he heard the car door slam. It startled him and broke apart a continuation of his earlier dream. This time, the woman was still immobile, but Lenny was about to get his pants off.

"What the…?"

He wanted to ask where they were, but Carver had left the car. There was a shack and a small pond, not much bigger than one of those Olympic swimming pools. The trees were dense in just about every direction except the road behind and the pond ahead. The place scared him, but he didn't have time to figure out why. The door he had been leaning against opened, and he almost fell out.

Two hands grabbed the back collar of his coat and dragged him out of the warmth of the car. His ass hit the frozen dirt hard, and he knew this wasn't going to be good. He reached out his hands toward the gym bag that had fallen out of the car too and the gun that was inside it.

"The problem, Lenny," Carver said, pushing him hard into the ground, "is that you have become a liability."

"A what?" Lenny said. A beating might be coming, but Carver might get distracted. Might take time out to answer a question or two.

"A liability, Lenny. It means you're more trouble than you're worth."

Carver stomped at Lenny's head as Lenny tried to sit up on the ground. The kick knocked Lenny sideways. There were a couple of quick kicks to Lenny's back.

"What did I do?" Lenny asked. He got another kick to the head as an answer, so he asked again.

"What did you do? Let me think," Carver said, but he really meant he was going to kick Lenny a couple more times and grind his heel into Lenny's hand when he put it on the ground trying to right himself.

"I haven't done anything," Lenny said. "I swear."

"You haven't talked to Ray Cruz?" Carver asked. Another kick. "You didn't hire two guys and now one of them is missing?" Another kick. "In the business world, they call that mismanagement, Lenny."

"I never talked to Ray. He doesn't know anything. I haven't said a word to him," Lenny said.

He had crawled a few feet from the car and his gym bag, and now he was getting to his knees. If Carver let him get to his feet, he'd rush the detective, knock him to the ground and beat the shit out of him with his bare fists.

"So, I didn't hear Ray talking about paying you?" Carver asked.

"But you came in before I said anything," Lenny answered.

"And if I hadn't come in? Would you have told about who hired you?" Another kick. This put Lenny on his ass again.

"What would I say?" Lenny asked. "I don't even know where he lives."

Carver looked up at the bits of sky showing between the bare branches above him. It looked to Lenny like he was calculating something. Concentrating. Maybe this was the best time to strike, but then, most likely the beating was over. Hadn't been too bad.

"I swear, I haven't said a word to Ray about anything," Lenny tried. The silence was beginning to creep him out a little. That and the fact that he was in the middle of a forest.

"You haven't said anything to Ray?"

"Nope. Nothing. Swear to god."

"How about to anyone else?"

"Nobody. Who am I going to tell? I've been in this business for years. You don't get to stick around this long if you talk. I'm telling you. I haven't said a word to anybody."

Carver looked up, then down again quickly.

"Good. I believe you."

He walked three steps to Lenny's gym bag, picked it up off the ground and unzipped it – looked inside.

"Looks like you were planning to go somewhere," Carver remarked.

Lenny was on his knees, his hands out in front of him. He was shrugging like he didn't see a problem with putting some distance between himself and the people his boss didn't want him talking to in the first place.

"Does he want me to stay?" he asked. "He want me to kill Ray?"

"Nope," Carver said.

He pulled Lenny's gun out of the bag and fired once, hitting him near the center of his sternum. Lenny fell backwards, his legs bent beneath him. He clutched his chest, but he couldn't take in another breath. Letting air out was much easier, and for a moment it seemed to relieve a pressure he felt.

Carver stood over Lenny, the gun in one hand, the gym bag in the other. He was ready to pull the trigger again if there was a need, but there wasn't one.

"I don't know if anyone uses this cabin anymore," Carver told Lenny. "But they probably won't until the spring. Then someone'll find you. Give you a proper burial. Unless the coyotes get to you."

When he was sure Lenny was dead, Detective Carver dragged his body a few feet into the brush. Then he wiped the gun off and put it in Lenny's hand. He didn't think that would fool anyone in law enforcement, but it would sure as hell distract a grand jury if there ever was one. He used a handkerchief to pick out a thousand dollars from the brick of bills Lenny had packed. He left those bills in the gym bag and took the rest.

Before getting back in his car, he made sure the dirt road was too hard-packed for footprints. Not that it made a difference. He had chosen the site because he'd heard it wasn't going to be used anytime soon. Lenny would be out there in the bushes for months unless someone started an immediate search for him and began asking hard questions of a lot of people. He couldn't imagine anyone would actually care enough to go through that effort.

CHAPTER ELEVEN

There was one place Ray wanted to go and ask questions, but he hadn't so far. After beating Nicky for a grand total of zero information, he figured he had nothing to lose. He went back to his apartment to prepare. He showered in the hottest water his building's boiler would put out and shaved though there were spots on his face he would rather have left untouched. He combed his hair gently, steering the comb away from the stitches that were still feeling raw and which he wouldn't doubt had popped in his run-in with Detective Carver.

He thought about getting himself into a suit – he owned one that he used for weddings and funerals alike. But he decided against it. Couldn't have gotten the cast through the sleeve without a hassle anyway. Clean jeans, a loose sweater and a heavier coat because he was tired of feeling like he was slipping into numbness from the cold. Besides, there were more pockets in the bigger coat. The revolver went with him in one of the zippered-up coat pockets because you never knew what to expect in a lawyer's office.

It probably would have been wise to drive to where Elena worked, but Ray was sick of wisdom – wanted to stretch his legs, get in a little leisurely walking, maybe feel good about having the use of his legs and lungs for a little while. Besides, if he needed a quick getaway, he was screwed anyway. He might be able to force a jog out of his body, but he couldn't get himself behind the wheel of his car all that easily.

It was a little after noon by the time he got to the lawyers' office. As he pulled open the glass door, his stomach begged him to get a sandwich first, but he ignored the plea and went in.

The young lady at the reception desk smiled at him, but was on the phone already. Ray stood patiently for about ten minutes while the person on the other end of the line refused to understand how his bill had been broken down. Sounded to Ray like the man just couldn't accept the fact that lawyers take a cut of whatever they win for you in court.

"Yes, sir," the receptionist said again and again. "Yes sir, I'll do that, but I think at this point you'll need to…. No, I don't think…. Well, I'll have Mr. Langan call you. As soon as he's in…. Later today…."

And so it went for a while before she finally got off the phone and started apologizing to Ray. He put up his good hand to stop her.

"I used to work in the business myself," Ray said. "Dealt with assholes like that all the time."

"Really?" the young lady said. "How'd you deal with them?"

"Oh, I'd smack them upside the head," Ray said, and he smiled while the receptionist giggled.

Ray explained what he wanted – to see a lawyer about a trip and fall accident at a department store. He was hoping to sue for millions. The receptionist took his name, Luis Aparicio, and said it might be a while to see someone. The four lawyers who worked there were either out or with other clients.

"Maybe you could come back tomorrow morning?" she asked.

Ray squirmed a little. He had figured that lawyers would be tripping over themselves to speak with him – if his story about falling down the escalator at Sears was true, and his broken arm, cuts, and bruises came from that, it had to be worth a good chunk of change to them.

"I'd really like to get started on this today," he said. "Maybe you can look up another law firm online?"

Not wanting to let a potential client slip away, she had him take a seat.

Just like she had told him, the wait was long and there really wasn't anything for him to do. Apparently, this office hadn't even thought about having magazines in the waiting area – either that or a client had swiped them. He dozed off for a few minutes, woke up with pain in his face.

"Any aspirin?" he asked the young lady.

She looked around in her desk drawers, but came up empty.

"They say a drink of water does the trick sometimes," she told him.

It sounded a little thin to him, but mention of the water made his hunger come back in full force and with reinforcements. His stomach grumbled loudly like he needed a plunger.

"I'll just step out for a minute or two, get something to eat and maybe find an aspirin," he told her. "Don't let anyone take my spot."

He wagged a finger at her, and she smiled at him again. She was a pretty girl. Ray wondered if she was flirting with him or really as nice as she seemed. On his way out he caught a dim reflection of himself in the glass door and figured she was as nice as he thought. Possibly the nicest girl left in the Bronx.

Lunch was hard to find. He didn't want to go back to the restaurant near the spot where his daughter had been savaged. It was the closest place to eat, but it would have been uncomfortable for him. He'd be thinking about the attack, not eating.

Across the street and farther down, there was a pizzeria. He'd eaten there before and didn't want to repeat the experience, but it was that or a bag of chips and a soda bought from a bodega. Pizzeria won.

If nothing else, the inside of the pizzeria was warm. Ray waited his turn, put in his order, then found a seat to wait till his slice was ready. He looked around – mostly teenagers avoiding school, but there was one man who caught his eye. A young man in suit and tie, a file open in front of him, his slice of pizza on a paper plate. He was stooped over the file, studying it like it might make a move. He moved his lips as he read. Ray pegged him for a lawyer.

His order came up, and Ray ate his slice and drank down a soda. In the whole time, the guy he was watching didn't touch his food or take his eyes off the contents of the file. It gave time for ideas to run wild in Ray's head.

What if this lawyer was the one who ordered Elena punished for what she had done to the company? Or what if he was the one who had started that speech while holding a gun to Ray's head? Hearing his voice and getting a closer look at his face – checking for lamp-shaped bruises, maybe – would help solve that one. But what if this lawyer knew something, anything, about the missing millions? Even if he had no role in what happened to Elena, it'd be worth finding out what he knew.

Ray cleared off his tray into a garbage can that was almost overflowing and walked over to the young man. He waited to be acknowledged, but it wasn't happening.

"Do I know you?" Ray asked.

The man looked up. No obvious bruising, but the look of concentration he had been using on the file melted away and turned almost to fear. Either that or disgust.

"I don't think so," the young man said. Didn't sound anything like the voice from the night before.

Ray squinted, trying to look like he was racking his brains for a moment. He looked down. The papers in the file all looked financial. Maybe a lawyer – maybe an accountant. He figured there was a good chance this man had nothing at all to say about what happened to Elena.

Ray was about to ask, straight out, "Are you a lawyer?" but the young man had changed his line of sight and stood up, held his hand out to someone just coming in from the cold.

"Mr. Meister," the young man said. He gave Ray a glance, and Ray walked off, the chance for asking questions gone.

Back in the law offices, Ray had to wait only a little while longer before being seen by a man about forty years old, with a collar and tie so tight around his neck that it looked like a tourniquet had been applied. His hair was in a buzz cut; his face was reddish like he'd been in the sun for too long in someplace tropical.

"My name is George Gates," the man said, his smile huge. "Come in, come in."

Ray wasn't even sure he wanted to talk to anyone anymore, but he went ahead with it.

"Sit," the man said.

He stood behind the desk waiting for Ray to take a seat, then he brushed the tie flat against his stomach as he sat.

"I passed by here many times," Ray started. He'd rehearsed this first part. "Is that girl at the front desk new?"

"Yes," the lawyer said. The smile was still on his face. "She's a temp."

"And there was a Hispanic girl that used to work here."

"Yes. Still does. She's taken a few days off. Is there something you wanted to talk to me about? An accident?"

"Yes," Ray said. He hadn't noticed any nervousness from the lawyer when talking about Elena. "Exactly. An accident."

The lawyer picked up a pen, hovered it over a legal pad.

"Where exactly are we talking about, Mr....?"

Ray tried to remember what he'd told the girl outside, used the lawyer's forgetfulness to mask his own. He remembered.

"Aparicio," Ray said. "Luis."

"Right. Wasn't there a baseball player with that same name? Played for the White Sox, I think."

"Yeah," Ray said. He had chosen the name out of thin air for the girl out front. Hadn't thought that he might need to talk to a baseball fan.

"Okay," the lawyer said when he saw Ray wasn't going to be saying anything else about the strange coincidence. "And where did you have this accident?"

Gates motioned toward Ray's broken hand and to his face in general. Even to save his own life, Ray couldn't think of the place he had mentioned to the receptionist.

"The restaurant a couple of doors down," Ray said.

"La Calidad?" Gates asked.

"Exactly."

La Calidad was the place near the alley where Elena had been attacked, and the only place that came to mind.

"There was ice last night as I was walking. I slipped, fell, tried to stop myself, but I hit my head on the fender of a car and on the sidewalk."

The lie came out quick and easy, and it sounded believable to Ray.

As long as the receptionist didn't put down anything different, he'd be fine.

The lawyer looked at the notepad in front of him.

"But it says here you fell down the escalator at Sears."

The lawyer looked at him with expectation all over his face. Ray opened his mouth and closed it. Nothing came to mind about how to smooth over the discrepancy. He'd never been good at lying. The silence between the two men lasted a full minute.

"Look. Mr. Aparicio or whatever. Obviously, you got hurt. You're entitled to compensation, maybe even substantial compensation from the looks of you, but I need you to level with me about the details here so we can come up with a strategy."

Ray moved to the edge of his seat. He was ready to get out of there, if only the lawyer was ready to stop talking.

"I should go. Feeling a little tired," Ray said when Gates paused for a breath.

"Well, maybe that's not a bad idea. Collect your thoughts, come back tomorrow, and we can sue the pants off of...whoever is responsible."

Ray stood up.

"Wait," Gates said. Ray stood still as the lawyer looked through one of his desk drawers and reached into the back of it. He pulled out a camera.

"Let me take a couple of photos of your arm and face. Evidence. It'll start healing by tomorrow, and...."

Ray left the lawyer's office as fast as his feet would carry him without him jarring his bones.

"Wait," Gates said behind him, but Ray was bolting.

At the doorway, he turned to the receptionist. She had a smile for him. He smiled back and waved. The door opened in front of him without him having to push. On the other side, the young man from the pizzeria was walking in with Mr. Meister.

The young man nodded to Ray with a weak smile, apparently glad Ray was leaving. Ray nodded back, would have liked to have sat down to chat with him, but Gates had a camera, and Ray had no intention of leaving a record of his visit to the place.

He felt for the gun in his coat pocket as he walked back toward his apartment. The last few minutes had sapped him of strength and nerve. He wished he had brought his car along. It was a one-minute drive, but he was feeling the weight of the last few days and of his stupid gamble. He expected Gates was probably on the phone to the police at just that moment, reporting an insurance scam artist.

Ray turned a corner on his way back home and was met with a stiff breeze. He put his head down against the wind and felt sorry he'd forgotten to buy aspirin earlier.

In his apartment, he wanted nothing more than sleep though it was still early afternoon, so he curled up under a quilt and was asleep in minutes with the revolver in hand.

CHAPTER TWELVE

Ray woke when it was dark, and he felt like staying in bed until morning, but he had only one solid lead, and he had to play it out.

Before dying, José had said Manny González was the one who arranged things, the leader. Paying Manny a visit was the only thing left for Ray to do, and that's where he was headed.

He knew it was colder than it had been; he could hear the wind outside, but he wore only a couple of sweaters this time. Manny might fight back and having a broken arm was enough of a disadvantage – he didn't need a thick coat limiting his movements. He packed his semiautomatic into his waist holster, the revolver went to an ankle holster, and he carried the gun he'd taken from his attackers in a brown paper bag. Even with all these preparations, he needed to make two stops before going after Manny.

★   ★   ★

On Bruckner Boulevard, about three miles from where Ray lived, there was a series of junkyards and scrap metal processing plants. No one lived there. By day there was the bustle of flatbed trucks bringing piles of old radiators or cast-iron tubs and of tow trucks bringing in wrecks their owners have given up on. By night there were only the sounds of strays that acted as security dogs – there really wasn't anything to keep from thieves unless they came prepared to haul away bulk metals that could be sold for pennies per pound. Bulldozers and cranes were disabled before the yards were closed for the night. The dogs didn't protect much – they just kind of showed up and got fed for snarling. Most of them wouldn't hurt you unless you hurt them first.

Some, not even then. Others were mean – used to staking out their territory. They'd chomp without warning.

Ray drove out to Bruckner to see Jerry Ramirez. Jerry worked late, took money home with him, carried a gun at all times. At any one time he had a half dozen dogs living off scraps he threw them. He made sure they were the type to run from a fight. If they snapped at him, he shot them.

Ray parked outside the fence, attracting all the dogs. He let himself in through a gate that had a padlock that hadn't been done up. Jerry came out of a trailer that was hidden behind a pile of squashed cars twenty feet high. He had a snub-nosed revolver in his right hand.

"It's me," Ray said. The dogs lost all interest in him as soon as Jerry came out into the yard.

"Me? Who?" Jerry squinted. "Ray Cruz?"

Ray nodded.

"What the hell happened to you?" Jerry asked.

"I ran into a door," Ray said.

Jerry took a look past Ray from the top step of the trailer.

"Let me guess, you got the door in the trunk of your car and you brought it here to beat the living shit out of it."

"Almost. Let's talk in the trailer."

Inside, it wasn't much warmer, but there was no wind. They worked out the details of what Ray needed.

"And when do you want the body found?" Jerry asked.

"Never."

Jerry squirmed in his chair. He was wearing coveralls and had his hands deep inside his pockets.

"But my guys shift the stuff in the yard around. I can have them work on one side and not another for a couple of days, maybe a week, but eventually, they'll find the body," Jerry said.

"I'm planning to bury him here, put some of your junk on top of the pile."

Jerry thought about it for a minute.

"Well, that could be done, but there are no guarantees. You

understand me? I mean, sooner or later, my guys are gonna need to shift whatever you pile on top. They might see the loose dirt. Even if they don't care, once they uncover that spot, the dogs might decide to dig. See what I mean?"

"I get it. But this'll buy me more time."

"Sure. But let me ask you. How are you going to dig? The dirt's all frozen."

"You got bulldozers here," Ray pointed out.

"Yeah, but I don't have backhoes. Even if I did, frozen dirt is like concrete."

Jerry took his right hand out of his pocket, held it out palm up.

It was Ray's turn to think. It took half a minute.

"Show me the best spot for getting rid of this guy."

Jerry's junkyard was about five acres of scrap metal and crushed cars and car parts piled twenty or thirty feet high. There was also a section of rubber tires that collected rainwater in the summertime and produced enough mosquitoes to choke a dog. There were other junkyards in each direction just as big. In the distance, there were apartment buildings. If it weren't for the piles, there'd be no privacy.

Jerry led Ray down a canyon of twisted steel and pointed out a spot next to one of the mountains of lightweight stuff – appliances and rotted piping.

"Right here. You shave away a bunch of the stuff to that side, dig your hole, do your thing, then push it all back. The boys won't be working in this area for a few days. We're supposed to be getting a shipment from Long Island tomorrow, dawn. If it's as big as they claim, that might give you an extra couple of days. But then, when my guys come here...well, you know. What they find is what they find."

The hard part for Ray was trying to get Jerry to wait for payment. A normal dump job was usually five hundred dollars. This wasn't a normal dump job. If the cops found the body buried under that metal, they'd put two and two together and suspect Jerry of being a willing accessory. He wanted ten times normal for that.

"I'll do better than that," Ray said. "I'll hand you ten thousand, but you have to wait for it."

"Wait for what? For you to get caught? You won't be paying me then, I think."

"Nope, you just gotta wait until the bank opens."

★   ★   ★

There was a stop at a gasoline station and one at a pharmacy. Ray's hand hurt and so did his face and a headache clawed its way up the back of his neck. He took three aspirin, then a fourth as he drove to Elena's apartment.

At Elena's, Ray was worried about how to get what he wanted without having to fight his daughter. As he made his way up the stairs, he figured it might be difficult, but it had to be done. If he could just get what he needed from Manny, he'd have all the pieces to the puzzle. Once he'd smashed the puzzle, no one would ever come after his child again.

There was no sound coming from inside the apartment. He rolled his eyes. He should have called ahead, should have gotten a guarantee from William that he'd be there.

He knocked and heard footsteps coming to the door. William opened. He didn't look happy.

"It's...." He looked at his wristwatch. "It's nine o'clock." The anger drained out of his voice. It was a bit early in the night to complain about the visit.

Ray looked at his own wristwatch.

"You're right," he said. "Look, can you come out?"

"Where?"

"Just yes or no, Willie."

"No."

"I found the guy that attacked Elena," Ray said. He kept his voice low.

William looked back into the apartment, patted his pants pocket for his keys, then stepped out, clicking the door behind him. He thought for a minute, looking down at the tilework.

"How do you know?" he asked.

"I know. Trust me, it took a lot to get the information, but it's rock solid. I know the guy, I know where he lives. I don't know who paid him or why, but I figured I'd ask him. You know, face to face."

William sighed loudly, rolled his eyes, then looked up to the ceiling. Ray only thought how bad William would be at poker.

"You're going to torture him?" William asked. He sounded like he thought it would be a bad thing.

"You could say that," Ray said.

"Then what? Kill him?"

Ray shrugged. "Look," he said. "These people almost killed Elena, they almost killed me. They wouldn't stop at killing you or Rosita. They want seven million dollars. You don't have it, I don't have it, and Elena doesn't have it. Want to take up a collection at the church?"

"Call the police," William said. He crossed his arms and waited for an answer.

"And what? Tell them my daughter stole millions of dollars from some hard-ass sons of bitches? What do you think the police are going to do? Protect her? How?"

"The FBI is working on the case," William said.

Ray waited a moment for the rest to come out, but William wasn't offering any more. The fact that the FBI was on the case was good enough for him.

"That's it? That's your plan for protecting your family? Let the FBI figure it out. How long they been looking for Jimmy Hoffa? How long they been looking for that guy that jumped off the plane with a million dollars? Wake up, Willie. The FBI hung her out to dry. She's alone on this."

The headache he had tried to ward off with aspirin came screaming back. He rubbed his forehead.

"Look. Just go back inside and forget I ever stopped by. Go read your books or watch your TV or whatever you were planning to do."

He turned to go, but William stopped him before he got to the stairway.

"Hold on," he said. "Let me get my coat."

He went back in, came out two minutes later. The neighbor from across the hall opened her door at the same time. An older woman – maybe fifty.

"I'll be back in about an hour," William said. "Just going to the store. Elena took a couple of sleeping pills, so she may not hear the baby…. Thank you so much, Mrs. Green."

The lady went into Elena's apartment with a few words about how it was nothing at all and a smile.

Ray shook his head.

"What?"

"You called a neighbor?" Ray said.

"What's wrong with that?"

Ray shook his head and decided to say nothing.

In the car, driving toward Manny's, William spoke.

"I'm not going to torture anyone. We could get into a lot of trouble, and Elena doesn't need anyone going to jail just now."

"Relax, Willie. I'll do all the talking. I just need you to make sure things go quietly."

"Am I going to need a weapon?"

"Not a bad idea. There's a paper bag under your seat with a revolver. Easy to use. Point and click like a camera."

Ray made the motion of pulling a trigger.

"And who is this…guy?" William said.

"Manny González. He's the one who attacked your wife. He's the one who brought along a friend. He's the one who got paid, and I want to know who paid him."

"And if he tells us?"

"I'll be happy."

"And if he doesn't?"

"Not really an option."

"You sure about that? What if he's tougher than you?"

"I'll kill him."

"But...."

There wasn't really a question. William knew this Manny person was dead either way. He wasn't sure how he felt about it.

"Or I can let him go, and he'll just forgive and forget and he won't come after Elena or Rosita or you because he'll have seen the error of his ways. Glory and hallelujah."

"Shit," was William's only response.

When Ray parked and was ready to go out, William put a hand on his arm.

"Your daughter," he said and stopped there.

"What about her?" Ray was frightened by the mention of Elena.

"She was drunk again tonight. Drank down most of a bottle of rum all by herself."

Ray sat back and thought about it for a minute. Here he was on a mission to save her, and there she was flushing her life away. He couldn't think of what to do except maybe kill more people faster. A vicious game of Whack-a-Mole.

"What do you want me to say?" Ray asked.

"Nothing. Everything is fine. How many times of her getting drunk did you say it took before we could call her a drunk? Three? This is just number two."

He got out of the car. Ray did the same and led him up the steps at the front of Manny's building.

★   ★   ★

On their way up the stairs, Ray gave William a wad of cash and told him to hold it up to the peephole when the time came.

"Tell him you've come from José Vargas. You've got a job for him. You've got to talk inside. If he won't let you in, say Lenny Acevedo recommended him. Got that?"

"A job? What does he do?"

"What do you think he does? He beats people, kills them if he has to. Rapes them if that's what you pay for."

William stopped on the stairs, tried to shake out of his head the depths of human depravity Ray had planted there. It didn't work.

They got to the door. There was loud music playing in two of the apartments, TVs blaring from two others, and a full-blown war of words between a mother and a daughter in another. There was a TV on in Manny's apartment, set at a regular level.

"As soon as that door opens, you put away the money. Understand me? Keep your hands in your pockets unless I tell you to do something. When I tell you, you jump to it. Believe me, I don't want you doing anything violent, that's my job, but if I say hold somebody, you do it or we might both die. Got it?"

William nodded and swallowed. "That's not much of a pep talk," he muttered, but Ray didn't hear him. He was moving into position on the left side of the door. He had the revolver in his good hand, and he was stooped, getting his center of gravity low.

William knocked. It took a second try for anyone to come to the door.

"Who?" a woman's voice asked. It sounded tired.

William held up the money as Ray had taught him.

"José sent me here about a job."

"José?"

"José Vargas."

There was silence for a half minute.

"I don't know no José Vargas," the lady said.

"Lenny Acevedo recommended you," William said. "But I can take my money elsewhere."

Another pause.

"How much?"

William looked at Ray. Ray mouthed, *"Ten."*

"Fifteen thousand," William said.

Ray shot him a look, but William ignored it. In another few seconds, the locks started to come undone. Just as the door cracked open, Ray threw his shoulder into it, ramming hard.

The woman on the other side got the edge of the door to her face, knocking her back into a hallway wall. Her arms splayed out from the impact, and she fell, sitting up against the wall. There was a gun in her left hand. Ray stomped her hand, then kicked her in the face. From where he was, he could see into the apartment's living room. There was Manny González, sitting on a sofa, watching TV, a beer in his hand. He leaned forward as Ray looked at him. He was stunned into doing nothing at all. Ray aimed at him.

"Take her gun," Ray said. "Bring her."

He moved into the living room, keeping his aim on Manny. Manny put his hands up, not letting go of the beer.

William pocketed the handgun and started to tug on the woman, hoping she'd come along peacefully. For about five steps, she did. Then a struggle started. He wanted her in the living room, she wanted to be free. She started to scream, and Manny's eyes started to shift. He looked toward another room. Ray took a quick glance, didn't see anyone but figured there was a gun hidden in a bedroom.

"Control her," Ray said.

"I'm trying," William answered.

The woman started to fight William like her life depended on it. She was kicking William, and he was half inclined to let her go.

Ray took three steps back, closer to William.

"I can't control her, Ray," William said, and to prove it, she struggled one of her arms free and started punching at him – mostly missing.

Ray whipped the gun in his hand at the top of her head, smacking her hard and loud. Sounded like a home run. She drooped to her knees. The fight had gone out of her.

"What do you guys want?" Manny asked. He still hadn't put down the beer.

William half dragged, half walked the woman to the sofa and plopped her next to Manny. Manny was young, twenty-five at most, with a buzz cut. He was wearing an undershirt that showed his lack of musculature and his paunch. His wife was probably ten years older or more and had a ragged bun of dark hair. She was thin, wiry, and loud.

"She your wife?" Ray asked.

Manny shrugged as though to say Ray's guess was close enough.

"Keep her quiet, or I'll pull the trigger and one of you will get hurt."

"What do you guys want?" Manny repeated.

"I've come to talk to you about a woman you beat. Her name was Elena Maldonado. Ring any bells?"

Manny's eyes widened and shifted, but he decided to play dumb.

"I don't know no Elena. I think you got me confused."

Ray wasn't buying the story, but he didn't have to. Manny's almost-wife spoke up.

"That bitch had it coming! Manny told me everything! That bitch deserved what she got!"

"You need to calm down, lady," Ray told her. It did nothing to quiet her.

"Anyway, what do you care about this girl?" Manny asked, though he had to shout to be heard over the voice of his wife.

"You admitting you attacked her?" Ray asked.

"She asked for it, that slut!" Manny's wife shouted. She tried getting off the sofa, but Ray waved the gun at her. It didn't stop her from shouting.

"She deserved it! Don't you wave that gun at me!"

"Shut her up," Ray told William.

"What am I supposed to do?" William asked. He looked lost and felt it.

"Keep her mouth from opening," Ray said. It was almost a shout – Manny and his wife wouldn't stop yelling at him. Manny moved forward in his seat. He still had the beer bottle in hand, and he was waving it about, gesturing with it.

"Shut her up!" Ray repeated to William.

William took a step toward Manny's wife. She kicked out at him – didn't hit him, but he jumped back. At the same time, Manny jumped out of his seat and made a move toward Ray. It was a tentative move, but Ray reacted. He jabbed the gun toward Manny's wife and pulled the trigger. Shot her right at the bottom of the sternum – center mass.

She sat back on the sofa in a semi-slump and moved her hand to the wound as though making sure it was really blood coming out of her.

Manny sat down again.

There was silence in the room at last. It lasted a full minute before William spoke.

"I should call an ambulance," he said.

Manny's wife was still looking at her bloody hand as though she found it hard to believe her blood could be anywhere other than inside of her where it had always been.

"Why?" Ray asked. "You sick?"

William didn't answer, didn't move. Manny did nothing but keep his eyes on Ray. Ray motioned to William.

"Get a towel for her," he said.

William took a moment to absorb what was being asked of him, then went looking for the towel. He opened one door, looked in, and went to another. The second door was the bathroom, and he quickly got what he was looking for, but he returned to the first room he had opened and took a closer look. He stepped inside, and came back to Ray in a hurry.

"There's a crib in there," he said.

"A what?"

"A baby crib."

"Is there a baby in it?"

"No," William said. "But it might be with a babysitter."

Ray looked up to the ceiling as though there might be answers there. There weren't any.

"Well," he said at last, "let's get out of here."

He signaled for Manny to stand, and he did.

"You give me trouble," Ray said. "And I'll shoot you. You think I won't do it, let me know now, and I'll show you."

Manny shook his head. No trouble.

"You gonna let me get some shoes on?" Manny asked.

"We're not going that far," Ray said.

"But I could step on glass," Manny pointed out.

"I wouldn't worry about that," Ray said.

"Are we going to leave the body here?" William asked.

Ray took his eyes off Manny for an instant to answer, but that was when Manny decided to use the beer bottle he'd been holding on to. He rushed at Ray and slashed at his head with the bottle. Ray put his broken arm up to defend himself. The pain almost blinded him, but he was already swinging his gun hand, jabbing the barrel of the gun into Manny's belly. Manny fell to his knees. Ray wanted to join him there, but kept his feet.

"Do that again," Ray said, "and I'll kill you."

William didn't know what else to do with himself. He asked again, "And the woman?"

"You mean the dead lady?"

"She's still…" William was going to say *"…breathing,"* but he took a look before finishing the sentence and found that the description no longer fit her.

"Do you have a baby?" Ray asked when they were at the car. The night was frigid and Manny was jogging in place to keep warm and to keep his bare feet off the asphalt. He shrugged.

"You don't know?" Ray said.

"We babysit for extra cash. You going to open the car door or not?" Manny answered.

On the way to the junkyard, Manny asked where they were headed.

Ray was in the back seat while Manny sat in the front passenger seat and William drove. Manny knew there was a gun pointed at his spine.

"A junkyard over on Bruckner," Ray answered.

"Shit. You going to kill me?"

"Depends," Ray said. "I have some questions, and if you give me some very good answers, you might make it back home again, safe. You don't answer, this is going to be very painful for you."

"Great," Manny said, but for the remaining minutes of the ride, he said nothing, just shivered.

★   ★   ★

Just like he had feared, Manny stepped on a shard of glass as Ray pushed him through the gates of Jerry's junkyard. William followed the two men. He would be the voice of reason if things got out of hand.

"Son of a bitch," Manny muttered to himself, hopping, then limping toward the section where Ray forced him to go.

Manny was carrying a red five-gallon plastic can of gasoline. He knew this wasn't going to be good for him, but couldn't figure out a way around doing what he was told. Ray had the gun and clearly wasn't shy about using it. Manny didn't even have shoes on or a coat.

"Stop here," Ray told him.

It was a section of the yard he and Jerry had cleared with a bulldozer earlier. Ray had Manny pour out the full canister onto a stretch of ground there, soaking it, making puddles. William crossed his arms and looked away. He didn't think this was going to go well for Manny, but then it might just be a mind game. Ray played a lot of those.

"Careful," Ray told him. "Don't get any on you."

"You going to burn me?" Manny asked.

"Nope. I need you alive."

Manny stood apart from the gas-soaked patch, his hands deep in his pants pockets. It didn't help much.

"I spoke with José Vargas, and he told me a lot of things about this beat-down job you guys did, so don't lie, and I won't have to hurt you, you understand me?"

Manny took a second to nod.

"Good. Now José says you called him up with the job, true?"

Manny nodded to this after thinking about it. His nodding was energetic, like it was part of his quivering from the cold.

"And that the both of you attacked her in an alley near a restaurant not too far from the Hunt's Point train station, true?"

Manny nodded again. This wasn't good enough for Ray; he wanted to hear the words.

"I beat her," Manny said.

Ray shot a glance at William. William's jaw muscles were working.

"And you beat her pretty good too, right?"

"I kicked her, I punched her, I tore up her clothes. So?"

Ray was going to spring the news about Elena being his daughter, but he didn't get that chance. William threw himself at Manny. Ray didn't think his son-in-law had it in him, but the first punch, straight to the jaw, was a solid one, and Manny's knees buckled. He fell to the ground, and William was on top of him. The second, third, fourth, and fifth punches were also right hands, and they all connected solidly. For the first few punches, Manny tried to fight back, but William wouldn't stop until about ten punches later. When he stopped, he got up to his feet slowly, and he was breathing hard.

"You don't know what you did to her," William said. He was crying. "You don't know what you did to my whole family."

He dusted himself off and straightened out his jacket and shirt. Manny tried to raise his head, but he couldn't hold it steady. He looked at Ray, and tried to prop himself up on his elbows, but it looked like he couldn't figure out where his elbows were anymore.

Ray pulled a book of matches out of a pocket and tossed them to William.

"Light up that gasoline puddle."

"We're going to kill him?" William asked, but now his voice sounded like he wanted to see this death, witness it.

"We'll see," Ray said. He squatted near Manny.

"Now, Manny. You can see we care a lot about this woman you attacked, so let's just get through the facts, okay? A few more questions. Why did you guys have to do this to her?"

"What?"

Ray repeated himself a little louder.

"She stole. She was…she was…supposed to give money to someone, but she didn't. She stole. That's what…the guy…that's what the guy said."

Manny was trying to catch his breath from the shellacking William had given him, trying to reorientate himself.

"Okay, and how much did they pay you?"

"Three. Three thousand. Two for me, one for José."

"And who gave you the money?"

"What?"

"I said, who handed you the cash?"

"My wife."

"No. Listen to me," Ray said. "Who gave you the three thousand dollars?"

"My wife."

"What do you mean?"

"My wife."

"Yeah, I heard that part already. What about her?"

"She's the one...she takes the money. She deals with the people who want me to work for them."

"Okay, so who hired you this time?" Ray asked.

"I don't know."

"What do you mean you don't know?"

"My wife does all that. I don't know who gave her the money. She just told me what I had to do and who I had to do it to."

Ray got out of his squat. He looked over at William and the fire that was still burning on a swath of dirt. William looked back. There was blood on his face. Ray motioned for him to wipe it off and he did.

"So you don't know anything about who paid you? Nothing at all?"

Manny found a way to sit up on the ground and shook his head.

"So even if I tell you that if you don't give me a name, I'm going to put you in that fire and burn you alive...?"

"Tony," Manny blurted out through teeth that were chattering loudly.

"Ah, Tony. Tony who?"

"Tony."

"Tony Tony? That doesn't sound right," Ray said.

"Tony...." Manny gave up at that point. He let out a sigh. He was trying to control his breathing, but the cold was forcing him to short, rapid breaths.

"You really don't know?" Ray said. He was a little surprised. "I

144 • STEVEN TORRES

mean, I will kill you. You understand that, right?"

"I got nothing," Manny said.

"Great."

Ray paced a little. The cold was getting to him too. The only warm person was William. He was closest to the spot where the gasoline had been poured. That patch was burning low and sporadic.

"So, you're just the muscle. Your wife was the brains?"

It looked like Manny nodded, but his whole body was shaking so it was hard to tell.

"Okay, so let me ask you this: did you or did you not come to my apartment and beat me with a baseball bat?"

Manny looked up at Ray like Ray was a madman.

"Why would I do that?"

"Maybe somebody paid you, asshole."

"I wish somebody had. Shit, I'd do it for fun now."

"So, you're saying no?"

"I ain't never seen you before tonight. Wish I still hadn't seen you."

"And you weren't with some guy that got a lamp smashed in his face?"

Manny looked up again.

"Looks to me like you got a lamp upside your head," he said.

"Funny," Ray said. "Wait right here."

He put the gun in his pocket and walked a few paces off to a pile of scrap and came back in less than a minute with a rag wrapped around a cast-iron shard.

"Willie," Ray said. "Go wait for me in the car."

William looked at his father-in-law a moment and decided it was best not to protest or ask questions. He trudged off, and the last he heard was Ray talking,

"Manny, you know how they say, 'This is going to hurt me, more than it hurts you'? Well, this is gonna hurt you a whole lot, *maricon*."

Sitting in the car, William kept his ear close to the window waiting to hear the fatal shot, but he missed it. A few minutes later, he heard the bulldozer working, then a crash of metal. Later, Ray came out of the junkyard, locked the gate behind him.

"You killed him?" William asked as Ray started up the car.

"Last I saw, he was alive," Ray said.

"But I heard the bulldozer," William answered. "I thought you buried him."

Ray shrugged.

"You buried him alive?" William asked.

"Last I saw he was alive. That's all you need to know. If the cops ever ask you about him, you tell them that's what I said. Less lying that way."

"You're worried about lying?"

"And getting caught in lies. Look, that guy attacked your wife for money and would have killed your daughter if someone asked him to. Don't cry for him."

CHAPTER THIRTEEN

William kept his face turned away as Ray headed toward Elena's apartment. He spent the drive shaking his head, pausing, then shaking his head again.

When Ray pulled over in front of the building, William said, "I don't understand you."

He moved to open the car door and get out. Ray stopped him.

"What part do you not understand?"

William thought for a minute, wanted to say, *"Forget it,"* but decided to speak his mind.

"This. This killing. We killed a human being today," he said. He gave the words time to sink in.

"We killed two today," Ray reminded him.

"This isn't a joke, Ray. I know these weren't the best people in the world, but they were human beings. There is a justice system in this country. There are laws, judges, police. We didn't give any of that a try. We just went in shooting and killing. That's not what I want for my daughter."

Ray nodded. He understood.

"I don't want that for your daughter either. I didn't want it for my daughter, but look what happened. Remember your wedding day and what I said to you?"

"What? When you pointed the gun in my face? I remember that."

"Remember I told you to take care of her?"

William didn't answer – could see this wasn't going to go his way.

"I think I even said, take care of her or I'll hurt you, right?"

"You said you'd kill me," William answered.

"Yeah. I'm thinking there was some kind of miscommunication, maybe you thought I was joking. Elena got beat black, blue and bloody. That happened while you were supposed to be protecting her. While the law, the judges, and the police were supposed to be helping you. And whoever had this done to her, they're still out there. They want their money back and she doesn't have it. Guess what happens when they don't get it. They hire people like me."

The words hung in the air. William turned away again, he shook his head and a smile crept over his face.

"You think this is funny?" Ray asked. "Think this is a game? Maybe. Maybe it is. But this is a game that I know how to play. And let me tell you one more thing, Willie. If these bad guys get to Elena and they kill her, don't think I'm letting you off the hook. If I lose Elena…. If I lose my daughter, what I did to Manny will look like mercy."

The two men sat side by side in the car for a moment. The smile on William's face had melted away, and he licked his lips.

"Get out of my car," Ray said, no anger behind the words. "And if Elena asks you where you were, tell her we went asking some drug dealers questions, and if she sees your knuckles, tell her you and me got into a fight."

William nodded then said, "But I haven't got any bruises on me or anything."

"Want some?" Ray offered.

Ray pulled away once William left and got inside his building. Creeping up the stairs to his landing, William could tell the door to his apartment was open. His heart nearly stopped inside him as he rushed the last steps and through the door. Inside the door, Elena stood with her arms crossed, waiting for him.

★   ★   ★

What Elena wanted to know, above all things, was what William had been doing out when Rosita needed him to be at home caring for her. The fact that he arranged for a babysitter didn't stand for much. Neither did the fact that she was the one who'd gotten drunk.

"Your father came by. He said he needed help trying to talk to some hoodlums, you know, somebody to back him up since he's got the cast on. We talked to a bunch of people, mostly lowlifes from the street. I stayed in the car most of the time."

"And your knuckles?" Elena asked.

William looked at his hands. Only the right hand had any marks on it but all the knuckles looked like he'd rubbed them on a cheese grater.

"I kind of got into a tussle."

"With who? One of the people you were questioning?"

William thought about his answer. Ray had told him to say it was a fight with him. But attacking his wife's father, who had a broken arm, didn't sound like a good lie to tell.

"Yes." He wanted to leave it at that.

"Who? A drug dealer?" Elena asked.

"I don't know his profession. Maybe. They all looked like drug dealers to me."

Elena thought for a moment. "Where?"

"What?"

"Where did you get into this fight?" She had her hands on her waist, her brow was furrowed, her hair tucked behind her ears.

"On the street," William answered. Then he added, "On Bruckner."

"A block from here?" Now, Elena was angry.

"What difference does it make?"

"Because drug dealers have memories. If you punched a drug dealer on Bruckner, how are we supposed to show our faces there? I can't believe this."

Neither one said anything for a minute.

"I'm going to wash up and go to bed," William said.

He went into the bathroom, locked the door behind him. Hadn't thought to check himself for other marks, but he was sure Manny had tried hitting him back. He used the bathroom mirror, but didn't find anything. Checked his pants and shirt as he took them off. No rips. He wasn't sure how to get around the fact that he'd given Bruckner as the site of the fistfight. He and Elena walked down that street every day. Maybe he could get Ray to say he'd scared the drug dealer off.

After his shower, he came out in a towel. Elena was waiting for him again, her arms crossed.

"You want to go over the details of your fight again?" she asked, and even with the fading bruises, every line on her face told William she was furious.

"Again?" he asked. He couldn't think of anything else.

"I talked to my dad," she said and waited.

"Maybe it wasn't Bruckner?" It came out like a question.

"And who, exactly, did you get into a fight with?"

"I didn't want to tell you that. You can see how it could be upsetting. I figured…me and Ray figured it would be better to leave out the fact that I got mad at him and punched him."

"You punched him?"

"Well, it was more of a glancing blow. Really, I scraped my knuckles on his coat more than anything."

Elena looked at her husband for a moment, fixed him with her stare. He let his hands drop to his sides.

"I didn't call my father," she said. "Maybe you want to tell me the truth this time."

William returned her stare for a moment, then slowly shook his head.

"The truth is a very, very bad thing," he said. Then he told her… some.

★   ★   ★

The phone ringing in the middle of the night sounded so far away in his sleep that it rang straight through to the message machine without Ray even opening his eyes. The sound of his daughter's voice did that for him. The voice dripped with anger and bile, and even though she said only that she needed to talk to him, the hour of the night – past midnight – and the fact that she made the message so short told him a lot. He had trusted William to at least get into the morning before telling her anything about Manny and his wife, but the only reason for the call was that William had told her something upsetting. He cursed his son-in-law and his own luck.

Then he wondered if something else might be the trouble. What if someone had called her with a threat? What if someone were lurking outside her door?

He listened to the recording a couple more times, trying to figure out whether there was any fear in her voice or if it was pure rage. Rage it was.

He wasn't sure he could see a point to calling her back, but she deserved to know from him whatever it was she wanted to know. It wouldn't bring Manny back, or his wife, or José. Still, she should hear from him what was being done to avenge her, even if she didn't care to hear it. Even if she only wanted to scold.

Ray got dressed, anticipating that she might want him to come over. Then he got himself a glass of water in case the call went on for a while and sat in a comfortable chair. The phone rang only once when he finally dialed. It was William on the other end.

"Elena?" he said. His voice was close to a whisper.

"No," Ray answered. "What do you mean?"

"She left, Ray. She caught me in a lie and she tried to call you. When she couldn't get through, she left."

"Left where?"

"How am I supposed to know?"

"You didn't go after her?" Ray asked. He was standing again.

"We have a four-year-old, Ray. I can't just leave her alone here."

Ray hung up and thought a few seconds about what to do: go out looking for her in the concrete heart of the city, or sit by the phone and hope she called again.

Outside, the world had turned to ice. There was a thin sheen on spots of the sidewalk. Ray didn't know what temperature the air was, but it made his breath catch. He used his jacket sleeve to wipe away frost from the windshield of his car while the engine warmed for a minute.

The distance between Ray's apartment and Elena's wasn't that great, but just like William, he had no idea where she had gone or why she'd left the warmth of the apartment. If he'd been angry with William, he'd have thrown William out into the cold. Women were hard to understand.

He drove, inspecting every person walking the sidewalks and going slowly through intersections, casting an eye down each lane he passed. There weren't many out at that hour and in that cold. He passed by a young couple walking arm in arm, their heads bowed into the night air. He remembered his own wife and the one occasion he thought she might walk out on him. He had come home expecting to find her, but Maria and Elena – maybe two years old then – were gone. He walked for an hour in the summer sun looking for them. He found Maria holding on to the child, both looking into the water below them on the Bruckner drawbridge.

"You want to jump?" Ray had asked back then. He hadn't planned on it, but he had startled Maria. She turned to him and her smile, the radiance of her face, soured. He was smiling at her, thinking he had been silly to think she had left him, and he tried to maintain his smile still when her reaction showed itself. He didn't want to show that he hurt.

"Wouldn't be such a bad idea," she had answered him. Her smile returned, weak, frustrated.

His smile wilted. He carried Elena back home. He and Maria said nothing at all for the whole walk.

He headed back to that same bridge, and there she was. Elena was looking down at the water, her elbows on the concrete parapet, her coat too thin for the weather, no hat on her head. He honked at her, and she got into the passenger seat next to him.

Ray got the car off the bridge and to a legal parking spot and turned on the heater.

"You want to talk?" he asked.

Elena shook her head, but started anyway.

"You killed that guy? Manny?"

Ray thought about lying, but didn't think it would work. "Yes."

"And his wife?"

"She was shouting at me, causing a scene. I just wanted Manny to give me some information."

"She didn't have to die," Elena said. It was a statement, an assessment.

"I tried knocking her out," Ray said. It didn't sound like much, but it was true and he didn't want to say William had been useless at keeping the woman quiet. Didn't want to mention William at all.

Elena nodded like she understood.

"Besides," Ray kept on, "a couple of people told me she was the criminal mastermind in that family. Worse than her husband."

Elena nodded again.

"Yep," she said.

Ray couldn't tell if she was agreeing absentmindedly or if she was hinting that she knew the dead woman personally and could vouch for how evil she was. He made a note to himself to bring this up again when Elena wasn't in the process of fuming.

"And the other guy? José?" Elena asked.

"I killed him too," Ray answered.

His voice was quiet. Until that moment, he had thought he'd been doing good things. Elena's silence told him he was missing some part of the moral equation.

"I've been trying to figure out who's behind all this," Ray said. "Whoever sent those two punks after you might send two more. They might kill you. They might kill William or me. They might even go after Rosita. If you just tell me—"

"Then they will definitely go after Rosita," Elena said. She pronounced the words slowly and carefully.

"Not if I get to them first," Ray answered.

Elena stared out the windshield, then shook her head.

"It's complicated," she said. It was almost a whisper.

Ray shook his head and pursed his lips.

"You know what?" he asked. Then he answered himself. "You're going to die because you think too much. You think this is complicated? This is as simple as it gets. This is life and death. That's it. Nothing more. You get out of this city. Far. You hide. You keep moving. You use only cash and fake names whenever you get a chance. You let me go after whoever needs going after. We'll get through this. Keep overthinking this, and you'll wind up...."

He stopped himself in time and looked out the side window.

"Okay," she said.

"Okay what?"

"Tomorrow Rosita gets out of daycare at noon. Anytime after that, we can get out of here. The day after tomorrow."

"She can miss daycare," Ray started, but Elena put up a hand to stop him. "Okay," he said, "okay. The day after tomorrow, you'll have plane tickets. Cash. Now. If you tell me who I should be talking to...."

Elena put her hand up again.

"I can't," she said.

"Honey, you don't have to worry about me," Ray said. "I can take care of myself."

"I don't know anymore," Elena said.

"You don't know what?"

"I...I used to be sure who did...this to me. Now I'm not."

"Just give me the names," Ray said, "and I'll sort them out."

"Like you sorted out Manny and José?" Elena said.

"Why? Did I get the wrong guys?"

It took Elena a moment to shake her head.

"Then what's so bad?"

"I'll just go. Me, William, Rosita. We'll go. When I have more information...when I'm sure again, I'll let you know."

"More information?" Ray asked. "How are you getting information? About what? Who?"

Elena put her hand up again. Ray accepted that he wasn't going to get the information he wanted, not yet. Still, the victory was huge. Making sure Elena was safe was what he had wanted most from the beginning.

He put the car in gear again and drove her home. Before she got out, he asked, "What were you doing on that bridge?"

"Just clearing my mind," she answered.

She stayed in the car a moment longer as though waiting for Ray to probe deeper, but he didn't. Just, "Take care of yourself, *mi'ja*. We'll get you through this."

She leaned over and gave him a kiss on the cheek, then she was out of the car and up the steps to her apartment.

Ray waited to make sure she got in all right, and a minute later, she came to one of the windows of her apartment and waved to him. He waved back, then drove home.

CHAPTER FOURTEEN

It was late when Ray got back to his own apartment building, but that didn't stop Detective Carver from being there waiting for him. Carver sat on the top step of the flight leading to Ray's apartment. Ray sighed when he saw him, but there wasn't much else to do.

"What now?" Ray asked.

He was standing a couple of steps below Carver, his good hand on the railing. Exhaustion had crept throughout his body and he hoped this was a short visit. He needed to finish his sleep.

"Just wanted to talk," Carver said.

Ray checked his watch.

"It's one in the morning."

Detective Carver shrugged.

"I know what time it is. Frankly, I was tempted to just have uniforms pick you up and hold you in a cell until morning, but I figured I'd cut you a break – talk to you like a man, face to face."

"And you're doing me this favor because...?"

Carver shrugged again.

"I like you," he said. Ray couldn't tell if he was serious or sarcastic.

The two men faced each other in silence for a moment before Ray pushed things.

"You gonna tell me what you want, or do I have to guess?"

Carver smiled. "I want to ask you about a guy named Luis."

"I'm gonna need a little more detail."

"This one ran out of a lawyer's office like the place was on fire. About your age, your height, your weight, your hair length, oh, and your scars, and your same cast. If I didn't know better, I'd be tempted to say you ignored my warning about leaving citizens alone."

"And what did this Luis, or whatever, do?"

"Well, that's the thing that's keeping you out of cuffs. The lawyer just mentioned it because I asked him to contact me if anything strange happened. He thought Luis was strange, not criminal."

"Sounds like you've got no real problem, then."

"If you go into that office or talk to anyone connected to it, I'm picking you up and holding you for twenty-four hours. Then I'm gonna ask that you get a psych eval. They can hold you for seventy-two hours while they try to figure out the cause of your, er, antisocial behavior."

"Well, I don't know any Luis that looks like me, so...."

"You just keep thinking it's all a big joke."

Detective Carver stared into Ray's face, looking for a tell, but couldn't find anything and broke the stare off.

"This is a nightmare," Carver muttered.

"What is?"

"Every time I deal with you. That's the nightmare. I got the guys in my squad calling me anytime your name pops up for any reason. Let me tell you, this is getting to be a full-time job."

"And you're keeping tabs on me because...?"

"Because I'm a detective. I spend my time sniffing for shit. You happen to have it all over you."

"Well, this one ain't mine. Do you want anything else from me?"

"I want you to stay the hell away from the lawyers your daughter worked with. In fact, stay away from all lawyers, okay?"

Ray nodded like he was listening, but he was already thinking about getting to bed.

Carver stood up to go. He tried one last time.

"Leave the citizens alone, Cruz. Just focus on your child."

"I've had two children in my life, detective. One is long dead, and the other I'm trying to keep alive."

Carver had read something about the long-dead child Ray had mentioned – the firstborn son of Ray Cruz, killed by a hit-and-run driver at the age of seven. The driver never identified.

"Riding his bike," Carver said out loud.

Ray shook his head as thoughts he didn't want started to creep into him. He wanted to end the conversation and get into his apartment and catch a few hours of sleep.

He asked, "Anything new on my daughter's case?"

Carver looked down. Nothing worse for a detective who isn't making progress than to ask him how the investigation's going.

"Nothing worth reporting."

"And Lenny? He didn't have anything good?"

"Dead end there. He didn't have shit. We cut him loose a few hours ago. Probably on his way out of town by now."

"And you put pressure on him?" Ray asked. He knew Carver didn't have the same kind of pressure tactics that he had, but a cop can be persuasive if he wants.

"Oh, I put all sorts of pressure on him. He just didn't have anything. A rumor that it might have been two guys doing the job. No details."

The two men stood silently on the stairs for a moment. Carver broke the silence.

"And you? Nothing for all your arm twisting?"

"Paid out about five or ten thousand for tips. I got less than you."

Ray shrugged. Carver put out his hand for a shake, and Ray took it.

"Here's to finding whoever did this," Carver said.

He turned to go. Ray wanted to stop him. Ask him about the FBI agent angle. He wanted to know if the detective had heard anything at all about this. He held his tongue. Figured he'd call the agent himself in the morning maybe, try to get a little more information out of her. He didn't need Carver to pry into that just yet, so he let the detective go.

Inside his apartment, he washed his hands and face and changed into sweats, hoping the warmth would help him get some sleep. He went into the kitchen for a drink of water and was soon asleep.

★   ★   ★

Sleep came easy for Ray. Waking up in the morning was harder. Even with his eyes wide open and his ears tuned to the noises of his neighbors getting ready for the day, Ray couldn't think of a reason to get out of bed. He had killed the attackers, but hadn't gotten any more information from them. Lenny also hadn't provided him with anything before leaving the city, and he didn't think Lenny would be back anytime soon. Not if he was smart.

He could try Elena's office again, but what could he say? He was a slip-and-fall client who would really like to know if anyone had threatened Elena Maldonado, the receptionist? A client who wanted to know if the firm had any internal troubles – other clients complaining that millions of dollars had been stolen?

He finally got out of bed because he had a trip to make to the bank and another one to the travel agency.

The bank was easy. The bank associate he spoke to was a young man, thin, blond, with a Christmas tie on. He warned Ray about early withdrawal penalties, tried to steer him out of making such a terrible mistake, but was quick and efficient once Ray made it clear what he needed to happen. The travel agency was different.

In the middle of a cold snap, everyone wants to get on a plane to the tropics. He had to take a seat and wait to see a travel agent, then he had to wait for her to go through a dozen possibilities on the computer, all of which would have worked if he had come in just a couple of days earlier. He nodded and mumbled about understanding and let her do her work. A half hour later, she smiled at him: a flight would take Elena, Rosita and William to Puerto Rico the next day. It would leave and arrive late, but it was better than waiting even longer because the coming weekend was booked solid.

"That'll be twelve hundred and thirty dollars," she said.

Ray pulled out thirteen hundreds from the envelope the guy in the bank had given him, but she shook her head.

"I should have said twelve thirty each ticket."

"What?"

"It's close to Christmas," she said to explain the gouging he felt.

Back at the bank to cash another certificate of deposit, the bank associate did the paperwork without asking questions or giving him any warnings this time. Didn't even ask what brought him back so quickly – there was an Off-Track Betting parlor not too far away, he was probably used to this kind of repeat business. Ray watched the other customers standing in line for a teller or filling out slips at the high desks with the pens chained to them. When he had his money, he got up to leave but turned back to the bank associate.

"Just out of curiosity, does this bank have any customers with a million dollars or more? You know. Any millionaires?"

The bank associate got a serious look on his face – thought for a minute, then the smile returned.

"This bank has several clients in that category. We are one of the most trusted banks in this section of the Bronx."

"Really?" Ray was surprised. "There are millionaires living in this area? Maybe people I meet every day?"

"Well, they don't have to live here to bank with us. They could have businesses here and live anywhere they want."

Ray stood in front of the associate's desk digesting the information.

"You planning to rob us?" the associate asked. He was smiling again, but there was a little nervousness in his face. He had said more than he should have about the assets and clients of the bank.

Ray held his broken hand up.

"Not today," he said. He smiled and the bank associate's confidence returned.

★   ★   ★

Passing by the travel agency again on his way to deliver the plane tickets and cash to his daughter, Ray almost ran into one of the lawyers from Elena's job. He was coming out of the agency, and Ray almost nodded to him in recognition. It was the same lawyer he had approached at the pizza parlor, but he couldn't remember the young man's name. He stopped himself from approaching him again. The first encounter hadn't been all that great – didn't want the guy to think he was being stalked.

★   ★   ★

There was no one home at Elena's place. Ray thought for a moment about slipping the plane tickets under the door, but then he'd have to do the same for the money he wanted to give her, and sitting in front of her door, feeding it hundred-dollar bills one at a time, didn't sound like much of a plan.

Instead, he got back into his car, dropped half the money and the tickets off at his apartment, and went out again with a gun under his coat to ask more questions. Mary Vargas was his first stop.

There was a moving van out in front of Mary's apartment building – La Rosa del Monte. They specialized in moves to Puerto Rico and the rest of the Caribbean. He had to wait for a sofa on its way down before he could reach Mary's apartment, the door taken off its hinges, Mary in work clothes and the baby in her arms. She had a bandana covering most of her hair and a smile on her face until she saw Ray.

"He hasn't contacted me," she said. Ray could tell she was afraid he was carrying a message from José. He put his hands out, palms up.

"I haven't heard from him either," Ray said. "I've heard a few rumors though."

"What?" she asked. There was concern on her face, and Ray knew it had nothing to do with José's well-being and everything to do with how the possibility of him being alive meant she wasn't yet free.

"Well…." Ray stepped aside to let another piece of furniture get carried by. He motioned to Mary that they should step inside and get out of the way.

The bedroom had already been completely cleared so they talked there.

"He's dead," Ray said.

Mary closed her eyes and hung her head low for a moment. She released the air in her lungs slowly before looking up again.

"You sure?" she asked.

"Yeah," Ray said. "One hundred per cent."

"And you're not lying to me?"

Ray shook his head. They were silent for a moment before Mary had another question for him.

"Were you his friend?"

"We knew each other. I worked with him a couple of times," Ray said.

"I hated him," Mary said.

"Yeah. He was a little bit of an asshole," Ray said.

"A little bit?" Mary asked.

Ray got to business.

"There might be a little more money owed to him, and as long as nobody leaks out that he's dead, I might be able to collect it for you if you want, but I need more information from you."

"I don't need the money," Mary said.

"Well, maybe I could keep some of it. It would help me out."

Mary nodded. "I don't know what kind of information I can tell you," she said.

"Well, I haven't been able to find Manny or his wife. I think they just up and left. Was there anyone else that José worked for recently? Did he mention any names? Anything at all?"

Mary shook her head. There was worry on her face. The baby started to move about in her arms. She switched him from one side of her to the other, his legs dangling about her hips.

"He didn't really tell me much about business. I know Manny used to call him. He roughed up a lot of people in the Hunt's Point area recently. You know. Store owners."

Ray knew all about it. He had worked the same type of protection business himself.

"Who did he do this for?" Ray asked.

Mary shook her head again. The baby started to whimper and Ray knew his time in control of Mary's attention was soon going to be over.

"That, I really don't know."

"He ever work with anyone else besides Manny?"

"And you? No, no one that I can.... Wait. He used to work with this guy named Lenny...."

"Lenny Acevedo? Guy with a broken nose? I know Lenny. Anybody else?"

Not that she knew of. The baby started to cry in earnest and the interview was over.

"When are you leaving?" Ray asked.

"Soon as I can," Mary said, and she unbuttoned her blouse and popped out a breast. Before Ray had turned to go, the baby had found what it wanted.

★   ★   ★

Not having gained any new clues yet, Ray drove over to pay off Jerry at the junkyard. On the way, he tried to think of who else he could squeeze information out of. There weren't too many people in his old line of work who he was still current with. It was mostly a young man's job and even two or three years out of the loop was a long time.

CHAPTER FIFTEEN

Detective Carver parked on the broad median under the Bruckner Expressway. The area was overgrown with weeds in the summertime, but now there were only a couple of rusting cars. Farther down, there was a bunch of plastic tarps and large cardboard boxes – refrigerator packing – that meant a shantytown was growing up.

"I've got a meeting with a CI on an old case," he told his partner. "Won't be more than fifteen or twenty minutes tops."

"Want me to come with you?" his partner asked.

Carver pretended to think about it for a moment before shaking his head.

"No need. Besides, I don't want to spook him. Just sit tight for twenty minutes. Won't be longer."

His partner, Joseph DiRaimo – sometimes called Fats – just nodded. He'd only been on the detective side of things for a few months, but already he wasn't liking his partner too much. Thought he was a cowboy – liked to work cases alone, and DiRaimo wasn't always sure what side of the law his partner was working. Carver got out and started walking.

El Don Juan, a strip bar that still advertised go-go girls with a sign that had been installed many years earlier at the start of the 1970s, was as shady a place as any in New York City, but the bouncer at the door waved Carver in without even needing to see his badge. He had it pretty much memorized. The inside of the bar was dark even for a topless bar, and the women – the ones he could see - weren't just topless. One of them, just inside the vestibule that screened the inside from passersby on the street, was bent over, her hands on the wall, and a guy in a suit and raincoat going at her from behind. He was about sixty and grunting, but the girl looked bored to Carver's eye. Three steps beyond the happy couple, there was a young Hispanic guy in polyester from the Seventies. A naked lady sat on either side of him as he stooped to snort lines off a table. Carver knew where to go if he ever needed to fulfill an arrest quota.

The man he wanted to meet was at a table right off the farthest end of the stage. In front of him, a young girl was trying to work the pole in just about nothing but heels that were way too high for her. It looked like she was just trying to keep from falling. Robert Meister waved Carver over.

"What kept you?"

"I have an actual job," Carver said.

"Anything I should be concerned about?" Meister said. He threw a glance at the girl on stage. She'd given up trying to keep her balance and was now crawling around on the stage, clawing the air in slow motion like some big cat on downers.

"Two other people were murdered in the precinct last night. Nothing to bother yourself with unless you killed one of them."

"Christ," Meister said. "These people are savages."

Carver didn't have an answer for that. He lit a cigarette. Took a look at the girl on stage. She was lying on her back. She was gyrating, maybe touching herself, but Carver thought it would only be a couple of minutes before she just fell asleep on stage. An older woman with her breasts out and a serving tray under her arm came near the table. Carver shooed her away before she could ask if he had an order. She took offense, flipped him off and headed to another table.

"You wanted to talk to me," Carver said after a minute.

"I wanted results," Meister said. "This whole thing has gone from bad to worse. I gave you ten grand, then I gave you ten more. I thought this was all going to be cleared up and I'd have my money by now."

Meister spoke in low tones, but he was angry. The muscles in his face were working hard, and he kept playing with a matchbook, splaying the matches and straightening them again. A couple had fallen off already.

"Well, I cleared up the Lenny issue," Carver said. "I can't find José or Manny. I'm guessing Ray Cruz found them first and they've gone to meet their makers."

"Cruz?"

"Yeah, he's Elena's father...."

"I can have him killed like that," Meister said. He snapped his fingers in the air. Then he did it again in case Carver didn't get the picture the first time.

"No, no. No need for that," Carver said. The last thing he wanted was for Ray Cruz to turn up dead when Cruz and his whole family had had a bunch of conversations with him already.

"I've dug around about him," the detective said. "He's a tough guy from way back. It's possible José and Manny are still alive, but I'd hate to think about what he's done to them."

"You gone to their houses?" Meister asked.

"I'll need to do more digging – they ain't at the address the NYPD has for them. I'll sort that out soon."

"And my money?"

Carver shrugged. The girl on the stage had stopped gyrating and a big guy with his shirt open most of the way to his navel came out from behind the curtains, got on stage with her and was stooping over her, saying something. Probably trying to wake her up. Another girl, in her twenties with pasties on, was looking out from behind the curtain, waiting for her turn.

"Don't ignore me when I'm asking about my money," Meister said. "You hear me? That bitch took seven million that were supposed to come to me. I had that deal set up, and she stepped in the middle. I need to get that money from her. Got it?"

"It's my understanding that she no longer has the money," Carver threw in.

"Bullshit!" Meister answered. If what passed for music in the place weren't so loud, everyone would have heard it.

"Bullshit! And on top of that, I don't care. I don't care where she put the money, I don't care if she has to pull it out of her ass, I need it. You understand me? I got people who—"

"What people?"

"People. Russian people."

"Russian mob types?" Carver asked.

"Serious people. Christ Almighty. What don't you understand? People. Who cares if they're Russian?"

Carver put his hands up as a sign of surrender, at the same time hoping the man would calm down.

"Look, I had patience with her, I told Lenny to take care of her. That didn't work. I'll kill her. I don't give a shit. You understand me? You understand that I have to put in my bid with the city on Monday, and I need a bank check with me. They don't go by good faith."

The two men were silent for a minute; Carver was wishing he hadn't shooed the waitress away. Meister worked his jaw.

"If I don't get my money, then I don't care," Meister said. "I'll kill her, I'll kill her husband, I'll kill her kid even. I don't give a shit. I'll kill her father too. I'm tired of the Bronx, all these spics and sambos running the place like…savages. I'd kill them all." A vein bulged in his forehead, and Carver tried to calm him. No good being overheard having a conversation like this, even if there really wasn't anyone in the bar who cared.

"Jesus, Meister, don't get yourself so worked up," Carver said.

"Haven't I told you not to use my name?" Meister said.

"Yeah, sorry, but you're shouting about murder here. Calm down a little. You're going to give yourself a heart attack."

"Big shit. I've had three already," Meister said.

"Today?" Carver asked.

Meister took a drink and calmed a little. He spoke more quietly anyway.

"Listen to me. Put some pressure on her, get her talking, kill someone if you have to, I'll pay, but find out where that money is and find out today."

Carver was about to explain how he had limits to what he could do, that Elena might well have gotten rid of the money or given it to someone who wasn't about to give it back, that if being attacked like she was didn't make her co-operative, he wasn't sure there was more to be done, but Meister wasn't listening. He put three twenties on the table and got up, starting to walk away.

"I've got a couple of leads, but this won't be easy," Carver said at his back.

Meister turned around. "If it was easy, I'd do it myself, asshole," he said. He kept walking.

Carver looked around, picked up one of the twenties and pocketed it, then he also walked out.

★　　★　　★

Back inside his car, Detective Carver wanted to tell his partner about how he was stuck between Elena's father, who was a certifiable nutjob who could leave a string of bodies all around the Tristate area, and Robert Meister, who was a bigger nutjob with a lot of money and venom for blood who might get even more people killed. Not that he cared all that much for most of the people who might be bumped off, but each of them might think they had a reason to kill him. They might even be right.

He looked at his partner's face for a few seconds before deciding that DiRaimo would be no help to him. He'd have to go this alone.

"Listen, I've got to take some personal time," Carver said.

"But you just took half an hour," DiRaimo pointed out like Carver might have forgotten.

"I know. I'm not saying I'll be gone all day. I just need an hour or two. Probably two. You just drop me off at the Hunt's Point subway station. I'll catch up with you at the station house after lunch."

"You cleared this with the captain?" DiRaimo asked.

"Jesus, what are you? My mother? Look, if the captain asks, tell him I needed personal time. Easy. I'll square it with him when I get back."

DiRaimo shrugged and put the car in gear. When he dropped his partner off at the subway stop, he noticed that Carver just stood there a moment, waiting for him to leave. DiRaimo thought about following his partner, but shook the idea out of his head. The day he started following his own partner was the day he quit the force. If you can't trust the guy who's covering your back, then you need to find a new profession.

Carver waited for his partner to drive out of sight before heading over to Elena's law firm at a quick walk. The day wasn't as cold as it had been the past week, but it was still freezing, and he'd spent a lot of time exposed to the elements. He thought of retirement as he walked. If he could just get Elena to do what everyone wanted her to do, he might be able to get himself to a beach.

At the law firm, the receptionist was a brand-new one, so he showed her his badge.

"I need to speak with Mark Langan," he said.

"May I ask who wants him?" the receptionist asked. She was pretty and young with curls that cascaded, but Carver figured her for dumb.

He took out his badge again, put it a foot from her face, and pointed at it with his free hand. She took the time to read the badge and ID card it came with carefully, then she took a note. When she was done, she looked back up at the detective.

"I'm afraid he's with a client right now. Can I take a message?"

"I'm not asking who he's with, sweetheart. I want to know *where* he is."

The receptionist checked a day calendar in front of her and looked up again.

"I don't have a note about that. He left with a client. Should be back by one-thirty or two, he said."

"Great. Any idea where he might have gone with a client?" Carver asked.

"This is only my second day temping here," the receptionist said. "I would figure he might go to a restaurant for an early lunch. Maybe La Calidad down the block?"

Carver thought about it a second. It wasn't a bad guess. For a better restaurant, the young lawyer would have to drive a long way. He checked his watch. Only a little past ten in the morning and La

Calidad didn't serve breakfast. Not that it mattered much. By law the bar he'd just come from wasn't supposed to open for almost another hour, but he knew for a fact it only closed its doors for a few hours in the early morning each day – patrons and dancing girls locked inside together doing whatever until the doors opened again.

"Thanks," Carver said. He was about to go out, but turned back.

"Langan didn't happen to leave here with a Hispanic man about forty-five or fifty with a cast on his arm?"

"No," the receptionist said. She was about to let Carver go, but figured if he was that far off the mark, he could use a hint. "He left with a woman," she said.

CHAPTER SIXTEEN

Mark Langan looked at the woman beside him and thought she wasn't quite beautiful – a bit too severe, looking like she'd just had her toes stepped on – but from the neck down, she was better than all right. He pulled the sheet down a little to reveal a nipple, brown and still perked. He moved to touch, but she slapped his hand away.

"You've got work to do," she said, and she slipped her body out from under the covers altogether, sat on the edge of the bed.

"We both have work to do," he said.

He sat up to get a better view of her. She obliged him without even knowing it, standing up and stretching a little before walking away from him and into the bathroom. He felt himself getting stiff again, but he knew she wasn't going to be up for any more loving. He wondered why that was. After all, he was the one with all the hard work to do. She just had to lie there.

She came back out of the bathroom still nude, panties in her hand. Her shape was a perfect hourglass. He could definitely have another go at her.

"I've called that Elena Maldonado a half dozen times in the last two days," she said. "Now she just hangs up on me. I need her to get back to work and undo what she did. She put that money in the wrong hands and she needs to put it in the right hands. The bureau needs her to do this or two years of work go down the drain and a lot of people, a lot of good agents, will have their careers ruined. Not to mention me. I'll be ruined. I'll be the laughingstock of the bureau, but that won't last long. Just long enough for the paperwork to go through on my dismissal. Understand me? I'm not losing my job because she got cold feet."

Langan smiled. She was looking at him for more of a reaction, so he sighed and shook his head like he couldn't believe everything that had happened. He'd heard this all before, wasn't stupid, hadn't forgotten it, so he found it hard to act interested. Especially when Agent Esposito was standing five feet away, naked.

"Well, not for nothing, you're in this mess too," she said. That got his attention. Any mention of himself would have.

"Me?" he asked, but he already knew what she was going to say and that she was right.

"You gave her the routing numbers, account numbers and all sorts of information. This was a service to your country, but if the operation doesn't work out, it probably won't look that way to others."

He smiled at her. She looked down at the little tent his erection was making under the sheets and held a hand up to stop him.

"We don't have time for that," she said. "Focus. Get dressed. We've got to get out of here."

She went back into the bathroom, left the door open and leaned over the sink to wash her face. A few seconds later, Mark Langan was behind her, groping her breasts and breathing on her neck.

She took hold of his right ring finger and pulled it back, not hard enough for actual pain, just a message.

"The bureau teaches this technique for incapacitating assailants who sneak up behind you," she said. "Want a taste?"

Langan let go.

*   *   *

Back in his apartment, Ray collected the cash and the plane tickets for Elena, and he was about to pick up the phone to call her when it rang. He answered on the second ring.

"Cruz?" He heard the voice and tried to place it.

"Yes," he said. "How can I help you?"

"This is Ramona Esposito with the FBI. I was hoping you had a little time to talk about your daughter's case."

Ray sat down, the receiver glued to his ear.

"Sure," he said. "On the phone?"

"Can you meet me?"

"When and where?"

There was the sound of papers shuffling on the other side for a moment.

"Can you make it to the Bronx Courthouse on Grand Concourse? We can meet on the front steps in about...let's say one hour."

"Got it. No problem. But if you don't mind me asking...."

Apparently she did mind because she had already hung up.

Ray called his daughter. No answer, so he left a message. It was short and didn't mention Esposito. Just said he'd try again later, was going out, and would be by sooner or later.

The courthouse was well known to Ray, as it was to most residents of the Bronx. It was not far from Yankee Stadium – an old building with a huge set of stairs at the front leading to an entrance of long columns and bronze doors. It was at the top of a hill and commanded a view. With the hundreds of cops, lawyers, court officers, defendants, victims, families on both sides, and reporters who went there every day, parking for an ordinary citizen was close to impossible. Getting there would mean two subway lines if he went by public transportation, but Ray dialed up a cab company.

The ride was quick, but since they were headed in the direction of the Stadium, the driver talked baseball all the way. Nothing really to talk about except how the Yankees might do given the fact that they'd tanked the season before. Ray didn't have much to say about any of that, and in the last block of the ride the driver switched to football. Ray tossed twenty dollars onto the front seat and opened the door before the car had come to a full stop.

From the top of the stairs, there was a lot to see, but no Agent Esposito. Ray wasn't surprised; he was a little more than a half hour early. He was kept company by pigeons and smokers. The hilltop position ensured a stiff breeze without letup. He thought about what he had wanted to ask the FBI lady.

Why couldn't she tell him stuff over the phone? In fact, now that he thought about it, the fact that his daughter had been out all day was not reassuring to him. What? Was she in the Witness Protection Program now? Or had something happened to her? What could be the break in the case? Was it possible that José's body had been found and the FBI wanted to trick him into talking with them about it?

No matter how he twisted the problem in his head over the next half hour, and he certainly did a lot of twisting, there was nothing good that could come out of this meeting on the courthouse steps. He was half inclined to just leave. Whatever news Esposito had could wait for another phone call, right?

He made a final survey of all the faces coming up and going down the stairs in front of the courthouse. There was no sign of Agent Esposito, but there were a few guys he had noticed waiting out in the cold even though they didn't have cigarettes to smoke. Were they cops? FBI?

He couldn't take waiting anymore. There were phones inside the building, but those required he go through security and a metal detector. That wouldn't have worked out well for him. Instead, he went back down to street level and headed toward the trains. He found a payphone outside a diner on the corner and called his daughter. Still no answer. That made him nervous. He tried to remember whether she had said anything about being out of the house for a few hours, but nothing came to mind.

He stepped to the curb and tried to get a look at the people climbing the courthouse steps. Didn't want to miss Esposito, though by his watch she was a few minutes late. A few minutes later and there was still no sign of her. He dug into one of his pockets and pulled out the business card she had left in his mailbox a few days earlier. He didn't expect her to pick up. He hoped she was on her way to meet him. He tried calling her anyway.

Disconnected.

CHAPTER SEVENTEEN

"How hard can it be?" Langan repeated to himself. "She's a little girl and everyone at that school is underpaid. Overworked. Too busy to even notice."

He had to rehearse this to himself because he knew that failure could only mean bad things. The plan was to walk straight into Rosita Maldonado's school, find the right classroom, and tell the teacher there had been a slight emergency with Elena and William, her parents. They wouldn't be able to pick her up and had sent him − note in hand with signature and everything − to pick her up for them. How hard could it be? Why would anyone doubt him? Why would they even care?

Of course, if for some reason he failed...the police might be the least of his troubles. He knew Elena. Liked her. But she'd tear his head off. Maybe he could handle her, calm her down, fight her off if it came to that. But Elena might not come after him alone. She had a husband, and William wasn't a small man.

Still, it had to be done and there was nothing but short notice. No time to find someone, no time to trick anyone into doing it. No better way. Not that he could think of at least.

The school was a low building, two stories tall, red brick. The windows had cutouts of fall leaves, made of oak tag and colored in, pasted on the inside. On the outside, the windows had metal gates. Langan could hear the children laughing and playing even before he opened the door.

"Can I help you?"

Security guard seated at a small desk right inside the door. Black man, maybe fifty, wearing a heavy coat and a baseball cap with some sort of embroidered gold badge on it. Probably sat at the door all day long. Langan was tempted to turn around and try to find another door.

"Can I help you?" the guard repeated; he sounded surly now.

"I'm looking for Rosa Maldonado," Langan said. "Any idea where I can find her?"

"She teach here?"

"No, no. She's a student."

Langan smiled, figured that had to help his case, but the thought crept in that talking about a little girl and smiling might make him look like a pervert. He let the smile dry up.

"Oh, I know who you're talking about. I know Rosita. I don't know all the kids, but I know her. What you want with her?"

"Well," Langan said; he tried to think quickly. He opted for, "That's private business."

"No. It isn't. You on school property and so is she. This is schooltime for her and that makes it school business. Now, what you want with her? You can tell me now, or I can ask you to leave."

"Her mother's not feeling well, and I...I'm a friend of the family, and she asked me to bring Rosita home."

The guard raised an eyebrow and looked like he had a half dozen more questions, but he didn't ask them. He rolled his eyes and sighed and filled out a hall pass.

"Go to the office. Room 104," he said. "Through those doors and turn left."

"Thank you," Langan said.

He took his pass, followed the directions and walked into the front room of the principal's office. He wanted to walk back out of there. He showed the pass to the secretary and told her what he wanted.

"And your name is...?" she asked.

"Leonard. Leonard Green."

He handed her the note he had forged. The secretary looked at him over her glasses as though trying to match the name to his face like they'd go together naturally. She had a sweater over her shoulders, and

Langan wondered if it was really that cold. Since he had just come from outside, the place felt stifling to him.

She looked at a chart and told him, "Room 209. Up the stairs and to your right."

The door to 209 had a large window, and Langan took a moment to find Rosita. There she was, all of three feet tall, working with clay at a table with other munchkins.

He scanned the room through the window to find the teacher. She found him first, was staring at him. Striking. Maybe twenty-five with dark hair, fine features, and an even finer figure. Her arms were crossed over her chest but that didn't hide much. And her legs. He wondered why he never had a teacher like that in all his school days straight through law school.

He motioned for her to come over and she did, saying something to the class over her shoulder as she walked. It took only a moment for Langan to tell the story a third time. It sounded even more convincing now that he was looking into her blue eyes and enjoying her smile up close. He wanted to reach out and touch her. Instead, he gave her his forged note to look over.

"And you went to Principal Wilder's office?" the teacher asked. She hadn't identified herself yet. He thought he might want to pretend not to be able to remember her name, force her to give it to him. Decided against that.

"Room 104," he said.

The teacher nodded.

"They sent me straight up," he added.

"Well, I'll tell her to get her things. Just wait right here."

She closed the classroom door again and walked toward Rosita, giving Langan a great view of her walking away. When this was all over and he had his share safely tucked away, he'd come back. She couldn't earn much teaching pre-kindergarteners, and he'd have plenty to throw around.

Rosita seemed about ready to balk at not being able to finish up with the clay, but after a few words from her teacher, she was putting on her coat and heading toward him.

"And this is Leonard Green, Rosita. Your mother asked him to pick you up and take you home today."

Langan tried to smile in a way he thought people might when they were picking up small children from school. He had never done it himself.

"No, it's not," Rosita said.

"Not what?" her teacher asked.

"That's not Leonard Green," Rosita said.

"What?" her teacher asked.

Langan could feel a bead of sweat roll straight down his back, and he had no idea what his smile looked like now, but it couldn't have been good.

"What do you mean?" her teacher asked. She stooped to Rosita's level.

"His name is Mark Langan. He works with my mom. I've seen him at her job."

The teacher straightened up to look Langan in the face and smiled at him. She was waiting for him to say something in his defense, but he didn't. Thought it was best to let the teacher think Rosita was just doing some of that pretend play that children were supposed to do.

"Can I see some ID?" Rosita's teacher asked after a moment.

"Uh, sure," Langan said.

He patted his pockets, found his wallet, pulled it out, but didn't know what to do next. It's not like he had fake ID ready for this. It's not like he wanted to show off his real ID either.

"You know what?" he said. "I left the ID in my other wallet. In the car. Let me just go down and get it. I'll be back."

"He's Mark Langan," Rosita repeated. It was more to herself than for anyone else to hear, but Langan took it as an accusation. When he got to the door that led to the stairs down, he pushed through roughly. It would have bounced back on him if he hadn't moved so fast through it. He heard the door open behind him as he reached the first landing and turned to go down to street level.

"Stop him!"

It was that bitch. Good looking, but she was taking the word of a four-year-old over his. He pretty much skipped down the last segment of stairs, taking them by twos and threes.

"Stop him!" the teacher shouted again.

The security guard rose up behind his desk as Langan was approaching. No way he would get out from behind the desk in time to get in his way, but that wasn't what the guard was thinking anyway.

He gave the desk a shove and got it in Langan's path, just clipping his thigh with it. Hurt like hell, but Langan shoved it back and kept going for the door to the outside.

"Stop him!" again, but it was too late. One good push and he was out of the building, on the sidewalk and sprinting for his car.

By the time the guard got out from behind his desk and through the door, Langan was in the car, pulling away. Langan was in on the passenger side, so there must have been a driver, but all the guard could say for sure was that it was a dark car, a sedan, and moving fast.

★   ★   ★

Ray raced to Elena's apartment. He didn't know what kind of FBI agent had her phone disconnected – he hadn't heard of the government failing to pay its phone bills – but it wasn't the type of agent he wanted his daughter dealing with and he imagined that's what Elena was doing. A rogue agent. Somebody who had gotten his daughter into deep trouble and was willing to sink her deeper before letting her out.

"Twenty dollars for every red light you go through," Ray called out to the driver.

The driver nodded slowly. He was a non-talker, but when the next light turned against them, he got into the oncoming traffic lane, went past eight waiting cars, and crossed through the intersection, nearly taking the red shopping cart out of the hands of a little old lady who was using it more for support than anything else.

In the end, the ride cost Ray almost two hundred dollars, but the cabby shaved ten minutes off what Ray thought it would take. Ray put the money in the man's hand, the man fanned the money out for a quick count and was off. Never said a word.

Upstairs, there was noise coming from Elena's apartment, and Ray put his hand on the gun at the small of his back.

He listened for a second. Elena's voice, but he couldn't make out the words. He damned his heart for beating so loudly in his ears. Then she laughed. That was clear. He exhaled, let go of the gun, and knocked.

"*Papi*," Elena said when she'd opened the door. She had a phone in her hand.

Ray followed her inside.

"See you in ten minutes?" she said into the phone then she gave an air kiss and pressed the button to shut it off.

"I've been trying to reach you," Ray said. He tried to make it sound nonchalant, but it came out worried.

"Shopping," Elena said. She pointed to a set of bags on the sofa as proof. "Rosita needs some new summer clothes if we're going to Puerto Rico – what she has doesn't fit her anymore. You know how it is."

She walked past her father and into the kitchen. He did know how it was. He remembered being with Maria and Elena in a shopping mall when Elena was ten. Her brother had died a few months before – hit-and-run, some said sedan, some said a station wagon, the police said they didn't know – and Elena needed new clothes for a new school year. Maria and Elena went through the store with smiles on their faces that Ray couldn't understand. At that point, he was still thinking he'd never smile again.

Elena came back out of the kitchen with a glass of soda in her hand.

"Want some?" she asked.

Ray shook his head.

"That was William on the phone. Said he'd be here in a few minutes. Got out of work early to help get ready for the trip."

She paused after the last word. It took Ray a moment to remember what he had originally wanted to see his daughter about. He reached for his inner coat pocket and pulled out the tickets and an envelope of cash.

"Here you go. Three tickets and a few thousand dollars. You use cash for everything once you get on the plane, you understand me? You need more money, I'll arrange for it, just give me a call."

Elena looked through the envelope and her eyes widened.

"How much?" she asked. The look on her face had become stern like she was thinking of rejecting the money. She had her pride and Ray knew all about it.

"About ten thousand. You can count it. I can give you a receipt if you want and you can pay me back later. Or not. Be frugal if that's what you want, you just never pay with anything but cash, understand?"

It took a moment, but Elena nodded. Then the phone rang.

The highlight of the conversation was Elena's repetition of the question,

"She's all right? She's all right?"

The lines of her face screamed terror. Ray knew it was Rosita she was inquiring about, but nothing came to his mind. What could happen to a four-year-old in school? A paper cut? Still, as his daughter put her hand to her forehead and started to pace, her face twisted, he found he had put his hand back on the gun at his waistband.

The phone call was a minute long, but it felt so much longer watching his daughter go through the gyrations of pain.

"What?" he asked. Tears were welling in his eyes; he didn't know why, but he knew they were appropriate.

Elena hung up, grabbed her coat and her keys.

"You have your car?" she asked. The words came out shrill. Like a demand, like she was the one holding a gun.

"No," Ray said. He felt stupid saying it. Clearly a car was needed and clearly he was failing his daughter. Again.

"We can get a cab," he said.

"Stay here," she told him. "Wait for William."

She headed for the door.

"Where are you going?" he asked.

"They tried to take Rosita," his daughter said. She wiped her nose with the back of her hand. There were tears streaming down her face and her eyes had turned red instantly. She opened the door.

"I'll come with you," Ray said.

She was out in the hallway.

"Someone has to wait for William," she said over her shoulder.

Ray looked around in the apartment for a second, found a scrap of paper, wrote GO TO THE SCHOOL on it in pencil. He pinched this with the door as he closed up, then he went out.

Elena was on the street when he caught sight of her again. She was half walking half jogging toward the school, and from a dozen steps behind her, Ray could make out that she was moaning like a wounded animal. He tried to jog to catch up to her. He wanted to touch her, share her pain. He also wanted to find out exactly what had happened.

The pain in his ribs and chest wouldn't let him go any faster. He started falling farther behind. He called for her. It made no difference. She was moving as fast as her legs could take her. She crossed the street straight through traffic, cars screeching to avoid her, horns blaring. She didn't hear it. Ray knew how she felt.

Traffic was flowing heavy when Elena got to the next intersection. She had to wait. This gave Ray just enough time to put a hand on her. She pulled away.

"Elena," he said. Wasn't sure what else to add. "What happened?"

His daughter was crying freely now, her shoulders shaking with the force of it. She didn't have the breath to tell him anything at the moment.

"Breathe," he said. "Breathe. And tell me what happened."

The light turned, and Elena was on her way again. Turning traffic had to wait for her; she wasn't stopping.

"Elena," Ray called. He was falling behind again, holding his side. "Elena, wait."

She turned half around, didn't stop or slow.

"They tried to take her. A man tried to take her out of the school," she yelled back. Agony dripped from her voice and tore into Ray's soul.

"Kidnap her?" Ray asked, but she was facing forward, walking fast and not paying him any attention. In another couple of minutes they'd be at the school, or at least she would. Ray wasn't sure he'd make it.

As she reached the next intersection, Ray had fallen four steps behind her. The light turned against her as she entered the crosswalk. A ten-wheel truck with a high cab lurched forward as she stepped in front. Ray watched as Elena put her hands up and arms out as though she could hold the truck back. Ray's hands went up to the hair at the sides of his head, and his legs went weak. He felt dizzy for a fraction of a second and the blood within him went cold to see his daughter collide with the machine.

The impact made Elena skid on the asphalt, the heels of her shoes snapped off, and she fell onto her back. The truck stopped, brakes squealing, driver sticking his head out to curse more effectively. Elena started to get up, and Ray breathed again. He rushed to her side, lifted her by the hand and didn't let go of her this time.

"What good are you to Rosita if you get killed?" he asked.

She was limping at his side, still crying, thinking nothing about the truck.

"They didn't take her," Ray continued. "They tried, but they didn't do it. Remember that. She's safe and tomorrow, she won't even be in this city anymore."

As they got to the block the school was on, Ray stopped her forcibly.

"Let me look at you. You look terrible," he said. She tried to pull away. "Straighten out your face a little. You don't want to scare her."

Elena used her sleeve to wipe her nose and her tears. It didn't do much. With the fading bruises and the smeared makeup, she looked like a Picasso.

"Now, when you go in there, you smile, you talk calmly, you stroke Rosita's hair, and you make believe you have the whole world under your control."

"But they almost took her, *Papi*."

"Yup. Almost. But you pretend like you're in control, you know why? Because you're the parent, and that's what parents do."

Elena muttered something about "friggin' Dr. Spock," and continued on to the school.

"You think they have metal detectors at this school?" Ray asked. Elena looked at him as she pulled open the door.

"It's a preschool," she said, leaving him to imagine what he wanted. He followed her.

★   ★   ★

Mark Langan stepped out of the getaway car about a mile from the school. He crossed the street to another sedan and got in.

"Where's the kid?" Agent Esposito asked.

"She recognized me."

"What?" Esposito was driving already. "What do you mean? How could she...?"

"I don't know how it happened, but I gave the teacher one name and the kid just said, 'He's Mark Langan. He works with Mommy.' I ran."

Esposito pulled over and turned off the car.

"What?" Langan asked. "What else was I supposed to do?"

"You were supposed to bring the girl."

"Well, what do you want me to do now?"

Esposito thought for a moment before answering.

"Get out."

"What?"

"Get. Out. Of. The. Car."

Langan laughed, but Esposito didn't. His smile disappeared.

"You can't be serious," he said.

Esposito pulled out her handgun and pointed it at him. He got the message and got out.

"Bitch," he said out loud as she drove away, and he tried to figure out where he was.

CHAPTER EIGHTEEN

William arrived at the school in his car only a few seconds after Ray and Elena. The security guard led them all to the principal's office. He kept his eyes down, ashamed he hadn't been able to stop the man who tried to take one of the kids.

"We've called the police," were the first words out of the principal's mouth as Elena knelt and hugged her daughter to her. Rosita had taken one look at her mother and started crying. "We had to, of course. We are taking this incident very seriously, but Rosita said something about this being a co-worker of yours."

"What?" Elena asked. She stood up, Rosita still clinging to her.

"Mark Langan. She said his name was Mark Langan. Said he works with you."

Principal Agnes Wilder was a tiny woman, about fifty, probably not quite five feet, not quite a hundred pounds.

"Sometimes parents do that, send friends to pick up their children, especially in emergency situations." She was talking to Ray now. "That's what he told us, he said Elena was sick. He had a note. Anyway, we wouldn't have called the police, but he gave a false name and then he bolted out of here when Rosita gave us his real name."

She stopped for a moment to catch her breath and to see if there was any reaction to what she'd said. Ray's attention was mostly on his daughter and granddaughter. She turned to William.

"Did we do the right thing? Should we have called the police?"

"We didn't send anyone," he said.

"Oh my."

Principal Wilder put a hand to cover her mouth and looked a little like she needed to take a seat to keep from falling.

"When did you call the police?" Ray asked.

"At the same time I was speaking with Elena, my secretary was on the phone with the police. They said they'd be right over. Oh my."

The principal took a seat next to her secretary's desk and looked like she was about to be sick.

"We almost let her go," she said. "We almost let her go."

Ray turned his attentions from the principal. Not much he could do for her. Besides, she had a secretary to help her.

"You know this Mark Langan?" he asked William.

William shook his head and moved in closer to his wife and daughter, rubbing both their backs to comfort them.

★   ★   ★

When the police came, Rosita was already calmed. The principal had found milk and cookies for the girl. The secretary, the schoolteacher, and the security guard each told Elena and the police every detail they could remember. It wasn't much, but the descriptions were more than enough to convince Elena that the man who had come to abduct her daughter was, in fact, Mark Langan, a lawyer at the firm she worked for.

"Any reason he might want to hurt your daughter besides the obvious?" a uniformed officer asked.

"What's the obvious reason?" Elena asked.

"Well, he could be a pervert," the officer answered.

"Can you just call Detective Carver here?" Elena said. She felt like she was wasting her time and didn't want to have to repeat herself.

The uniformed officer moved a couple of steps away from Elena and Rosita, who were sitting side by side on plastic chairs in the principal's office. A raft of uniformed officers and even a couple of TV news vans had invaded the school area. Parents were picking up their children and asking questions. A representative from the board of education was on his way from Brooklyn to handle the press.

Ray wanted to be gone before Detective Carver arrived. Now

that he had a solid name, he didn't think he needed the police. He could handle Langan, of that he was sure. And Langan would tell him everything he knew. But he didn't feel right leaving Elena and her family while Langan might be close by, and who knew what he had in mind?

Carver's partner, Joseph DiRaimo, showed up first, told everyone Detective Carver would be by shortly. DiRaimo got all the details, had a fax of Mark Langan's driver's license sent to the school, then, once Elena and Rosita identified him, had the photo sent to every precinct in the city, and sent uniformed officers out to his place of residence and his office.

"Like a regular manhunt," Ray remarked.

"Exactly what it is," DiRaimo answered. "We catch the bastard and a lot of people can sleep easier."

DiRaimo had run out of things to say when Detective Carver finally arrived. He reeked of cigarette smoke, and Ray was almost positive there was a hint of alcohol floating in the air as he entered. Carver spoke with his partner alone for a few moments, took a look at the fax of Langan's license, then looked up for a half minute, calculating.

"Any place I can talk with Mrs. Maldonado?" he asked the school principal. She pointed out the door to her inner office.

William, Ray, and DiRaimo all got up to go with Carver and Elena, but he waved them off.

"Sensitive discussion," he said as Elena went through the door ahead of him.

"But I'm her husband," William said.

"Yeah," Carver answered as he closed the door behind him.

"We've got to talk," he said to Elena once the door was closed. "You never said a word to me about this Langan guy."

"I would never in a hundred years have thought he would do something like this," she answered.

"You mean the kidnapping thing or the assault thing?" Carver asked. He meant to be mean – wanted to force her to talk. Her shoulders slumped, but she tried to put on a bright face.

"You always such an asshole?" she asked.

Carver tossed his palms up like he couldn't understand the root of her anger.

"Look, if I understand this all correctly, this Langan guy has gone through a lot of trouble to hurt you. It's more than just personal. I'm guessing if all he wanted was a little payback for something, he could have had you fired, right?"

Elena tried to figure out the technicalities of Langan getting her fired, but there wasn't all that much to consider.

"Yes," she said.

"So why go the extra mile? What did you do to him?"

Elena looked down at her broken shoes. She would have loved to have told Carver what she thought was Langan's motive – that she had taken money and maybe the FBI was involved and someone, a client of the firm, was out seven million dollars. The way she figured it quickly, Langan was probably working on behalf of the client. She couldn't see the upside to telling. Sure, she might land herself in jail – no matter how right she thought she was – but telling Carver everything wouldn't do anything to help. There was already a manhunt for Langan. She shook her head.

"So, you can't think of any reason?" Carver pressed. "He's just some sick psycho picking on the innocent?"

"Looks like it," she said.

Carver sighed. "Let me tell you something. You may think this is the smart way to do things, but it won't work. You're lying to me now and I know it. You're endangering your family, your daughter, and for nothing. When we catch Langan, we're going to squeeze him, and I guarantee you, he will squeal like a pig. He will give his side of the story and you know what? By the time that lawyer is done smoothing everything over, no one is really going to care what you have to say. After all, you never even filed a report. According to you, nothing happened to you a few days ago and you have no idea why Langan came here today. Not smart. What do you think of that?"

Elena shook her head. "I think you should come back to talk to me after you catch Langan. For now, I'm tired, and I want to take my baby home."

Carver sighed and opened the door for her to step through.

★   ★   ★

It was almost four o'clock before they were able to leave Rosita's school. Her teacher was in tears as they filed out of her classroom. Ray knew the tears were real and the teacher would help where she could, but there wasn't much to be done. Not by a schoolteacher.

"Shit!" Willie yelled out as soon as he reached the car.

"What?" Ray asked.

"Damn kids," Willie said. He was pointing at the front passenger-side wheel on the car. It was flat.

Ray looked and pointed at the rear passenger-side wheel. It also was flat. He went around to the street side of the car. Two more flats.

"Wasn't kids," Ray said out loud.

"What was that?" his daughter asked. He didn't want to scare her. Puncturing the tires was a tactic he had used a few times himself. Usually got people walking. At the very least, they'd be waiting for a cab to come. Either way, they were vulnerable. Ray looked at the near houses and cars. Plenty of places to hide, but no evidence that Langan or others were doing that.

"We should call the police," Willie said.

"Let's just go," Elena said. "I don't want to wait here." Ray looked at her and could see in her eyes that she knew what was happening. She knew that the punctures were on purpose. There were ten other cars parked on that same street and all were fine. No coincidences.

Still, it was a large group — three adults and a child. There could be a drive-by shooting planned, mow them all down, but Ray didn't think so. It was still light out and the street was busy. You didn't set up a drive-by on a street where you might get caught in traffic.

"Let's walk," Ray suggested. "Too cold to stay out here forever."

From Rosita's school to Elena's apartment was a five-minute walk to the Bruckner Drawbridge over the Bronx River, then another five minutes or so home. Certainly less than half an hour even at Rosita's pace, and there was the chance of finding an unoccupied gypsy cab though that chance was slim – cold days saw the cabs snapped up pretty quickly.

"Walk?" Rosita asked. Her voice told the grown-ups that she had never considered walking such a distance in the cold.

"Don't worry, sweetie, your father will carry you," Ray said.

Elena laughed at this and so did Willie, but after a few seconds, Elena's laughter turned into tears. Ray thought it might be pain in her ribs, but he went to her and she put an arm around his neck and whispered in his ear.

"I can't do this," she said softly.

"Sure you can, Elenita," Ray said to her just as soft. "It's only a few minutes. Then you can rest."

"No, *Papi*, I can't go on like this. I can't be hunted. I...I can't do this, all of this. That's what I'm talking about."

"I know, sweetheart. I know what you're talking about, but in a few minutes, you'll get to rest, you'll feel better, then you'll have the strength to finish this day and you'll find the strength to start tomorrow. One foot in front of the other. *Entiendes*?"

Elena nodded. She wiped her nose on her father's shoulder. This made him laugh, but the look on her face was the saddest he had ever seen it, and it nearly broke him. He wanted to tell her about being strong for her daughter or about telling him who had done all this, but it wasn't the place or time. When they turned back to Rosita and Willie, they were hugging each other and watching Ray and Elena. Rosita's face was troubled. She wanted to cry even if she wasn't sure why.

"Let's go," Ray said and he started out a few feet ahead of the others as an example, and to make sure the path before them was clear of people waiting behind garbage bins or around corners. He had quietly pulled the revolver from the holster clipped to his waistband, and held on to it in the right-hand pocket of his jacket.

They set a good pace to keep warm, passing a small public park where teenagers were necking even though it was only ten degrees out. If there was going to be a surprise, Ray figured it would have come there since there were plenty of bushes to hide attackers, but they passed the park in peace. At the end of that block they were about halfway home.

Ray had taken a couple dozen steps on the bridge when he heard a shriek and wasn't sure who it had come from. He spun around. Elena had one hand to her mouth and with the other she was pointing. Her eyes were wide with terror. Ray took a step toward her; Willie was standing right behind her, holding Rosita to him. Ray followed her pointed finger. A white van was passing by. The passenger, a young Hispanic man, was drawing a finger across his neck. Ray saw the threat, brought his gun hand out of the jacket pocket and tried to aim. The van sped up as he kneeled to steady himself and try to read the license plate number. *XTA* was all he was sure of. That and that the van had New York plates. If they hadn't been taken off some other car, he'd track it down for sure and maybe have a solid lead. These were his thoughts when he turned back to his daughter.

Willie was saying something, holding Rosita even closer, but Elena wasn't where Ray had seen her. He turned a little more and found her − one foot on the base of the low concrete parapet, one on the sidewalk, both hands on the top of the wall − if she wanted, a few inches more and she would be over it. In Ray's mind, he saw the clear image of her dropping over the side of the bridge, over the four-foot-high concrete barrier. Ten feet away from him, but there was nothing he would be able to do except take a step closer to the barrier and watch as she hit the ice forty feet below. The impact, imaginary as it was, shook his soul.

He stepped onto the base of the barrier beside his daughter at the wall. She was staring down at the forty feet of empty air beneath her. Ray looked down and saw her as she might be − dead at the bottom. There she was on top of the ice chunks that had clogged the area around the pilings, not moving, and what would he do? He thought for a moment that if she jumped, he'd go after her – following her over the side and into oblivion - but they both noticed something move off to the side of them. Rosita was struggling to get away from Willie, who was holding her as tight as he could – her face turned in to him, keeping her eyes from watching her mother. Willie's eyes were streaming, his face was twisted like someone had melted it for him.

Ray closed his eyes and wished he had the courage to blow his own brains out. It could not have hurt as much to die as it did to live just then as he felt his heart expand in his chest, squeezing his lungs and stopping his breath and sinking as though it had turned to stone.

"You want to go over together?" he asked his daughter.

He was serious and she knew it. When she turned to him, her face had been ruined with tears that burned a path down her cheeks. Her lower lip trembled. Ray hadn't seen that in a decade. He knew when he saw her that he shouldn't have asked the question. She might say yes.

"I want to live, *Papi*," she said. "But it's so hard."

He put his hand on hers. Not to stop her if she decided to die but to remind her of the warmth of life.

"It's so hard," she repeated.

"I know it, sweetheart. It's like the sign says: 'Life's a Bitch.' That ain't even half the truth."

They were silent on the edge of the bridge for a full minute, and Ray was thankful his son-in-law didn't feel the need to come any closer. Probably thought Ray had the situation in hand. That couldn't have been farther from the truth.

Ray spoke.

"I've wanted to die many times in my life. You might not remember when your brother died – you were very young...."

He paused and looked at her to see her reaction.

"I remember," she said.

"I hope I hid it from you, but if I didn't do a good enough job, I'm sorry. I wanted to die every day for a year. Maybe more."

"Then you went to prison."

"Best thing for me. For your mother too. I was about ready to give up on everything. On life. Couldn't get my mind off the bad. Know what I mean?"

"Believe me," Elena said. "I know."

"But what kind of father gives up?"

"Yeah," his daughter said.

Ray let the affirmation hang in the air.

"Want to step away from the wall? Your daughter's watching."

Elena took a quick look where William was still holding Rosita, shielding her.

"Yeah," she said again. Then she stepped back from the wall.

★   ★   ★

Ray hadn't felt the weakening of his legs, but he found himself sitting on the cold concrete of the bridge sidewalk, his back against the barrier that wasn't high enough – he'd have to write a letter to the mayor or something. He didn't remember putting his gun back in his pocket, but that's where it was. Willie had put Rosita in his arms and was on his phone with the police. Elena stood off to one side, hugging herself to keep warm.

"Grandpa," Rosita said.

Tears had streamed down her face already, her cheeks red from the cold, her brow twisted in fear, sadness, confusion and anything else a child might feel having seen her mother on the verge of jumping from a bridge.

"Grandpa, stop crying," Rosita said. "What did Mommy do?" She patted Ray on the cheeks with both hands. "What did Mommy do?"

"I don't know," Ray was able to answer. It was the truth, but it came out strangled.

Rosita started to cry again.

"Don't cry, sweetheart," Ray told her, and he held her tighter. "Look at your mommy. She's okay now. Don't cry, sweetheart," he told her again. It was all he had.

★   ★   ★

"Look," Detective Carver said. "I'm very sorry about...how this is working out. Nobody wants this. Nobody. But I need to get some information."

He was talking to Ray, who had finally been able to stand again. Another officer was talking to Elena and a different one was talking to William. Ray looked up the road and back down again. He wouldn't have looked off the side of the bridge for any money.

"What do you need to know?" There was an edge in his voice as he asked the question. With a daughter who had almost jumped off a bridge in broad daylight and in front of her own child, he didn't think there was anything Detective Carver needed to know. There wasn't a piece of information in the universe that would heal Elena or make it so that she hadn't been wounded so deeply that she almost killed herself in front of her family.

Carver ignored the tone and asked, "William Maldonado says your daughter was pointing at a van that passed by. When it passed, she... she almost jumped."

Carver waited. Ray waited too, then he slumped his shoulders.

"Did you see this van? Anything you can tell me about it? Who was in it?"

Ray looked up and down the street again. He wanted to laugh, tell Carver to get lost.

"If I knew," Ray said. "If I knew who was in the van...."

He didn't finish the sentence – didn't have to.

Carver shook his head. "Cruz," he said. "Let me tell you – this stinks. Stinks like shit."

Ray didn't disagree.

"Well, let me just ask – there really was a van, right? And she pointed like your son-in-law said?"

"Yes. Because, you know...."

"You think Willie maybe had something to do with it?" Ray asked.

"Well, it's not unusual. And women, sometimes they cover up for the husband. You know. Especially if there's a kid involved."

Ray smiled weakly.

"What's so funny?" Carver asked. He had put away his little notepad.

"I was just thinking about a joke," Ray said. "Something about a detective who couldn't find his own ass with a flashlight. Can't remember the rest."

Detective Carver stepped up to Ray, spoke to him from two inches away.

"You think this is funny? Not so funny if I start to look your way for all your daughter's troubles. For all I know, you beat her yourself."

Carver pulled away a few inches to gauge the reaction on Ray's face. There wasn't one that he could find. After a second, Carver started to back away slowly, maintaining eye contact. Ray smiled and froze the detective for a moment, then he bobbed his head as though he were going to deliver a head-butt. Carver stutter-stepped a few feet away.

"Thought so," Ray said.

"Animal," Carver muttered as he turned away. He turned back.

"One thing, Cruz. This investigation I'm doing into the attack on your daughter – it's all but closed now. As far as the NYPD knows, nothing happened to your daughter, and today, she just decided to walk across a bridge. We'll be looking for this Langan guy, don't worry about that. But I'm gonna be keeping an eye on you for the next few days. You start asking questions, bothering citizens, and I will come down on you like a hammer and send your ass back inside. Go home. Grieve. But stop going around asking questions. You get me?"

Ray thought for a moment, then he nodded and turned to where William and Elena were standing with Rosita, and went toward his family while the detective went to his car.

★   ★   ★

Ramona Esposito sat at the edge of her bed and sipped from a bottle of rum. Something simple had gotten complicated very quickly and she didn't like it. She had the rest of the day to fix things comfortably. The weekend if she needed it, but she hoped she wouldn't.

She picked up the phone next to her bed and dialed her father's number. He picked up on the third ring.

"What's the matter?" he asked after the niceties.

"It didn't work out."

"What? She's a four-year-old. What do you mean it didn't work out?"

"Langan screwed up. He screwed up. Nearly got caught. The girl identified him."

There was silence for a moment. Esposito wasn't sure her father was still on the line.

"*Papi?*"

"One minute. I'm thinking."

Then a half minute later, he said, "This doesn't have to be so bad. This Langan dope can be your fall guy. If you can get Elena to give you the codes you need, you can let Langan take the blame for everything. On top of that, you can cut him out of anything you were going to let him have in the first place."

"He was never going to get anything," Esposito answered.

"Good. But now, to make it official, I have no doubt Ray's going to kill this Langan."

Esposito tried to think as optimistically as her father, but couldn't.

"What if Langan tells him our plan?"

"Oh. Well, you deny everything. And once you have the money, you run."

After the call, she took several more sips from the bottle and started to pack a gym bag. She thought about wiping her fingerprints from the apartment and even started the task in her bedroom, but gave it up after a minute. She walked through other parts of the apartment and looked at the mess.

"Stupid girl," she said to herself. Then she got her gym bag and headed out.

CHAPTER NINETEEN

The rest of the trip to Elena's apartment was completely uneventful – a squad car drove William, Elena and Rosita. Detectives Carver and DiRaimo took Ray. They said absolutely nothing along the way.

In the apartment, Rosita was so tired that she couldn't fall asleep, and even though Ray wanted to hug Elena to himself and hold her there, he couldn't. His granddaughter needed attention and Elena and William gave it to her. When things had calmed a little, he spoke up, put his hand on Elena's shoulder.

"You won't have to worry about anything like that after tomorrow. You get on that plane tomorrow evening and don't even look back."

Elena shook her head. He wanted to ask why she looked sad, why she couldn't believe that she could put her troubles behind her. With Rosita there, he didn't. Instead, he sat in an armchair and watched the family console each other. It took a while before they noticed him again.

"What are we going to do about the car?" William said.

"What car?"

"Our car. The one with all the flat tires."

Ray was tempted to say that they could just leave it where it was. The worst that could happen was that it'd be towed away – maybe it'd be stripped for parts once the sun went down. Hell, maybe it was stripped already. Write it off as a loss and get a new one. He knew they had bought it used, but he also knew the ten thousand dollars they'd spent was a lot to them, and they couldn't afford to let it go. He sighed.

"I'll get it towed to a garage. Tell them to get new tires on it. You'll have it back tonight."

He was going to add that this plan would work if the car hadn't already been cannibalized. He didn't. He just held his hand out for the keys.

"Thanks, *Papi*," his daughter said as he went out the door.

★   ★   ★

Just like Ray thought, there were two men trying to take parts off Elena's car when he made it back to the school. One was inside, on the driver's-side seat, trying to pry the radio out of the dashboard, the other was under the hood working on getting the car battery. The hubcaps were gone already. The actual wheels would probably be last since the tires were flat – there was still some value in the rims though.

"Hey!" Ray roared. He had his handgun out. The guy under the hood ran away empty-handed. The guy inside the car tried to give the radio a couple more tugs.

"I'll shoot your ass if you don't get out of that car," Ray shouted. The guy got the point. He stepped out of the car and backed away, his hands up, the wire cutter he should have used still in one of them.

Ray closed the hood on the car and got in. The car started on the first try. The radio wouldn't play. His plan was to drive the car on its flat tires at about two miles an hour and bring it to Sammy's fixit shop. Four flats would take less than an hour to repair or replace.

It was near five o'clock by the time Ray got to the garage. A light snow was being whipped up by wind, tossed in every direction except straight down. Sammy was out front of his shop, bringing down a heavy metal gate with a chain pulley. When he noticed Ray's headlights on him, he turned and shook his head. He tried to wave Ray off, not recognizing him. He continued bringing down the gate, and Ray honked at him.

"Closed!" Sammy shouted and went back to work shutting down the shop.

Ray got out of the car, walked over and tapped Sammy on the shoulder.

"We're closed," Sammy said.

He turned to look at Ray, and his eyes went wide. So did Ray's. Sammy Ortiz had a bruise that covered half his face. Both men froze for a moment. Sammy moved first. He ran the few steps to a wooden door next to the roll-down gate. This would lead him back into the shop where he could barricade himself in and call for the police.

He got the door open and half his body inside. Ray slammed into the door, pinning him in the threshold. Sammy struggled. He was a large man and didn't have a broken arm to worry about. Not yet, anyway. He tried pushing himself off from the doorpost and with each frantic push he got another inch of his body inside the garage. Four or five more pushes and he'd be safe again. Ray put his handgun to the back of Sammy's head with a sharp rap. Sammy stopped moving.

"How'd you get that bruise, Sammy?" Ray asked.

Sammy didn't know what to say.

"It wouldn't have been someone slamming you in the face with a lamp in the middle of the night, would it? Because I know someone is walking the streets of this city with a bruise just like yours – somebody who put a gun to my head and tried to kill me."

Sammy closed his eyes and tilted his head up. Being crushed by a door in the freezing air of the city, having a gun at the back of his head – this wasn't the way he wanted to die. Not that he had given it that much thought, but he was thinking about it now.

"Answer me, you asshole," Ray said, and he pressed against the door even harder.

"I...I...I..." Sammy said. Nothing was coming to him.

"That's all you got?" Ray asked. "I should pull the trigger now. You think I won't?"

"I...I..." Sammy said.

"Really," Ray said. "That's interesting." And with the barrel of the gun up against the back of Sammy's head, Ray pulled the trigger. The round went straight up into the air, but the noise was enough to make Sammy's whole body go flaccid. The only thing holding him up was the door that pinned him.

Ray let go of the door and quickly pushed Sammy inside, following behind him. He grabbed Sammy by the back of his coat and dragged him past the tiny anteroom that the door let into and brought him to the garage bay, the same one where he'd had his chat with Israel.

He let Sammy go in the middle of the garage floor. Sammy tried to get onto all fours, but even though Ray did nothing to stop him, that task was too much for him at the moment.

"We got a lot to talk about, Sammy. A lot of catching up to do."

Ray paced his way around Sammy then back again. During Ray's third trip around the garage owner, Sammy made a weak lunge, trying to grab at Ray's legs with one hand. He missed, but Ray stopped his pacing.

"Are you kidding me?" Ray asked Sammy.

He stomped down with his heel on the hand that Sammy had on the floor supporting him. Sammy didn't make a sound as he clutched the wounded hand to his chest, but he wanted to. Ray crouched down next to him.

"I got five bullets left in this gun," he said. "That means I can shoot you five times, but I can do that without killing you. You understand me? You know that guy on the number two train that has no legs so he goes around sitting on a skateboard begging for money?"

Sammy didn't even acknowledge the question, but Ray went on anyway.

"How do you think that guy got that way?"

He cocked the gun in front of Sammy's eyes, and Sammy's face twisted as though he were crying even though no tears flowed. He opened his mouth but no sound came out.

"It's okay to cry," Ray said, straightening up again. "I've been crying for days now, and you're going to tell me why that had to be."

*　　*　　*

Detective Carver was quiet in the car as his partner pulled up in front of the station house. Police cars were parked facing every direction on the street since the precinct didn't have a parking lot of its own. The two men had interviewed a dozen people who knew Mark Langan, including his co-workers and his neighbors. No one knew of any connection to him and children, or of him and Elena, except that they worked in the same office and so would know each other as a lawyer knows a paralegal or receptionist. No animus between them. In fact, if anything, people suggested that Langan had an eye for the ladies as a young man with good looks and money to spend might have. Elena was young and beautiful – maybe there was a connection there, no?

One of his neighbors, an older woman, asked if Elena was a woman of about thirty with short hair and a trench coat. She was shown a picture which she took her glasses off to look at.

"That's not the one. At least, not the one I've seen."

"So, there is a woman he's with?" DiRaimo asked.

"Yes," she said, then she shut the door.

"Know anything about this woman?" DiRaimo asked his partner.

"How the hell am I supposed to know?" Carver asked. "I don't know this Langan guy any more than you do."

"Okay," DiRaimo said. They were getting back into the car. "Just seems like there are a lot of things in this case that you know about. Thought this might be one of them."

Carver was inclined to argue – maybe challenge his junior partner to clarify. But then DiRaimo might take him up on it and that wasn't likely to work out well. He stayed silent on the trip to the station house.

"I'm gonna need the car for a little bit," Carver said.

He was standing outside of the car with his hand extended, waiting for the keys. It was just beginning to snow and the wind was driving flakes crazily. DiRaimo hesitated.

"You want to tell me anything?" DiRaimo asked.

"Yeah, I want to tell you to give me the goddamned keys and mind your business. I'll be back in a few minutes. We'll report to the captain together."

DiRaimo handed over the keys.

"Case related?" he asked as Carver got into the driver's seat, but the senior detective ignored him, shut the door, and drove away.

A mile or two later, Carver parked a few doors down from Langan's place of work. The streets, usually busy until at least five-thirty as people walked to the subways, were empty. The sudden snow had made people either rush or stay indoors until the squall was over. Carver rushed into La Calidad restaurant, shook the snow off as he got inside. There were no customers though the place was usually loud with them. A waitress, a young Latina in white shirt and tight black pants with her hair pulled back and hoop earrings dangling, approached him. She had a menu in her hand and pasted on a smile for him.

"Table for one?" she asked. The English was accented, and Carver knew she had probably only been in the country for a couple of years.

"I need to speak with your boss," he said.

"Mr. Meister?" she asked.

"That's the one."

"He's not here. Table for one?"

"No. Then I need to get him on the phone."

The young girl shrugged. People had all kinds of needs. Not everything was an issue she could help with. This thing about getting Mr. Meister on the phone was one of those things.

"Jesus Christ," Carver muttered. He looked beyond the girl. There were two other waitresses and a busboy, all looking at him. "Great. Look, sweetheart. Where's his office?"

"You can call him from there," she said, pointing to a payphone near the front door.

"Right," he said. Then he walked past her deeper into the restaurant and toward where he knew he'd find either an office or a kitchen. The waitress followed him, telling him he couldn't go back there. He turned to her.

"*Soy la Migra*," he said. "I'm immigration."

The young lady slowed down and said nothing else to him – let him wander on his own.

The back area turned out to be both, first a kitchen to his left-hand side and then a corridor with a janitor's closet, a couple of bathrooms then a storage room and, to the side of that, the manager's office. He heard noise coming from there so he opened it.

There was Meister, standing by his desk, pants around his ankles, one of his waitresses lying on his desk, her legs in the air, her shirt still on, her pants nowhere near.

Meister was grunting, pushing into the girl. He took a quick look over his shoulder at Carver. The girl looked at the same time, tried to cover herself up, started to squirm.

"Keep your legs up," Meister told her, and she did as ordered.

Carver looked away. "We have to talk," he said.

"Can it wait a minute?" Meister said, still pushing.

Carver stepped out again and closed the door. It was a few minutes before the young lady came out in a rush, her pants back on, her shirt tucked in. Carver smiled at her as she passed by. After all, he thought, the whole episode was embarrassing for him as well. She didn't notice him.

Meister zipped up his pants.

"Those girls," he said, waving at the door where the girl had just left. "They have no morals really. All I have to say is I'll get immigration on them or wave a few dollars at them, and I've got the keys to the kingdom."

He looked past Carver at the door as though his mind were outside the office somewhere.

"Good underneath you, these brown girls, but no sense of morals. My wife wouldn't be so damned easy, I can tell you that much."

Carver wasn't sure he wanted to say anything in response. He just shook his head. Meister waved his hand at the door again and took his seat behind the desk.

"What is it we have to talk about?" he asked.

"Langan."

"What about him?"

"He just tried to kidnap Elena Maldonado's daughter from her school."

"Shit."

"Yeah, shit. Wouldn't have been such a bad plan, but he had to run out of the school without the kid and now all of the NYPD is looking for him."

"Shit."

"Yep, still shit. Now, what I need to know is if you sent him to do this, because this needs to be controlled and there's no time like right now to start."

"Did I send him?"

"You got it."

Carver waited a moment, was about to ask again.

"No, I didn't send him. I wouldn't send a lawyer to do rough work. That's not what I pay him for."

"Great, so he just got creative on his own."

"Shit."

"That's well established, Mr. Meister. Now, there's also the question of a young woman, good looking with short dark hair, that Langan apparently has in tow. Know anything about her?"

Meister looked confused.

"A young woman?" he asked.

"That's what I said. What is it? Is there an echo in here? Listen, I don't have time for this. If I'm gonna cover your tracks, I've gotta move right now and work through the night, so just tell me, do you know the woman I'm talking about?"

Meister looked at the office door again as though wishing he could go out right through it and not look back at Carver and all the trouble he was bringing with him.

"I didn't send Langan, and I don't know this woman. He likes the ladies – a couple of times he's been here and sampled the girls a little, but I don't know about his love life. Didn't even know he had one."

"Great. That's all I need from you right now. I've got your home number. I might need to call you later tonight, maybe a couple of times. You be sitting right by that phone, because the first time I get an answering machine, I'm no longer working for you, you understand me?"

"But my wife and I are supposed to go out to a friend's house tonight."

"Cancel it. It's snowing out. Travel's going to be a bitch."

Carver put his hand on the doorknob to go out, but turned back to Meister.

"Oh, and remember the fee we discussed? It's double now."

Meister opened his mouth to say something, but Carver went out the door and shut it behind him. On his way out, he recognized the girl who had been under Meister, but she was folding napkins and didn't look up.

CHAPTER TWENTY

The last thing Ray wanted to do with Sammy Ortiz was kill him. He'd done that with Manny's wife, and it had cost him time and effort. The woman's body had been found already, the newspapers reported, and might soon be connected to him. He'd go to jail for her or at least be harassed by the police, yet he hadn't gotten anything useful from her or her husband. He wasn't going to make the same mistake with Sammy. He knew for a fact Sammy had information he wanted. If nothing else, he knew who he was with when he came into Ray's apartment a couple of nights before and tried to shoot him in the head. But Ray had a feeling Sammy had more to say than just that.

"You don't want to talk anymore?" Ray asked.

Sammy had admitted to putting a gun to Ray's head, but he didn't want to say who was with him or who had sent him. He spent a lot of time crying and complaining that his head felt like it was splitting in two.

"I can't," Sammy cried. There were real tears now, and this was the tenth or twentieth time he'd said this.

"You're more afraid of them than you are of me?" Ray asked.

This was almost always the problem when he was trying to get information. The people he worked on were often more afraid of someone who was miles away than they were of him, even if he was only inches from them – hell, even when he was actually stepping on them.

"No," Sammy blubbered.

He shifted his weight so that he was sitting with his legs crooked in front of him. He held his knees with his arms.

"I don't know," Sammy said. He sounded grumpy.

"You've said that before. You don't know what? Who was with you? I find that hard to believe. What are you telling me? Two complete strangers decided to try and kill me at the same time?"

Ray paced a little more. He'd done a lot of that in the past twenty minutes. He decided to take a different line of questioning.

"Okay, forget who was with you. Why were you there?"

"Why?" Sammy asked.

"Exactly. Why were you there? Money? For fun? Because you hate my guts? Was it some girl that dared you to do this? Why?"

Sammy kept his head down, but Ray was almost certain there had been a reaction to the mention of a girl. Was Sammy involved with Elena's assault?

"So, what was your reason?" Ray asked. He crouched down next to Sammy, invading his space.

Sammy looked him in the eye and opened his mouth, then he lunged at Ray, knocking him to the floor. In half a second, Sammy was on top of Ray, holding Ray's gun hand pinned to the concrete with his left hand and punching Ray in the face with his right. Ray bucked under him, but Sammy was a larger man. He tried flexing his wrist to aim the gun at Sammy, but it wouldn't angle anywhere near him.

"You think this is going to work out for you?" Ray shouted at Sammy between the fourth and fifth punch.

The fifth punch landed and the fist went back up in the air. Ray used his cast as a club as the fist came down and Sammy lowered his body and head to put everything he had into the punch. The cast caught Sammy on the lips, cutting them, crushing them against his teeth. The fist that was flying to Ray's face didn't make it. Instead, it retracted and flew to Sammy's lips to try to salve the injury. Ray used his cast again with Sammy leaning a bit back, bringing the cast down on Sammy's crotch.

Sammy rolled off of Ray, still holding his mouth. He got to his feet and tried for the door Ray had dragged him in through. From his back, Ray aimed his gun at Sammy's moving legs. He emptied out the remaining five rounds. Only the last bullet hit Sammy at all, lodging in his femur. Sammy collapsed onto his back like a felled tree.

It took Ray a full minute to get up off the floor. He felt nearly deaf from the sound of the gunshots in the enclosed garage, his face felt like half of it had been pureed, and his cast hand was throbbing. None of this helped make him feel kindly toward Sammy. If he weren't out of bullets, he might have used just one more for Sammy's head and left things at that.

He limped toward Sammy, who was on the floor holding his leg and crying. Ray felt like he'd popped a muscle in his right calf in his struggle to get out from under Sammy.

"You shouldn't have done that," Ray said. He tried to make sure he wasn't shouting. There was a ringing in his ears and he wasn't sure if Sammy was suffering from the same problem.

"I need an ambulance!" Sammy was shouting.

Ray nodded to him.

"Understatement," he said.

"What?"

"Understatement," Ray repeated, then he slapped Sammy in the ear with the gun.

Sammy rolled half onto his side, holding the ear. Ray limped over to a workbench, tucked the gun into his waistband, and found a length of chain about twenty feet long. He approached Sammy with the chain and Sammy said something.

"What?"

"I said the other person was a lawyer."

"A lawyer? What he look like?"

Sammy grimaced in place of shrugging.

"About my age, short haircut. Dark hair. Dark eyes, too. Always smiling. Langan is his name. Mark Langan. I got his business card."

Ray stood in the shop with the chain dangling from his hands. He was trying to piece together the information he had, see how it fit. That Langan was bad was no surprise to him at this point, but what had Elena done to him to deserve all this? And if Langan was hiring people, why would he risk coming to his apartment in the middle of the night with a baseball bat?

"Why?" Ray asked.

"Why what?"

"Why did you come to my apartment?"

"To kill you," Sammy said. "I wish I had."

"But why?" Ray repeated. "Was he paying you?"

"A million dollars," Sammy said.

"He was going to pay you a million dollars to kill me?"

Sammy had just enough strength for a couple of short laughs.

"What am I missing?"

"The whole neighborhood," Sammy said. "He wasn't going to pay me. He was going to get me the rest of this block."

"I don't get it. Real estate? He was going to give you some abandoned buildings and empty lots?"

Two more short laughs from Sammy. Ray started to swing the chain he had in his hand as though he were preparing to use it as a whip. Sammy sobered up.

"Land is the only thing god isn't making any more," Sammy said. "And New York City land is some of the most valuable land in the world."

"And Langan owns all this property?" Ray asked.

Sammy grimaced again.

"You got yourself involved with this Langan guy, you were ready to pop a bullet into my brain, and you're not even sure he had the property you wanted?"

This time Sammy had the strength to move his shoulders in a shrug.

"I'd have killed you for nothing," he said. "And I'm not the only one. It was basically you that killed Israel. You got Marla killed."

"Who the hell's Marla?" Ray asked. As he said the name, he remembered.

"Prostitute. Israel told you about her...."

Ray cut him off with a nod. He hadn't thought about Marla since

Carver had mentioned her; seemed like weeks ago. He wondered who else he had talked with was dead or dying now.

"Who killed her? Langan?"

Sammy shook his head. "The kind of shit you do comes back to haunt you," he said.

Ray nodded in agreement. He hadn't thought he was talking with an auto-mechanic philosopher.

"Now tell me about what happened with Elena."

"Who?" Sammy answered.

Ray started swinging the chain again. "That's not a good answer," he said.

★　　★　　★

Detective Carver made sure he straightened his tie and his hair before appearing at the station house. He didn't know his partner too well, but he knew DiRaimo was a straight arrow, and straight arrows might spread gossip about clandestine meetings and personal time taken in the middle of a murder investigation and other bullshit like that. Nothing too damning, but it wasn't like he needed someone paying close attention to him at the moment. Meister had offered him a hundred thousand to help get info out of Elena and generally tie up loose ends – there were plenty of those; now that fee was doubled, and there was no way he was going to lose that. He had bills to pay.

He nodded to DiRaimo, who was sitting at his desk in a hall filled with desks and detectives working phones or typing reports or eating Chinese food from containers. DiRaimo got up with a notepad in hand. It reminded Carver to get his notepad out as well. Best to look diligent even if they had no new information.

The two men walked toward the back of the detectives' area toward the office of their captain, Captain Lowe. Lowe was a big man, scary, but on his way out of the department. The one thing he didn't want in his last year on the job was to be embarrassed. He stayed connected to each major case that came in to the squad, and had even come out to Rosita's school to stand behind the officials higher up the food chain who had to answer questions for the TV cameras.

"Anything I should know about the case?" Carver asked his partner before opening the door to Lowe's office.

"I followed up a rumor about the prostitute, Marla."

"What about her?"

"People say her boyfriend killed her, but there's no body. He's still at large."

Carver and DiRaimo walked into the office, and Captain Lowe motioned for them to close the door behind them.

"This Langan guy turn up?" Lowe asked.

As the senior detective, eyes were on Carver. He shook his head.

"Canvassed. Work, home, nobody knows anything."

"And anything on a motive?" Lowe asked. He turned to DiRaimo for variety.

"Nothing yet. Perp knows the kid's mother, Elena Maldonado. She turned up beat to hell a few days back. We're thinking something like maybe the two of them had an affair, she pissed him off somehow, he attacked her and he's not satisfied with what he's done to her. Came after the kid for some more revenge."

"And you spoke to this Elena woman about that angle?" Captain Lowe asked. He was still looking at DiRaimo.

"Well, Carver talked to her," DiRaimo said.

Carver shrugged.

"I've talked with her, but she won't say a word about the assault, and she won't say anything about Langan either."

"Doesn't want to press charges?"

Carver tossed his hands up and let them fall slack to his sides.

"I think she'd go for charges on the kidnap thing, but definitely not on the assault. If it turns out that the two things are related, she might not even go for that."

Lowe swiveled in his chair for a moment and bit at his thumbnail.

"Well, we just gotta find Langan," Captain Lowe said. "You did a thorough canvas?"

"We were about to do that just now." Carver took charge.

"Then don't let me keep you," Captain Lowe said. He waved them out the door, but then called them back.

"Normally, I'd say be careful with the lawyer – we don't need more lawsuits – but this guy tried to grab up a four-year-old, so bring him down whichever way you can."

"We didn't need to be told," Carver grumbled as he closed the door on his way out of the office.

★   ★   ★

There is nothing easy about changing a flat tire when your arm is throbbing and in a cast. Sammy's garage had all the equipment needed to lift the car, take the tires off, and screw the nuts on tight once the new tires had been put in place. He also had a complete set of four tires that fit perfectly, brand new and with a warranty for sixty thousand miles.

The problem was hoisting the tires onto the bolts. The whole operation took more than an hour. It didn't help to have Sammy whining about his leg every few minutes.

"I need a doctor," Sammy said again as Ray tightened up the last new wheel.

"You're going to get one," Ray told him. "And when you go in and they see the bruising around your neck, they're going to ask questions and they're going to want to bring in the police. You know what to tell them, right?"

"The bullet was from a mugging, the bruising on the neck too. Two guys waited for me to close up my shop, they took a few hundred dollars – my receipts for today."

"Good. The doctors won't believe you and the police won't either, but if you don't get too crazy on the details, it won't matter. You're not dead, so they won't really care. Now where are your receipts for today?"

"Why?"

"I gotta take them," Ray said. "It won't do any good if you say you got shot and mugged, but you still make a deposit."

"But I got credit card information in there," Sammy said. "And almost a thousand in cash."

"I'll pay you back every dime," Ray said.

"I don't believe you," Sammy answered.

"I don't give a shit. You put a gun to my head. Trust me, you're getting off easy."

Ray collected the receipt envelope, a purple rubberized pouch with a zipper and lock. He found a small knife on Sammy's desk and cut open the envelope. He pocketed the cash, put the rest on the front seat of his car. He put the heavy length of chain he had wrapped twice around Sammy's neck in the trunk of his car. He collected the lead he had fired in the shop as well. He didn't need any of it coming back to haunt him.

Finally, he helped Sammy get to his feet and into his own car. It was still snowing outside, but the wind had died and the flakes drifted down slowly, almost as though they hadn't quite made up their mind to fall.

"You okay to drive?" Ray asked.

"Just give me the keys. If I wait any longer, I'll pass out."

Sammy hadn't bled out all that much, but his face had become pale. He started up his car.

"Remember," Ray said through the passenger-side door. "If you talk about me to the police, they'll find me, and I'll tell them everything you told me tonight. I might spend twenty years in jail, but you'll spend ten. Trust me, you don't want that."

Sammy pulled away without answering, the car fishtailing a little in the snow as he made a right-hand turn at the intersection. Ray stood watching, then he listened for the sound of a crash he was sure would come, but it didn't.

"No way he makes it," he said to himself.

He went back into the garage and pulled William's car out onto the driveway and rolled down the heavy gate, locking it and wiping down the lock to be sure.

A few minutes later, Ray was parked near the East River. He got out and tossed the handgun as far as he could throw – didn't even hear the splash when it hit the water.

Not far from there some homeless guys were warming themselves with a scrap wood fire burning in a fifty-five-gallon drum. Ray tossed in the sliced-open pouch with its credit card receipts. One of the homeless men offered him a drink from an open bottle he'd been keeping warm at his armpit. Ray thanked him, but declined. Even if he had wanted a drink, he didn't have time for it. He had forced Sammy to arrange a meeting with Mark Langan in Upper Manhattan. "I know how we can frame Ray Cruz for everything, but I need your help," Sammy had said. Langan was reluctant but agreed to the rendezvous. Ray had only a few hours to prepare his ambush.

CHAPTER TWENTY-ONE

Carver made a phone call to Robert Meister from a payphone around the corner from the police station. Meister picked up on the first ring.

"Any word from Langan?" Carver said.

"What? No. I tried calling his number a couple of times, but nothing. He's a smart young man – probably headed for Mexico by now."

A light went off in Carver's head.

"How do you know he's smart?" he asked.

"He's a lawyer, for Christ's sake. Went to Columbia, went to Yale. He's no idiot."

"Right," Carver said. "You stay by that phone. I might need you again."

"My wife will get suspicious. The maid usually picks up the phone."

"Yeah, deal with that," Carver told him then hung up.

He walked back to the car, where DiRaimo was waiting behind the wheel. He was deep in thought and stood by the door a few seconds before pulling it open.

"Something wrong?" DiRaimo asked.

"Nope. Things might be coming out right for once. Let me ask you something. What do you know about Langan? I mean his personal shit."

"Not much. We heard he likes the ladies, but the only one he hangs with in particular is still a blank. He started working at the firm he's at about eighteen months—"

"Yeah, when did he graduate from law school?" Carver asked.

"I'd have to go back inside for the files to be sure, but I think I remember something like three years ago. Why?"

"And what schools did he go to?"

"If I remember right, Yale for undergraduate stuff and Columbia Law. What's up?"

DiRaimo turned in his seat though the steering wheel ate into his gut. He wasn't going to be answering any more questions without some kind of payoff on the horizon.

"One more thing," Carver said. "The other lawyers in the firm, any of them Ivy Leaguers?"

DiRaimo shrugged. "I didn't question the other guys, didn't do any background check on them. Not yet anyway."

"Well, I can tell you, the head honcho there, I talked to him a couple of times about the Elena Maldonado thing. His degree says he went to Pace. Not a bad school, mind you, but it's no Yale, it's no Columbia."

"So?"

"So what the hell is this Ivy League lawyer – slick, young, smart, real go-getter – what the hell is he doing in a nickel-and-dime place in the South Bronx?"

DiRaimo faced forward to think about it a moment. He wanted to say the guy could be doing his good deed or could be paying off debts or could be doing some kind of penance, but none of that fit with the one thing he was sure about with Langan. The man had tried to abduct a four-year-old girl. The daughter of a woman who'd been assaulted recently but was afraid to talk.

"So what do we do?" DiRaimo asked.

"I say we get his boss on the phone, tell him we need access to Langan's things or we're thinking of getting a warrant for the law offices – he won't like that so he'll meet with us. We check his diplomas – most likely fake."

"And what does that get us?" DiRaimo asked. "I mean, let's assume they're fake right now and cut to the chase."

Carver didn't really have much to say about that for a moment. DiRaimo was pretty much right. Knowing Langan was a liar – being able to prove it – was nice, but it didn't get them very far.

DiRaimo filled in the silence. "Of course, we might find clues to his real identity, aliases, fake addresses, shit like that."

"Brilliant," Carver said. "Now, you go and make that phone call to Langan's boss. I'll take the car and tie up a couple of other details."

Carver waved at his partner as though telling him to scoot out of the car.

"But shouldn't we do this together?" DiRaimo asked.

"Langan's still out there, and god only knows if he's looking at some other four-year-old right now. If we split up, we work faster."

"Okay, but what are you going to be working on?"

"Look," Carver said, "I can't carry your weight for the entire investigation. You're going to have to do some work here. Believe me. There are loose ends, and I need to handle them. Now get out, and let me drive."

DiRaimo got out of the car and watched as his partner got into the driver's seat and pulled away, then he walked back to the station house.

*　　*　　*

There was only one rule to detective work when you had to talk with people who didn't want any part of your investigation. If you shook the tree long enough and hard enough, you always got what you wanted – as long as you had the right tree. If he could get his hands on Mark Langan, Carver would shake until answers came out, but the little shit was on the run. DiRaimo had checked to make sure he didn't have a passport, but if he faked the diplomas on his office walls, he might have faked a passport and who knew what else. One way or the other, that tree wasn't going to be shaken.

Elena Maldonado was still in town, and she was fragile. Most of the shaking had been done already thanks to Robert Meister and the goons he had hired. Langan had helped there as well. The woman was on the verge of something – probably a nervous breakdown, but maybe she could be finessed into just telling him where the money was. Pressure tactics hadn't worked yet. She was stubborn. Maybe taking the pressure off would do the trick.

He rang her doorbell and the husband answered. The tired look on his face turned to something closer to anger.

"Have you found that Mark Langan?" William asked.

"Not yet, but, in fact, that's what I wanted to talk to your wife about, if she could just step out for a minute."

"She's not stepping out," William answered.

"Listen," Carver said. "If you want to keep your wife and your daughter safe, I need to speak to your wife."

"You've spoken to her a bunch of times," William said. He crossed his arms. "None of that talk has done a damn thing for us so far. Maybe you should just let me handle Elena's safety. And another thing—"

Elena came up from behind her husband and put a hand on his shoulder, stopping him. He turned to her, and she nodded.

"It's all right, William," she said. "It won't hurt to talk a few minutes. Come in, detective."

"I was hoping to talk to you in private, Mrs. Maldonado. If you don't mind."

Elena thought about the situation. If Carver had something to say about her attack, then she didn't need to hear about it in front of her husband. She looked at William.

"Go ahead and finish what we were doing," she told him. "I'll only be a few minutes, right, detective?"

"Five. Tops," he answered.

She stepped out and the detective escorted her ten feet from the front door of the apartment. They spoke in a near whisper.

"Look, I know about the money. Millions of dollars went through your hands and it didn't get to where it was supposed to go. I'm guessing Mark Langan helped you set up a phony account."

Carver paused there, hoping to get confirmation from Elena, but she didn't react. He wondered if he'd have to speak louder.

"Well, by doing what Langan wanted, you helped rip off someone who probably deserves it, but this man is a terrible man, and he'll do terrible things to get the money back. In fact, he's done terrible things. You know what I'm referring to."

He waited again for confirmation, but it wasn't coming.

"Well, I know who this man is, but right now, there isn't a whole lot I can do against him. There simply isn't enough evidence. Even if you testified against him, there wouldn't be enough evidence to keep us from getting laughed out of court."

Another pause. Elena crossed her arms, and Carver could almost swear she was seconds away from rolling her eyes at him in boredom. The badass attitude must run in the family.

"Anyway, if I can't put this guy away, I'm thinking that maybe, just maybe, I can get him to back off from you. If you can, anonymously of course, get half the money into an account, he could access it. Then, this paper trail would keep him from bothering you again because if he did, I'd bust him for receipt of these misappropriated...uh, funds. Now...nobody wants him to go to jail over this because it would come out that you helped him with his theft. You see? Both of you would be stuck with just leaving each other alone."

There was more silence and Carver wondered if he had explained it right, but replaying it in his head, it sounded good – she keeps half the money and Meister is out of her life for good. Of course, once Elena accessed the money, Carver was sure he'd be able to get the rest out of her.

"So what do you say?" Carver pressed. Elena was smaller than him by a lot, and she was still badly bruised though the marks were fading, but her silence and her look of contempt or disdain or both unnerved him.

Elena straightened up and counted off on her fingers.

"Number one," she said. "I don't have the money. And number two, I thought by now you would have figured a few things out, but you don't know anything about any of this. Sad, really. Pathetic."

With that she walked back to her apartment door and let herself in without looking back or waiting for a response.

Carver felt like punching something as the door clicked shut.

★   ★   ★

"Where's your partner?" Captain Lowe came up behind Detective DiRaimo, startled him a little.

"Hell if I know," was his answer.

"Trouble?"

"Probably," DiRaimo answered. He was in no mood to protect Carver. He amended his statement. "He's out tying up some loose ends on the Maldonado thing."

"And you?"

"I'll be checking on a couple of loose ends. Carver got it in his head that Langan may be a fraud – fake law degree, that sort of thing."

"Make the calls," Captain Lowe said, and he left.

DiRaimo started dialing.

CHAPTER TWENTY-TWO

After speaking with Detective Carver, Elena sat quietly on her living room sofa for twenty minutes. William came out of the bedroom where he had been packing a suitcase and looked at her for one of those minutes, then he went back to work.

For the full twenty minutes, she tried to practice not feeling anything, not thinking anything. Mostly it worked, but when her time on the sofa ended, she went to the kitchen in search of rum.

William heard the cabinets opening and closing and stopped in the middle of folding a shirt. He was positive that soon he'd be summoned to the kitchen. Elena would find a plastic bag with three bottles he had emptied into the sink and rinsed out, and she'd want to know why he had done that. He considered telling her that he was just preparing for the trip to Puerto Rico, but that didn't make sense. If you were leaving, you threw away the things that could spoil like meat or milk, but how long would they have to stay away for the rum to go bad?

He heard Elena leave the kitchen and enter the bedroom. He tried to think, but only telling her the truth made any sense to him. He was afraid she'd get drunk for the third time that week. Elena went to the opposite side of the bed, picked up a shirt and folded it. She didn't ask him anything, didn't give him the evil eye. He still felt like explaining his decision, but kept it to himself.

Elena was still folding clothes when the phone rang. William and she looked at each other. On the second ring, Elena put down what she was doing and went into the living room to answer it. Two minutes later, she walked out of the apartment. William rushed to find his keys to the apartment, put on shoes and his coat, and left Rosita behind, sleeping. He hurried down the stairs after his wife, calling her name, but she didn't answer. He could hear her footsteps taking the steps as fast as she could; she was a flight and a half ahead of him. By the time he made it out to the street, all there was for him to see were the red taillights of a retreating sedan and the silhouette of Elena riding in the front passenger seat.

★   ★   ★

Detective Carver looked at his watch while waiting for a light to turn at the intersection of Tiffany Avenue and Southern Boulevard. He had promised his partner he'd be back at the station house in an hour. There were fifteen minutes left for him to keep that promise, but he didn't think that would be likely. A minute later he was parking in front of the same store where he had once dropped Lenny off.

The store owner behind his plexiglas stood up a moment, thinking the detective might be a customer, but recognized him and sat again. Nicky was on his customary seat at the back of the store. His bodyguards no longer had seats. Carver looked at the three of them and their matching bruises.

"Let me guess, the three of you got into a lovers' quarrel," Carver said. He figured he'd get a smile out of one of them, but it didn't work out that way.

"Detective Carver," Nicky said. He paused for effect. "You want to remind me why I'm cutting you in for one K a month for the past two years if some punk can walk in here and beat the shit out of me?"

Carver looked at the guards – busted lips, purpled noses, hangdog expressions.

"Ray Cruz?" Carver asked. Had to be.

"Damn straight. Now what you gonna do about it?"

"What did you tell him?"

"The hell was I supposed to tell him? I'm the only one that don't know shit about shit and he gotta come in here and bust my ass for that? I'da told him anything. That man's crazy."

Carver looked at Nicky until he went on talking.

"I told him Lenny was here, Lenny bought from me, and Lenny was leaving the city. I told him you were going to take him out to the train station, like Grand Central Station or something. That's it. S'all he wanted to know."

Nicky held his hands out, palms up like he was inviting Carver to search him.

"You've been playing with fire, my friend," Carver said. "Any ideas where I can find this 'crazy man'?"

"Don't you worry about Ray Cruz," Nicky said. "I got people out there looking for him right now."

"Let me guess. Two guys in a white van?"

Nicky nodded.

"They're not the only ones."

★   ★   ★

Ray made his way to Elena's apartment to drop off the car. Fatigue came close to overwhelming him. His head hurt, his broken hand alternated between throbbing and stabbing him with pain, and his ribs were sore. His back felt tight, like it might spasm on him, and his face felt like it had been beaten, which it had. He told himself that he had only a day more of troubles ahead of him, and if he could survive to see his daughter get onto the plane, he could rest.

As he parked, he saw his son-in-law walking toward the apartment building. Ray got out of the car and caught up to him.

"What happened to you?"

William was breathing hard. There was a plaster of snow on the chest of his coat and a small trickle of blood running from his chin.

"I fell," William answered. Standing out in front of his building, he rested his palms on his knees, stooped low and sucked in air.

"Why are you out?" Ray asked. He already feared the answer.

"Elena left. Walked out while I was packing. I tried," William said.

"You tried what?" Ray asked.

"I tried to follow her, but I wasn't fast enough. I slipped on ice about a block down. By the time I got up, the car was gone."

"What car?" Ray asked.

He grabbed William by the upper arms and forced him to straighten up, then William explained what had happened. When Ray heard how his daughter had disappeared – gotten into a strange car of her own free will – he didn't know what to do. He wanted to get into the car and drive around, but the Bronx went on for miles, and in five minutes Elena and her driver could be anywhere.

He raised his fist. He wanted to punch his son-in-law, tell him he had managed to sink to a new low, but none of that would help.

"I'm the stupidest man alive," Ray said, then he went up the stairs at the front of the building.

As William led the way up to the apartment door, Ray thought that he had come within only a few hours of finally figuring out why his daughter had been attacked, why his granddaughter had been threatened, but at the same time he had lost his daughter altogether.

He tried to tell himself that maybe the sedan meant nothing, maybe the phone call meant nothing, but it didn't work. He wanted to believe that a random girlfriend had called her, and Elena had gone down to meet her. He couldn't. He tried to tell himself that maybe it wasn't Langan in the car, maybe it was as simple as Detective Carver wanting to chat or maybe that FBI lady, Esposito. The cops or the Feds might use all kinds of pressure tactics, but they didn't actually hurt or kill the victims they wanted testimony and evidence from. He prayed his daughter might be with someone as harmless, then he prayed for the faith to believe.

"Carver was here," William said.

Ray nodded. This helped.

"They talked a few minutes, then Elena came in and sat for a while, thinking."

William said the last word like it was a bad one.

Ray opened his mouth to propose that William stay with Rosita

224 • STEVEN TORRES

while he go out in the car to look around. He didn't get to say anything. The phone rang. Ray was sitting on the sofa next to it. He picked up before William could take a step or reach out his hand.

"Elena?"

"*Papi*," his daughter called out to him and her voice was broken as it had been some days ago right after the attack. The sound nearly shredded his heart. "I need you now. Agent Esposito. She's crazy. Come and get me."

She lowered her voice for these last few phrases, but Ray could make them out.

"Where are you, sweetheart? I'll be there in—" he was saying. There was a noise in the background, sharp and loud. Another ear might not have known what it was, but Ray jumped from the edge of his seat to his feet – actually lost contact with the floor – when he heard the shot. He fell back onto the sofa.

"Sweetie?" he said into the phone. The answer was another shot, closer.

"Jesus Christ!" he shouted into the receiver. Another shot. And, not as close, the sound of a car passing over the rough metal grating of the Bruckner Drawbridge.

Ray shoved the phone in his son-in-law's direction. He wanted to say something like *"keep talking to her"* but he was breathing out snot and spit, and the tears in his eyes made him unsure William was even in the room with him. The entire rest of the world had slipped away from him, so why not his son-in-law?

He went into the kitchen and pulled out a carving knife. It was the only weapon he had. He came back to the living room.

"I'm going to the Bruckner Drawbridge. Sounds like she's there. I...I...."

"There's just a dial tone," William said. He held the phone out to Ray as proof.

"Call the police. Call Carver. Tell them where she is. Call 911. Esposito's got her," Ray said. He had his hand on the doorknob.

"Esposito?" William asked, but Ray was gone.

*　　*　　*

The drive to the bridge was torture. After three minutes on the road Ray inhaled, and for all he knew it was his first breath since hearing the gunshot. Ray's blood pounded in his ears. The streets were still slick, and stopping for lights and starting up again was work. At one stoplight, with the bridge in sight, Ray took his eyes off the road, searching the sidewalk for pedestrians. When the light turned, he floored the gas, spun on ice, and clipped a parked car with the back end of his. Foot still on the gas, he overcorrected and clipped the front end too. Somebody'd be surprised in the morning.

At the corner before heading onto the bridge, he pulled over a moment. Wanted to check for footprints. The noise of a car going over the bridge's grated surface made him drive again. A squad car came around the corner, roof lights on but no siren. A semi-emergency. Ray followed it onto the bridge. Another squad car rounded the same corner and pulled up behind Ray for a moment before moving to pass him. The squad cars parked on the bridge.

Ray pulled to a park and put on the hazard lights, left the engine running. There was a half inch of snow but no footprints on his side of the street; he crossed against traffic. Plenty of footprints on the other side – a whole area where it seemed like someone had rolled around, mashing the snow. The police officers were out of their vehicles but not moving anywhere, just standing, chatting, probably had orders to just be there. One of them looked at Ray, deciding whether to stop him or let him be. It took a second for him to say something about Ray moving along. Ray ignored him.

There was a spot on the concrete wall that kept drunks from driving off the bridge where the snow had been wiped away or pressed down. For the second time that day, Ray approached the wall and looked over the side. This time, there was no mistake. On the ice forty feet below, his daughter.

"You can't be here," the police officer shouted at his back.

He had no idea how true his words were. If Ray had the strength, he would have rushed at the officer with the knife in his pocket drawn out – forced him to shoot. Instead, he crumpled where he was, fell to his knees, scraping his forehead against the rough concrete of the wall. The tears that fell from his face melted dots into the snow beneath him, and what use was the air that blew if he couldn't breathe for the fist inside his throat twisting itself and strangling him? The officer behind Ray was joined by others and they mumbled something. He didn't hear it and didn't care anymore. He felt he was about to lose consciousness and wished for it as a mercy.

"Why? Why? Why?" he said in a hushed tone as air found its way out of him.

"What was that, sir?" one officer asked.

"Why?" Ray said. "Why can't I just die?"

★   ★   ★

There was no safe way down to the water directly from the bridge. Teenagers wanting to graffiti the side of the bridge could get down part of the way, all the way to the underside of the bridge if they were careful and strong enough, but it was still over thirty feet from there to the water. A false move meant a dead graffiti artist.

The police and fire departments both had men by the side of the river within ten minutes of Willie's call. An ambulance crew also waited. It took a half hour longer to get Elena out.

★   ★   ★

"Sir?" One of the uniformed officers tapped Ray on the shoulder. "You said you're the father?"

Ray nodded. His throat was in such pain, he couldn't trust himself to say a word.

"We're gonna need you to identify the body." The officer stayed stooped over Ray where he sat in the snow. "Whenever you're ready."

Ray almost laughed at that. Ready to identify the corpse of his child. He'd done that once before and it nearly killed him. The world was a hard place and he was a hard man, but damn it if he wasn't about ready to crack.

The officer straightened up and waited, hovering. Ray worked himself to his feet, motioned for the officer to lead the way.

The EMTs leaning against the back end of the ambulance, their hands in their pockets, waiting for Ray, stood up straight when he neared, smiles dropping off their faces, left over from whatever conversation they were having. Ray took a breath and nodded to the one closest to him. He looked very grave and nodded back, then he reached for the sheet that covered Elena and pulled it back a foot using both hands. Ray looked up to the stars first, the few of them that had started to show through the clouds. He would have said a prayer, but he didn't know one that fit. Then he looked down to the gurney.

The face was mashed, bloody, torn, but it didn't matter. Nothing mattered. Nothing could matter. It wasn't Elena on the gurney. The prayer he didn't know how to pray had been answered. Ray laughed, laughed right into the face of Ramona Esposito. The sound came from his throat like a dog's bark. He laughed again into her face as though she might hear him. The EMT covered over the body again, offended.

"What?" he said.

Ray was already walking away, waving a hand as if to say he had more important things to attend to. He did. Detective Carver was there now with his partner.

★   ★   ★

Ray was smiling at the detectives. With the stitches and bruises on his face, it wasn't the prettiest sight.

"Not your daughter?" DiRaimo asked.

"Nope."

"Know who she is?"

"Ramona Esposito," Ray said. He hadn't thought about deceiving the police on this issue – didn't think he'd get the chance to say it was anyone other than his daughter. He wanted to retract the name as soon as he said it.

"And Ramona Esposito is…?" Carver asked, but his partner looked like he'd swallowed a roach. Carver turned to him.

"What?"

"I know that name."

"She's an FBI agent," Ray said. He knew cops didn't like to hear about one of their own getting hurt. Figured he'd probably get hauled in even though he had nothing to do with her death and it looked to him like Ramona Esposito deserved what she got.

"FBI agent?" Carver asked.

DiRaimo pulled a photograph out of a coat pocket and stalked over to where the EMTs were closing the door on the ambulance that would take Ramona to the morgue.

Carver repeated his question.

"Yeah, she said she had been working with Elena on something. Very sketchy. Anyway, I figure she got tired of playing it straight and went crooked."

"And what makes you think that?" Carver said. He crossed his arms.

"She tried to kill my daughter," Ray answered.

Carver didn't have an answer for that. Tried another question.

"So your daughter killed her first?"

"I didn't see what happened," Ray said. "Anybody could have killed your FBI girl. This is the Bronx, baby. Only the strong survive."

"You quoting t-shirts at me now? Now? When we're talking about murder?"

DiRaimo came back before Ray could answer. Good thing, since Ray didn't have a comeback ready. Carver and DiRaimo took a few paces away from Ray. Ray didn't bother trying to listen in. He didn't care what they had to say.

Carver and DiRaimo walked over to the ambulance, talked with the EMTs and several of the uniformed officers and the rescue workers who had fished Ramona off the ice. Ray stood in the snow, his good hand dug deep into a pocket, his cast hand tucked under his jacket. It was an hour before the detectives came back to him.

Carver finally called him over to his unmarked car.

"Let's go," he said.

"Where?"

"Station house. You got a lot of questions to answer."

"About what?"

"That woman ain't no Ramona Esposito, ain't no FBI agent, and you knew all about where she'd be. That means questions."

"I've got to find my daughter."

"Yeah, don't worry about that. She'll be found. The whole precinct is looking for her."

CHAPTER TWENTY-THREE

It was a half hour to midnight when Ray finally opened the door to his apartment. He knew he was exhausted, but at the moment he felt light like a rough wind would be enough to lift him off the ground. Life was hard and the world was bad, but none of that mattered because his daughter was alive somewhere. The police were hunting for her like a criminal, but that was nothing too. She was a smart girl. She'd handle a confrontation with the police and come out all right. In fact, if he could just get her to JFK the next day, things would be better than all right.

As soon as he entered the apartment, he turned on a light and headed for the phone.

"William, you know the plans for tomorrow?"

"Sure, but where's Elena? What happened? I've been waiting here for hours."

"The plans for tomorrow are still good," Ray said. He gave William a minute to think about what that meant.

"Oh. Good. Thank god. But why are we talking in codes?"

"Because your phone might be bugged. Or maybe mine is. One way or the other, the less we say, the better. Now get some sleep. I'll be over first thing in the morning."

"And Elena too?" William asked. Ray hung up on him.

He went into the kitchen. Peanut butter and jelly chased down by rum and Coke to give him strength for meeting with Mark Langan. Made his sandwich, made his drink, and turned with them in hand to carry them out to the dining area, but the sight shocked him so that he spilled the drink and the sandwich flipped in the air before landing on the plate again. There was his daughter – wet hair and clothes, fresh bruises on her face.

"*Papi*," she said.

She was about to cry and held her arms open for a hug. Ray emptied his hands and pressed his daughter against him, held her tight, burying his nose in the nape of her neck, sniffing in hard to get all of her, tears running from eyes that had grown swollen in the past few hours.

"How did you get in?" Ray asked after a minute.

"The super knows me."

"Ah. And you want to talk about what happened?" He didn't want to add that the first kill can be the hardest.

"I want to tell you everything," Elena answered.

★   ★   ★

The plan was supposed to be simple. The law firm she worked for was supposed to administer seven million dollars in disbursements made by the city to several nonprofit housing and education organizations. The money was hijacked; it never was transferred correctly and instead went to one account. Since the city had bungled this small matter, the federal government was stepping in to make sure the money was taken back from the account it had gone into and that it went to the proper accounts. Steal back what had been stolen and give it to those it was intended for. Simple.

At the same time, the federal government was overseeing an auction of properties that had been seized around the city in the past year. The bids were already in, but whoever had stolen the seven million (an identity masked by false names and encrypted account numbers) had apparently rigged the bidding. Rightful high-bidders replaced with one bidder for twelve of the properties all centered in the Hunt's Point area. These bids needed to be re-rigged – the rightful high-bidders would get their deeds.

This is where Elena came in. Mark Langan, working on behalf of the firm and Ramona Esposito, representing the federal government by way of the FBI, approached her, explained the situation, and asked for her help in this delicate matter. She agreed. Who doesn't want better housing for the poor, better schools for children?

"So you were supposed to do what?" her father asked.

"I was supposed to take money from one account and put it in another which Mark and Ramona told me about."

"And about the property?"

"That was still under investigation – maybe someone in the law firm was involved, maybe not. Anyway, I was supposed to make sure that the sales were all made in one name – a fake name so that essentially the government sold the buildings and lots back to themselves. This would buy them time so they could hunt for the guilty. Then they could offer the properties again in a clean auction."

Ray had a half dozen questions he could ask, but he narrowed it down to the one he cared about most at the moment.

"So you did what they asked you to?"

"At first. I switched all the paperwork. Agent Esposito gave me a false ID so none of it would come back to me. That night I changed my mind."

"Why?"

"It dawned on me. If they knew where the money was – even if they couldn't identify who the owner of the account was – why not just transfer it into the right accounts?"

"So…?"

"So, the next morning, bright and early, I went into the office and did just that."

"Shit," Ray said. "For all we know that fake account belonged to a mobster. Now it's empty."

"Oh, it's worse than that," Elena said. "I reworked the auction bids too. Figured if they were wrong about one thing, they'd be wrong about the other."

"Reworked the auction?" Ray said.

"Easy, just slips of paper in envelopes in Langan's office. I replaced them with other slips."

"Aw shit," Ray said a little louder.

"What?"

"What? Langan was running a scam on someone about this auction thing. Slips of paper in envelopes, that sounds a little unofficial to me."

"Well, he might have been scamming someone but it's too late now. I filed those papers the same morning. It was all done by the time Langan came in."

"Does he know you changed the slips?"

"I figure he'll find out on Monday when the results of the auction are released," Elena said. "You think Langan will try to hurt me again? I mean, he should be running from the police now, right?"

Ray said, "You did the right thing, *mi'ja*. In everything you did, you did the right thing. Don't forget that. But I wouldn't worry about Langan anymore. There's still someone out there missing seven million that they were expecting, but who knows, maybe that's also Langan."

Elena looked down, her face turning to sadness. Ray figured he knew what was on her mind – the cost she had paid, the cost her family was paying for her trying to do the right thing.

"What about the FBI lady?" Ray asked. He'd learned a lot from Carver and DiRaimo, but wanted to hear what his daughter knew.

"She just wanted the money. As crooked as they come," Elena said. "Once I got in the car, she started talking about needing access to the money. When I told her what I did with it, she pulled her gun out."

"And what did you do?"

"Grabbed the steering wheel and pulled. We hit a parked car and her airbag went off. I got out of there."

Elena said the last sentence like she was surprised at herself and at the fact she was still alive. Then her hands started to shake.

"We fought on the bridge," Elena said. "I killed her."

She cleared her throat.

"I gave her a right cross like you taught me. Then I kicked her in the gut, and she stumbled back against the wall, and I just...."

"She got what was coming to her. She was a murderess and a con artist. Never an FBI agent at all."

"How do you know this?"

"First time I saw her I knew she looked familiar, but I couldn't place her. Hadn't seen her in years, and she grew up. I used to work for a guy named Fat Tommy – not a nice guy. It was about ten years ago that her mother took her to live in Florida. When I saw her up close and dead, I was pretty sure. When Detective Carver gave me her real name, it made sense. She's wanted in New Jersey and Pennsylvania for fraud…she *was* wanted."

"Isn't Fat Tommy going to come after us?" Elena asked.

"Don't worry about him. If I know him, he'll be on the run about now. I'll catch up with him." Ray looked at his watch and kissed his daughter on the forehead. "Listen. I've gotta go. I'll be back."

He went into the bedroom and brought out the last gun in his possession, a .9mm Smith & Wesson. He made sure a round was chambered and got a second magazine as well. He took everything to where his daughter was sitting.

"Here," he said. "This is the safety, now it's on, now it's off. On, off. On again. See? Someone tries to come through that door? You take the safety off, you hold the gun with both hands, and you aim for the belly button. You understand me?"

Elena smiled at him like he was an idiot in need of her sympathy.

"No one is going to look for me here," she said.

"Maybe not," Ray answered. "But they might look for me. Did I tell you someone beat the shit out of me with a baseball bat and put a gun to my head right in this apartment?"

Elena's smile dried up, and she put her hand out for the gun.

★   ★   ★

It was close to the meeting time of 1 a.m. when Ray finally drove into the area of Columbia University. He parked around the corner from the meeting place at the south end of a small park, but he could see that Mark Langan, in a dark overcoat and with a knapsack hanging from one shoulder, was waiting there already. That wasn't how Ray had wanted things to go. He wanted to be there first, stake out the place, watch Langan approach, surprise him as he arrived. Wasn't going to happen.

He didn't shut off the motor, didn't fully close his door. He got out the blackjack he'd brought along, carried it close to his right thigh, and hugged the side of the park fencing as he made his way to the corner and around. Langan had his back to him only ten paces away. He was doing a little dance to keep warm. As long as the dance didn't involve turning around, things might turn out all right. Five paces away, Langan turned. He froze; Ray didn't. He kept striding, getting into position before Langan knew what was happening. He raised the blackjack, and just one step from slapping Langan his right foot went out from under him on ice. Ray was on his back, the blackjack still raised as though his body hadn't yet realized he had fallen.

Langan took two steps away, running, then turned back. No traction problems for him. He kicked Ray in the ribs then he did it again.

"You stupid bastard," he shouted.

He raised his leg to kick again and Ray smacked the foot he was standing on right out from under him with the blackjack. Langan fell straight to the concrete with a scream and clutched at his leg, not really wanting to touch it but feeling like he had no choice.

"What the hell was that?" he yelled at Ray. Ray slapped at him again, still on his back. Not much leverage, but he broke the hand Langan had been using to soothe his leg pain.

"Jesus! Stop that!"

Ray stood up and made sure he was on a firm footing.

"Don't hit me again!" Langan shouted. Lights turned on in an apartment across the street.

"Shut up," Ray said, and he gave Langan a whack to the face that caved in his two front teeth and broke his nose. The blow sent Langan onto his back. He was still moving, but not with any purpose.

★   ★   ★

Inside the car, it was quiet. Langan either didn't know what was going to happen to him or didn't care or Ray had hit him harder than he thought.

Ray drove north to a building on 153rd Street near Trinity Cemetery, the Amtrak train lines and the Hudson River. The building was fully occupied with working-class families who didn't want any trouble, but Ray knew the passageways in the basement led to a large room with double-thick walls and soundproofing so effective that forty men could scream and shout and cheer on fighting dogs as they tore each other's ears off and no one in the building would suspect a thing.

Dogfighting was not a sport Ray enjoyed. It seemed cruel. But that didn't mean the Pit didn't have its uses. He'd been there on business several times and the place never failed. If they had seen a live dogfight, the toughest cases cried at the thought of being taken there. If they hadn't seen one, it only took showing them a warm-up exercise – a poodle thrown to a pit bull.

Marcos Howard was waiting for Ray outside the building, leaning against the thick stone handrail of the building's front steps. He was a big man, six foot four or more, and he said he was three hundred pounds because his bathroom scale refused to go any further than that. Nobody would have been surprised if he told them he weighed four hundred. He stepped over to Ray's side of the car, stooped down to the window, and put his hand in to shake.

"Who's the punk?" he asked.

"Guy I need to have a talk with," Ray answered.

Marcos took a closer look at Langan, his nice clothes, couldn't imagine a man like that needing a visit to the Pit. Would have thought he'd cave with just a threat – he looked worked over already. Maybe he was tougher than he seemed.

"All right. Let's get this show on the road," he said as he straightened up.

★   ★   ★

Ray pushed Langan along ahead of him down a cinder-block-walled hallway with bare dim bulbs hanging every ten feet. Langan was holding his broken hand and limping so bad that he scraped along the wall for support.

"I thought you was out of the game," Marcos asked Ray.

Marcos was at the back of the line, his bulk taking up the whole passageway.

"Just a little side job," Ray said.

There was silence for a few more steps.

"I heard about what you did to Nicky up on Longwood. He the one broke your arm?"

"Part of the same side job," Ray answered.

"Who's Nicky?" Langan asked, jumping into the conversation.

They came to a half turn in the hallway and a padlocked door. Marcos passed the key to Ray – there was no way he'd have been able to sidle past the other two men in the narrow passage. Ray took off the lock and passed that with the key back to Marcos.

"Where is this?" Langan asked.

"Don't you ever shut up?" Ray asked back at him.

Langan didn't have an answer.

"Now, I don't care what you do, but at the end of an hour, I want this shit cleaned up – you know where the hose is at. I need to sleep and I ain't getting paid enough."

With the last words, he put out his hand. Ray fished into his pocket and pulled out a wad of twenty-five hundreds. Marcos counted them. He nodded and Ray opened the door and pushed Langan inside. Marcos turned on a light.

"Now. They's four dogs in there, but, you know, if you release more than one at a time, sometimes they just start to fight each other, and it's extra if one of them kills another, you understand me?"

"Dogs?" Langan asked.

Marcos pointed. There was a ring about twenty-five feet wide, sunken into the floor of the basement and with a four-foot-high wall around it all. There were gates visible in the wall – four of them – and behind one, Langan could see an American pit bull, its ears cropped, scars on its face. It was watching the men silently. The concrete walls and floor of the ring were brown, not gray, and at the center of the floor, there was a drain. Above the drain, a chain on a pulley with what was left of a rubber tire dangling. Another chain was attached to the first one in order to pull whatever was hanging over the ring to safety. Marcos gave the chain a tug, brought the tire over and undid a clasp that was holding it. The tire dropped with a thud at his feet.

"Oh shit," Langan said calmly.

"You got that right," Ray said. "Look. I'm gonna hang you by the hands where that tire was. You answer my questions, and I won't have to let loose any dogs."

"I think you broke my hand," Langan said.

"You want me to hang you by the neck?"

Langan seemed to think it over a moment.

"Are all the dogs going to be dangerous ones?" he asked.

Ray wasn't even sure he'd heard right.

"Because that one over there is a pit bull. That's a dangerous breed."

Ray looked at Marcos. Was Langan bluffing? Playing the tough guy? Stupid?

"You on drugs?" Ray asked.

"Not in a while," Langan answered.

"How long?"

"What time is it now?" Langan asked. "I haven't taken a thing since a little after midnight. You know. Just a little something to take the edge off."

"Sure," Ray said. "There's going to be plenty of edge in a minute."

"Anything else?" Marcos asked as Ray tied the chain around Langan's wrists.

"Yeah. How do you get the dogs to stop biting?"

"To stop? Oh, I know what you mean. Like to get them back in their cages. I got something for that."

Marcos went to a three-foot-high cabinet where he kept gauze, needle, thread, and a Super Soaker.

"A water gun?" Ray asked. Seemed strange that such a fierce animal would be afraid of water, but then everything was afraid of something.

"Not water," Marcos said. "Ammonia. A good spray to the face and they'll probably let go."

"Probably?"

"They's dogs, man. I can't guarantee how they'll react. They might go after you. I don't know. It's never happened before, but it might."

Marcos left and Ray asked Langan if he was comfy. The man seemed about ready to fall asleep. Whatever he had taken was kicking in, but Ray figured that effect would fade in a minute.

"Why don't you just ask me what you want to know?" Langan asked. It was a good question.

"I'll get to that," Ray said. Then he gave several pulls on his end of the chain, and as it worked its way through the pulley system, it began to lift Langan's hands.

"Wait," Langan said. "I'll tell you everything."

"I don't doubt that," Ray answered. A few more pulls and Langan had his hands above his head.

"This is really hurting," Langan said.

A few more pulls and he was on the tips of his toes; then with a couple more pulls, he was dangling, trying to get his footing on the concrete wall, not wanting to go into the pit. Ray tied off the chain on a cleat.

The pain from his broken hand was almost too much for Langan. He was twisting from his wrists, and when he opened his eyes he could see all four cages, each with a dog waiting patiently, but with tension in every muscle, for the training exercise to begin. There was about a foot and a half between his toes and the drain beneath him.

"I said I would tell you everything," he repeated. Breathing was hard, hanging the way he was. Speech came out in bursts.

Ray waited for Langan to stop swinging, then he went to the cage Langan was looking at. He was standing to the side of the cage. The gate to the cage was fastened at the top with a screwdriver. Pull the screwdriver out and there was nothing to keep the dog from rushing at Langan and grabbing a hold of whatever part it could with massive jaws and waggling its head playfully, ripping and shredding him.

"Look at me, Langan. I take this screwdriver from here, and the dog in the cage will come after you. I want you to pay attention. You answer all my questions, and I don't need to pull out the screwdriver."

"I said I'd talk," Langan tried to shout, but it came out weak.

"Good. Two men attacked Elena Maldonado a few days ago," Ray said. "Who sent those men and where can I find this person?"

"His name is Meister, Robert Meister, he lives in Westchester County, Scarsdale. He owns La Calidad restaurant. He owns a few other buildings. He's an old guy. Older than you. White hair." He didn't know what else to say. If there was anything that would have helped, he would have said it.

"Good, good," Ray reassured him. "Now tell me about the FBI agent, and no lying because I've spoken with her."

"The FBI agent? Oh, Ramona, she's in love with me."

"You two planning to run off with everybody's money? The deeds to a dozen pieces of property?"

"Money yes. The deeds, the auction, that's all fake. I just wanted to have something as bait."

"And when all of this came out, when all these angry people came after you?" Ray asked.

"They weren't going to come after me," Langan answered. He was almost smiling again.

"Right. The police and all those angry people were going to come after my daughter."

Langan was clear-headed enough to know there was nothing he could say that would make Ray happy.

"And you tried to take my granddaughter out of school. What was that supposed to do? Make Elena give you account codes?"

"We figured if we had the little girl, there was no way she'd keep hiding the account."

"She wasn't hiding it," Ray said.

"What?"

"The account. There's no hidden account. She just gave the money to the people it belonged to."

Langan was quiet a while, thinking.

"All of it?" he said. "Why would she do that?"

Ray thought about explaining the word *honesty* or *integrity*, but he remembered that he was talking to a lawyer and gave up. The blood was ringing in his ears. His daughter made thirty thousand dollars a year and had to work with idiots. She was smarter than the piece of meat he had hanging over the drain of the pit. He was tempted to release at least one dog just to hear Langan scream, didn't doubt it would be loud, the mess would be bloody. But he was tired of the noise and the blood. He wanted to kill Langan quickly, painlessly.

"And you're sure you had nothing to do with my daughter being beaten?" Ray put his hand on the screwdriver as he asked.

"I swear to you. That was Meister. You saw Meister. You came up to me in the pizzeria. I remember you. He was sitting with me."

Ray remembered of course. Would recognize the man. Knew where to find him. The owner of a restaurant can't just disappear – not without selling it off first. He didn't doubt Meister was a client. But....

"How do I know you didn't just choose that name at random?" Ray asked.

"Just let me down, and I'll take you to the office. I'll show you all kinds of paperwork."

"Stay right there," Ray said. His head was starting to pound with the puzzle in front of him – how to decide if there really was a separate person responsible for the attack on Elena. He needed a little fresh air. Not that it was that much better in the hallway, but the smell of blood and dog was getting to him.

"Where are you going?" Langan asked.

Ray ignored him.

He opened the door to the hallway and took one step out. The air was cooler and cleaner, and from the far end of the hallway, Detective Carver was charging his way.

"Hold it right there, Cruz!" Carver shouted from twenty feet away.

Ray turned back into the room and moved as fast as he could to the cage facing Langan and pulled out the screwdriver holding the dog back. The sound of the metal scraping as he pulled alerted all the dogs in their cages, and the one that was released burst into the pit running for Langan.

Langan kicked at the dog and screamed. The first kick hit the dog square in the face and knocked him onto his back, but Langan was twirling in the air now, unable to control his movements. The dog came at him again as Carver came into the room, his gun in hand.

"Holy shit!" Carver said when he saw what was happening.

He ran to the edge of the pit next to one of the cages to get a better look at what he was dealing with, but the dog inside that cage was trying to break out and Carver backed off a step.

The dog missed with his next jump, came down on all fours, jumped and missed again. Langan was still screaming and kept his legs up in a crunch as much as he could, but the dog was jumping high enough to reach any part of his lower half.

"Cruz! That guy's not a *piñata*! Control that dog or I'll shoot it," Carver yelled out above Langan's screams.

Ray shrugged.

"Shoot it if you want."

Carver tried to take aim at the dog but at just that moment the dog chomped onto the center of Langan's right thigh and hung there, shaking his head, trying to get a piece the size of a large grapefruit to come off. Langan and the dog were twirling and there was no shot to take.

"What's the command?" Carver said.

"What command?" Ray shouted back.

"Make it stop, heel."

The water gun with ammonia was on the wall near Carver. Ray pointed to it from his position near the dog's cage. Carver holstered his weapon, picked up the water gun, primed it and squirted. The stench of the ammonia made him turn away, but his aim was good enough. The dog yelped and went back to his cage with his tail between his legs.

With the Super Soaker in hand, Carver followed the chain to the cleat. He'd have to lower Langan a little to have enough slack to pull him out of the ring.

"Want me to reel him in while you lower him?" Ray asked.

Carver nodded.

"You try any funny stuff, I will shoot you dead."

"I don't have a gun," Ray said, and he moved to the side of the ring with the chain to bring Langan out.

Carver lowered, and Ray pulled. Langan was whimpering and shaking and still curled up with his knees near his chest as Ray lowered him to the floor. Carver started to come near.

"I need more slack to undo his hands," Ray said.

Carver turned back to the chain he'd been working, and Ray pulled out the screwdriver he'd put in a jacket pocket – stabbed Langan three times, fast – liver, lung, and near the heart – before Carver was able to turn, aim and fire.

The bullet from Carver's gun hit Ray in the spine and lodged there. He fell on Langan and rolled onto his back.

"You stupid bastard," Carver said.

"Meister," Ray said. He couldn't find Carver with his eyes as things started to get dark in the room.

"Yeah, I know Meister. He wanted you dead days ago. God knows what he'll do to your family now."

Above the sound of the dogs barking, Carver thought he heard police officers announcing themselves out in the hallway. He took two steps from Ray and fired at him again.

"Freeze!" shouted two uniformed officers in tandem.

Carver raised his hands over his head, the gun still in the right hand.

"I'm on the job!" he shouted back. "I'm putting the gun down."

Two more officers came into the room. One of them searched Carver and found his badge.

"You okay, detective?" one of the officers asked.

"Me? A little shaken up, but I'm just peachy," Carver answered. He tried to smile. "Better than those two anyway."

CHAPTER TWENTY-FOUR

Carver was taken to the same hospital as Langan and Ray, but he got to ride in the back of a squad car. He had a shaky right hand and some blood spattered on his shoe. It was department policy that he be seen by a doctor. In the past, officers involved in shootings had suffered all sorts of wounds without recognizing it because of the shock they were in. Carver quickly received a clean bill of health and a small prescription of relatively weak tranquilizers.

"How are these with booze?" he asked.

"Don't take them with booze," the doctor responded.

"Guess that answers my question."

When asked by Captain Lowe if he wanted a union rep before being debriefed, he waved off the idea.

"It's simple. I got a tip that Cruz was going to kill Langan. I followed up, caught him in the act with a knife or screwdriver in his hand. Cruz turned on me, and I had to kill him. He wouldn't stop even though he was on his stomach, so I shot him dead."

Carver motioned with his hand, pulling an imaginary trigger at the floor.

"Well, you didn't shoot him dead."

"What?"

"Cruz. He's still alive. Maybe not for long, but the doctors are working on him," Lowe said.

"Oh," Carver said. "Good, good."

"And what about this tip you got?" Lowe asked. "How'd you know where Cruz was going to be?"

"Oh, Cruz smacked down a drug dealer over on Longwood yesterday morning. Guy named Nicky. He had his feelers out looking for a little payback. The guy at the dog ring called him up when Ray contacted him, and Nicky told me."

"Nicky Gomez?" Captain Lowe asked. "I know all about him. Piece of work, that guy. Well, he got his payback."

"Another satisfied customer," Carver said. He wanted it to sound funny, but the captain just looked at him for a long moment.

"Anyway," Lowe said. "We can chalk one up for the good guys. Official report and IAD can probably wait 'til tomorrow, but if you're game...."

Carver shook his head. He didn't feel like talking with anyone else just then. Captain Lowe left him for a moment to arrange a squad car to take him home.

As he was getting into the car, he saw Elena, William and Rosita rushing into the hospital – Rosita asleep in her father's arms.

* * *

"If it weren't for the first bullet, the bullet to his gut, I'd give him a pretty good chance of surviving," a doctor said. "Probably paralyzed, but alive."

"So, you're giving him a bad chance of surviving?" Elena asked.

The doctor thought for a moment, struggled to find the right words, and settled on, "Yes." She was young but tired and seemed genuinely sorry she couldn't share better news.

"The bullet to the abdomen hit a couple of organs and there's been plenty of blood loss. The next few hours should give us a better picture."

The doctor put out a hand to Elena's shoulder.

"I'm truly sorry I don't have better news for you."

"Can I see him?"

The doctor thought about this too. She couldn't see the harm.

Ray opened his eyes as his family entered the room. He had a plastic mask pushing oxygen into his nostrils. He took it off with his good hand.

"Packed?" he asked his daughter. He sounded weak.

"All packed," she said. There were tears in her eyes. He tried to move his hand to wipe them away, but his arm was too heavy for the motion. She stooped down to kiss his cheek.

"I have always loved you," he told his daughter. His eyes rolled in his head. He wanted to stay focused, but it was hard. "I'm proud of you. You did good."

"I got you killed," she said. A laugh escaped her, bitter.

Ray shook his head. It was a weak movement.

"*Mi'ja*, it's what parents do. It's love. My pleasure."

He wasn't sure he was making sense anymore, and he had much to say, so he got to the business of telling her about Meister.

"Kill him or get on the plane," he finished.

"But once he knows he lost…" Elena started.

"He'll be really mad," Ray finished for her. "Kill him or get on the plane," he repeated. "One or the other."

"Or maybe both," Elena said.

"Even better," Ray said.

★　★　★

That night, lying in a new room, Ray got the news of Robert Meister, businessman from Scarsdale, dead in his car, a single gunshot wound to his head.

Ray had no idea whether his daughter did it or Meister killed himself or if someone else did it, maybe even the same crooked cop who had shot him twice. It didn't matter. His daughter was safe; her whole family was safe. Everyone he loved in the world was safe. He smiled to himself then closed his eyes at peace.

FLAME TREE PRESS
FICTION WITHOUT FRONTIERS
Award-Winning Authors & Original Voices

Flame Tree Press is the trade fiction imprint of Flame Tree Publishing, focusing on excellent writing in horror and the supernatural, crime and mystery, science fiction and fantasy. Our aim is to explore beyond the boundaries of the everyday, with tales from both award-winning authors and original voices.

•

You may also enjoy:
The Sentient by Nadia Afifi
Junction by Daniel M. Bensen
Interchange by Daniel M. Bensen
American Dreams by Kenneth Bromberg
Second Lives by P.D. Cacek
The City Among the Stars by Francis Carsac
Vulcan's Forge by Robert Mitchell Evans
The Widening Gyre by Michael R. Johnston
The Blood-Dimmed Tide by Michael R. Johnston
The Goblets Immortal by Beth Overmyer
The Apocalypse Strain by Jason Parent
The Gemini Experiment by Brian Pinkerton
The Nirvana Effect by Brian Pinkerton
A Killing Fire by Faye Snowden
Fearless by Allen Stroud
The Bad Neighbor by David Tallerman
A Savage Generation by David Tallerman
Screams from the Void by Anne Tibbets
Ten Thousand Thunders by Brian Trent
Two Lives: Tales of Life, Love & Crime by A Yi

Horror and suspense titles available include:
Snowball by Gregory Bastianelli
The Wise Friend by Ramsey Campbell
Somebody's Voice by Ramsey Campbell
The Haunting of Henderson Close by Catherine Cavendish
The Garden of Bewitchment by Catherine Cavendish
One By One by D.W. Gillespie
Black Wings by Megan Hart

•

Join our mailing list for free short stories, new release details, news about our authors and special promotions:

flametreepress.com